P9-DTD-962

BROWN LORD
OF THE MOUNTAIN

*The cover photograph, taken on the coast road near Clifden,
Co. Galway, is by Pat O'Dea, and is reproduced by kind
permission of the Irish Tourist Board*

By the same author in Pan Books

SEEK THE FAIR LAND
THE SILENT PEOPLE
THE SCORCHING WIND
RAIN ON THE WIND

WALTER MACKEN

BROWN LORD
OF THE MOUNTAIN

UNABRIDGED

PAN BOOKS LTD · LONDON

First published 1967 by Macmillan and Company Ltd.
This edition published 1970 by Pan Books Ltd.
33 Tothill Street, London, S.W.1

330 02481 7

Printed in Great Britain by
Cox & Wyman Ltd, London, Reading and Fakenham

The Beginning of the Story

IF YOU want to begin any story at its proper beginning you would have to go back to the time of Adam and start from there. Wiser men have done this and taken the story into recognizable times. So the story of man has to begin at a point of time in the memory of the man who tells the tale.

So this one begins on a stormy night in the Mountain at the wedding feast of Donn Donnshleibhe.

Built in a scoop of the hills, the village of the Mountain on this night in September was being peeled by the west wind and scoured by the slanting rain. People whose front doors faced into the wind had sodden sacks outside their front lintels to stop the rain flooding their kitchens.

This was the kind of night it was, but it didn't stop them from going to the feast of the only son of the Lord of the Mountain.

There the house was at the end of the road, built like the gowleog you would use for a catapult, a long low branch to the left where they lived, the bit in the middle where the porch was that led into the shop, and the long room on the right, with the lights blazing inside and all the window glass befogged and dripping with the breath and the sweat of the rejoicing people.

It was hard to get in there. Many young men stood at the doorway looking into the big room. There were three oil lamps hanging from the ceiling clouded with waves of blue tobacco smoke. At the far end there was a wooden table with three tapped half-barrels of porter on it.

The fiddler and the melodeon player were hidden behind this table. Sometimes they were silent, but when the music came the young people went to the centre of the room and they danced. There were very few sober people in this room, because it was now nearly midnight, the talk was loud, the sound of hobnailed boots on the concrete floor was harsh and in one corner drunken men were in a huddle singing come-all-ye's, out of key, in opposition to all the other noise.

5

The young Donn was backed up against the wall watching all this. He could see it all, because he was very tall and powerful. He was not drunk. He might have been better off if he was. From his height he looked around him at all this and it brought him no joy. He looked at his father, a man as tall as himself, a big rangy man with thick white hair combed back over a well-shaped head. He was sitting on a high stool. He was shouting at times, singing at times, clapping people on the back at times, turning now and again to put his huge arm around the frail shoulders of Martin MacGerr, the father of the bride. This man's hair was thin, his eyes were very blue, and they made an odd contrast, the big lusty-looking Donnshleibhe and the scholarly-looking MacGerr, a wisp of man with dreamy eyes, more bewildered by his surroundings than by the whiskey that was being forced on him by his new and unexpected relation.

Donn moved his tongue in his mouth. It was dry. He would have to make up his mind soon. When a girl put her hand on his chest and asked him to dance, he remembered to smile down at her and shake his head. But always his eyes went back to his father. The resentment rose in him, the longer he looked at him.

He knew the title Lord of the Mountain was derisive as it was used now, but the old man made it his own. He was a lord of his own choice, who saw no opinion but his own. His judgements were decisive and without appeal. This feast should not be here in this house of his, but down in the small cottage at the foot of the hills where MacGerr lived his life with his books and the copybooks of his scholars.

His hands were clenched behind his back. He felt them hurting him and took them and looked at them. They were big hands and the nails had made deep indentations in the palms.

Suddenly he pushed himself away from the wall and started to move out of the room. He had to force his way. He heard the banter over the noise and the sweat and the fumes, but it glanced off him. He wanted to get out into the air. The faces of all the young people he knew refused to come into focus. He just smiled and said 'Yes! Yes! Yes!' Their shouts and encouragements were slightly obscene, but this wasn't unusual.

6

He broke through them, went off by the porch and stood in the rain.

It was drenching rain. He was wearing a new navy-blue suit and a white shirt. In seconds he felt the water pouring from his hair and down his face into the collar of the shirt. He rubbed his face with his hand.

He knew that the thought in his mind was terrible, but he didn't see how he could do anything else.

Abruptly he walked to the right, where the family rooms stretched and he went to the window of one room and looked in. There were lace curtains. He could see vaguely through them, but where they were parted in the centre he had a clearer view.

His mother was there and some of the ladies, and Meela, his new wife, was there, in her neat blue dress with the white collar. She was right opposite him. He could see her clearly if he wanted to. He didn't let his eyes drop below her forehead. He had found himself doing that, even when they were being married in the Chapel of Ease at the foot of the hill this morning, not looking into her eyes, just looking at her forehead where it curved out from under the jet-black hair. Nor now, nor now, because don't mind father, don't mind circumstances, she was the focal point of his resentment. The others would only be wounded in their pride, but it would be different with her.

He tried to tell himself that she deserved it. She wasn't the force that had brought the marriage into being. He could have said no, couldn't he? If he had been courageous, he could have even shouted down the roarings of his father. He hadn't done so, and what had been love and affection seemed stale now and brought the taste of his mouth, the dry bitter taste. His mother wouldn't mind. She was there with her flowered blouse held by a cameo brooch, a plump woman with no lines on her face, insensitive to suffering, insensitive to life, who loved wounded birds and helpless things. She would have something to nurse now.

He pulled away from the window, and thought.

He went back to the porch.

The young men were jammed in the doorway, looking in,

7

shouting, hurrooing. He passed by the back of them and tried the door to the shop. It was open. He went in. It was feebly lighted by candles stuck in bottles. All the oil lamps were in the big room. The place smelled of spices and food and stale spilt drink.

He went behind the counter.

He pulled out the drawer with the brass handle that was built under the lower shelf. He felt in here. There was money in it. He didn't take it all, just a fistful of pound notes. He stuffed those into his trouser pocket, turned and left the place, got by the backs of the young men without being noticed and went out into the rain.

He pulled up the collar of his jacket, and grunted ruefully at its ineffectiveness.

Bicycles were thrown against the wall in untidy heaps. He picked the one nearest to him, freed it from its neighbour, and wheeled it out to the road.

He stopped a little here. His eyes went back to the room where Meela sat, obediently drinking tea and eating porter cake, wondering no doubt why Donn hadn't appeared to see her in hours. She was a blurred picture to him as he looked, then he mounted the bicycle and headed down the road from the Mountain with the heavy gale at his back.

It was a bad road. He seemed to be flying. From here the road went down and down, winding and twisting, the dirt greasy with the rain, like riding on a river, wobbling in the ruts made by all the cartwheels.

When he tried the brakes he found that there were no brakes.

He was glad. It was a wild ride. He could have fallen on any yard of it for six miles, before it became reasonable where it got near to the main road into the town.

A grand way to start the mi na meala, the month of honey, they would say. No month of honey for him. They would all know that the month of honey had been before it should have been. He had had a terrible desire to cry out in the church: Yes, yes, it is as you suspect, if we waited this could have been a christening. He heard the voice of his father roaring in his ears, while he just stood and said hypocrite, hypocrite under

8

his breath. He was lacking in courage. Was he lacking in courage? He could have said like others said before him: Well, I wasn't the only one. There was no law. But he hadn't because he knew that this wasn't true.

He was twenty-one. He had a mind of his own.

The water weeped from him as he cycled along the road to the big town.

He would leave the bicycle there at the railway station.

He tried to console himself that it was her fault, that she ought to have known. She ought to have begged him not to go through with it. He would have been for ever up there in the Mountain, like a sheaf of oats under his father's flail. Wouldn't she know that? He couldn't do it. She ought to have used her intelligence.

It wasn't running away. He would prove this. That it wasn't a lack of courage. Just that they pushed him into a corner, all of them pushed him into a corner. What time did he get to think?

Well, there would be plenty of time to think now.

There was a war breaking out in Europe wasn't there?

That would be the place where you could prove what you were made of, provide a feeble reason to them, for his flight in the night of the storm.

He didn't care.

His big jaw was tight as he saw the faint yellow of the lights of the town. He imagined the gleaming steel rails running away from it, and beyond over the sea, where he would be free, and leave them behind him, for ever and ever and ever.

He was his own man, for ever and ever and ever.

But while a man lives there is no for ever.

One

HE SAILED into the Bay on an April evening.

He leaned against the wheelhouse of the Spanish trawler, not conscious now of the throb of the diesel engine under his boots. The sea was calm. When he turned his head left he could see the sun sinking beyond the islands, a great red-coloured orb reflecting itself as far as the wake of the boat. The far-away mountains were coloured blue and purple, and some of the windows of the houses that faced that way were winking redly at the dying sun.

He felt the presence of the man beside him. It was José.

'This is yours, eh?' he asked in Spanish.

'Not this, beyond,' Donn said, pointing towards the hill that rose out of the town.

'It is good to come home,' José said. 'Always I like to go home.'

Donn didn't answer.

José had a home, on the Atlantic coast, in a small village mainly consisting of a row of houses going down to the harbour, with its mass of rocking masts, a littered garage, two bars with the odd smell in them, a few shops and all the time in the world. José had a wife, and she was Irish, and three small children. His wife had been so pleased to see Donn, to talk English, but it was frustrating too because he did not know the place she came from and so could not tell her about such a one or such a one. She was disappointed in him.

'You see your father, your mother?' José asked.

'I don't know,' said Donn.

'A long time since you see them, no?' he asked.

Donn thought. He remembered the wild bicycle ride down the wet road, sitting in the train waiting for it to move; the absurd feeling that any minute his father would come running along the platform shouting: Hey you! Come back you!

'It must be about sixteen years,' he said.

José tsk-tsk-tsked.

'This is too long,' he said. 'Life is short, no?'

'Sometimes life is long,' said Donn.

A bell tinkled below. Manuel shoved his big head out of the wheelhouse and shouted something at José. José said: 'Yes, yes, Manuel!' and went back.

'So we bring you home, Senor Don Don!' Manuel shouted.

Donn laughed. He had a hard job getting them used to his name, Donn with two n's. It was an impossible task for them so they settled for Don Don, and tacked on a Senor for good measure.

'And made me work hard for my passage,' said Donn.

Manuel laughed.

'A big fellow like you,' he said. 'If we do not work you then your joints rust up like idle iron.'

Donn laughed. His Spanish was not good. Bog Spanish like they used to say bog Latin when they were at school. But he gave them great occasions for laughter with his pronunciations.

'Soon now,' said Manuel, 'you will be in front of a fire in your father's house and you will kiss your Momma and Poppa.'

Donn thought of kissing Poppa. He had to laugh.

'Yes, yes, Manuel,' he said. They were nice simple people. If they had character complications he didn't know of them. They had very good manners and families were important to them. They could hardly be expected to understand his.

'Soon, soon,' said Manuel, going back to his task.

The engine had slowed. They were gliding past the island with the lighthouse on it, already beginning to flash its beam at the hills and the island-broken horizon. He felt the muscles of his stomach tightening. He wondered why in the name of God he was coming home. Only partly home, he decided then. He could go to the town, and after that he didn't have to go any farther if he didn't want to.

Why? What instinct was it? He had been sitting in the warm sun on the many-thousand-year-old bricks at Ostia when the thought had come into his head. Here in this town dug out of the past, with its houses, temples, long, long chariot roads, it suddenly seemed to him looking at it that the life span of a man was very short. He was imagining this nobleman's house with its stately halls peopled by ladies and children and servants in light whispering robes, and there at the end of the hall was a small room with a toilet built over what had been a drain, and the toilet seat was made of shaped marble. So little difference to modern life. Men and women who had lived that long ago, and to them at that time life was important too, and there seemed no end to it, that it would go on for ever. Now they were dust and their marble toilet seat remained.

As he went back to Rome, he felt the call of the hills and this place that had been his home. It was like no other place in the world for that reason, and the thought had come to him: It is time to go home. He argued against it, fervently, but he kept being pushed.

It took him until March to make his way out of Italy, across France and down into Spain. But he was a seasoned traveller by now, and he found this trawler that would call at the port for supplies in the middle of their long fishing expedition.

He was almost disappointed because he would never have bought a ticket with home as its destination. He just played the cards and they fell out this way, and now he was nearly home.

The boat was turned in towards the dock.

He left the deck and went below to the cramped quarters. There was nobody there, so he put the last of his things into the big duffle bag. He looked around. He had to keep bending. They had photographs tacked up, of wives and children, all smiling in the sunshine, and dark-haired black-eyed smiling girls who were the *novias* of young Juan and Gonzalo. Looking at them made Donn feel very old and very experienced and very sad.

He went up on deck again.

He went to the raised prow of the ship and stood near the winch. He saw the feeble lights of the dock fighting against the afterglow. He could feel the boat yaw a bit as they met the stream of the river. But she righted herself powerfully and edged in towards the pier where men were waiting to catch the ropes that were coiled by José and Gonzalo. They heaved, the men ran to the bollards, the side of the ship nudged and then snuggled against the iron-bound wooden baulks, and she came to rest.

This was the part Donn didn't like, saying goodbye to the men of the trawler. He reflected that this was always a trouble when you had wandered as far as he had. In wars it was separation by death, or feebly waving hands from stretchers. People were the raw meat of the world, feeding it. His inclination was to swarm up the ladder and run down the pier. But he couldn't. They came around him. All of them had to look up at him.

'You were very kind to me,' he said. 'I thank you. I hope we will meet again.'

'If God wills it,' Manuel said, shaking his hand. 'It was a good diversion for us to have you with us.'

'But we are not your family,' José said. 'We hope you will be warm in their embrace. They will be joyed to see you.'

'That's right,' said Donn.

Juan and Gonzalo clapped him on the back.

It was dark now. He could not see their faces, just their eyes in their dark faces reflecting the dock lights. He abruptly swung away from them and climbed the iron ladder. The tide was full, so he didn't have far to go.

He was blocked by a blue-uniformed figure at the top.

'Hello,' he said, 'trying to get ashore without searching?'

'Oh,' said Donn, 'is there no place without you?'

'You are not a Spaniard?' the other said in surprise.

'No,' said Donn, 'nine-carat Irish.'

'Let's see your bag,' he said. Donn handed it to him. He followed him over under a light.

'Brandy, tobacco, wine, cigarettes?' he asked.

'No,' said Donn.

'Most unusual,' he said, squeezing the bag expertly. 'No solids in here anyhow. Have you a passport?'

'Yes,' said Donn, taking it from his hip pocket. It was well tattered.

The man glanced at it, whistled as he ruffled through the pages. 'It's nearly stamped to death,' he said. 'You have been around.'

'I have been around,' Donn agreed.

'Most unusual,' he said, 'but I suppose it's all right, otherwise you'd have to see the police. Are you from here, or where?'

'From near here,' said Donn.

'All right,' he said, looking at him curiously. He had to look up at him, a big fellow with unshaven face, thick brown hair, wearing a sailor's jersey. He wondered about him. There was no clue in his face. He went to the side then and, bending, shouted down 'Hola, Manuel, and what are you trying to smuggle this time?'

Manuel shouted something up at him in Spanish and he laughed, and Donn shouldered his duffle bag and walked away.

Home is the sailor, home from the sea, he thought. No flags out. The docks were deserted. One small ship had been unloading fertilizer. He could smell it as he passed, his boots were powdered by it as he walked the quay. No bands playing *Here the Conquering Hero Comes*. He was a hero, he thought, grinning wryly. He had medals to prove it. But then they were foreign medals which would cause no wonder at home. If he told them they would just say: Ah, so, and tell me did you hear that Bartley Folan lost a sow in 1939, the year of the war?

At the end of the docks, he paused indecisively. If he wanted now he could go home, at once. It wasn't that far. He could hire a hackney or if it went to that he could walk it. He would be there before the dawn. Now that he could do it, he didn't want to. It would take a bit of thinking out.

So he turned left and went up one street and into another one and turned out of that and mounted the broad stone steps into the hotel. There was only one young girl with fair hair at the reception desk.

'I want a room,' he said, and she raised her head, and having seen him couldn't hide the disquiet that came into her eyes.

'I can pay for it, in advance if necessary. Does my appearance shock you?'

Now she was confused.

'Oh, no, sir! No, sir!' she said, looking around, hoping that somebody in authority might appear.

'You just imagine me shaved, and washed and wearing a collar and tie,' he said, leaning on the counter, 'and you'd be writing me fan-mail.'

She was very young. She thought over what he had said, and then she giggled.

'So?' he asked.

'Yes, sir,' she said, giving him the book to sign. She watched him as he signed it. His face was bronzed. In April? He had very regular features. For her he was very old, over thirty, she imagined, but he was interesting. She giggled again, and then rang a bell.

'You'll have to stop giggling,' he said. 'You will never make a cool receptionist. You must be slightly stern, with a little condescension, a touch of hauteur, crushing insolence with a glance.'

She blushed. So they still do that, he thought.

'I am joking,' he said.

There was a little uniformed fellow beside him. He was looking from the duffle bag to the big man, with his mouth open.

'Will you be able to carry that?' Donn asked.

'Why the hell wouldn't I? I mean yes, sir,' he said, lifting it in his arms.

Donn laughed. 'On our way,' he said.

The little fellow was too young to quell his curiosity.

'Are you off a ship?' he asked.

'Yes,' said Donn, 'a submarine that got wrecked off the coast. I'm the only survivor.'

'Go on,' he said, 'do you think I'm a kid, or what?'

'What makes you doubt my story?' Donn asked.

'Arrah, we'd ha' heard about it,' he said. 'Did you really come off a ship?'

'Can't you smell?' Donn asked. They were in close proximity in the lift. The little fellow used his nose, actively.

'Fish,' he said.

'Well, there you are,' said Donn.

'A bloody oul trawler,' he said. 'I knew there was no submarines.'

'Ah, but you were hoping there was,' said Donn.

'I'm not an oul eejit,' he said, scornfully. 'Submarine, me eye!'

'You are growing old too young,' said Donn.

But the half-crown pleased him and he grunted thanks as he closed the door.

Donn sat on the edge of the bed. He had been in many hotel rooms. They were as impersonal as an undertaker's. He wondered why he had come. He thought of the Spanish fishermen, and how attached to them he had become. He thought of many other people to whom he had become attached. Why? Looking for somebody close, clinging to them because they could never become really personal. A father was a father whatever kind of a father, a mother was a mother, a home was a home and, this was the thought that disturbed him more acutely, a wife was a wife – or was she?

He started to strip. Now he could smell the fish himself off his clothes. He shaved the bristles off his face, painfully, and he washed himself in the bath, and as he dried himself in the steamed-up room he saw himself in the mirror. He looked at his big body briefly. It was carved with the machine-gun bullet that had ploughed down his chest and the knife wound that had skittered along his left rib cage. Not pretty. They made him feel old and scarred. What had he learned from them? That it was good to be alive? What was good about it? That was what he had set out to see. He was impervious to sentiment, he thought, and what was this but sentiment that was bringing him home?

But he didn't have to go home.

He kept this thought in his mind. He dressed himself in the white shirt, tie, and the lightweight suit, and the shoes. He piled the other, fishy, clothes in the bag. They would have to be cleaned, some time somewhere.

He paused at the desk in his glory and waited until he had attracted the girl's eyes.

'Well?' he asked, turning for her inspection.

She blushed again, he noticed, but she was more courageous now.

'You're gorgeous,' she said, smiling, and then put her small hands in front of her mouth to stop a giggle.

'Never judge the book by the cover,' he said, laughing, and went into the dining-room.

His dilemma was with him as he ate. He didn't notice the other diners. It was with him when he went into the bar and drank. This didn't solve it for him. It was with him when he went to his room and looked out at the star-studded sky. It was with him when he slept. It was with him during the night when he awoke, and thought over it, and had to smoke several cigarettes before he could sleep again. The trouble is that I have cut myself so completely off, he thought. Body and soul. You don't do a thing like I did then stroll back and say: Well, I'm home! What a situation. What would be the reaction? He sweated as he thought about it.

Finally, he thought. I will leave it until the morning, and then it will be the train or the road.

Two

He stood halfway between the station and the bus.

He couldn't make up his mind. He was in a state of anger with his own indecision. On each side of him there were people running for the train and people running for the buses.

He said: Make up your mind, stupid.

Why had he come this far just to turn around and go away again? He went suddenly and swung on to the bus. It wasn't filled. He threw his bag on an empty seat. He felt better. He let the tension drain out of his body. He wiped sweat off his eyebrows with his forefinger. Just shows you. It was a pleasant morning. There were shafts of sunlight shining through white fleecy clouds. His clothes were light.

The conductor pressed a bell and they moved slowly from their stand and into the town.

He sat back. I am committed now, he thought. He put his head back and closed his eyes. It was an old bus. It rattled. There was no heat. They went down through the town, stopped to pick up two more passengers, which made three in all and himself. They stopped once more and then they were out of the town and into the countryside.

He tried to keep his mind a blank. He didn't want to think. All the places he passed had associations for him. He didn't want to think about them.

He paid his few shillings.

The conductor talked as he pinged his ticket on the little machine he wore.

'Tourist?' he asked.

'Native,' said Donn.

'Home on a holiday?' he asked.

Donn grunted.

He passed on.

The fields looked good. They were wearing the new green of spring. The turned earth of the ploughed fields looked fresh and wholesome. The lakes were reflecting the blue of the clear sky. So what? Everywhere you went there were green fields and blue skies with lakes reflecting the sky. He had seen skies that were limitless on the great plains; lakes that were like inland seas. You couldn't see the shores of them, and fields of wheat where twenty combine-harvesters would be lost in their vastness.

He craned his head to try to see where the mountains began. He could get glimpses of them as the road started to wind. The bus was very bumpy. Every imperfection of the road jolted his body. It was like a very aged man.

Even the gentle greening bushes were familiar to him. They were just a little larger, he supposed. The blackthorn bushes were white with blossoms.

Imperceptibly the bus started to climb and he could feel it in his thighs. How many times had he cycled this road, sometimes at three o'clock in the morning home from dances in the big town.

They stopped in a street town. The conductor got down to deliver bags and newspapers. He knew every shop in the place. There were four of them. There seemed to be no people he could see, or who might recognize him.

Several miles later the bus stopped again. He got his bag and stepped on to the road. He paused for a few seconds, then hoisted the bag to his shoulder, walked from the tarmac to the dirt road that set off into the hills, and didn't look back.

Big surly bastard, the conductor thought as he pressed the bell.

The road was well pot-holed. The pot-holes were filled with water. The rain of last night had not yet time to soak away. The road rose ahead of him in a series of lazy inclines. There were a few houses near the roadside. The front doors were closed and smoke rose from the chimneys. He saw no people, but he was sure he wasn't passing unknownst to them. They would speculate about him, talk about him. He was an odd figure to see on the road of an early April morning but still only a dog came over a wall and barked at him. Like all sheep dogs he was barking with his mouth and wagging his tail at the same time.

He was soon clear of the houses and the green fields until

on each side of him there were only the bogs stretching away towards the hills, and beyond these were more hills. The boglands were broken up by outcrops of giant granite boulders.

It was a very bleak land and yet it was attractive. His eyes were adjusting to its oddness. He knew that in another four miles the road would cut to the right, towards the ever-rising hills, and there he would walk the road into his own place, about another four miles where it seemed to the eye that no road had a right to be. He became impatient to get there and stepped up his pace.

What was the quality that made up the desire for your own place, he wondered? He had met men weeping into their beer on three continents who were crying because they were separated from their own place. They had the opportunity and the means to go back, but they didn't. Maybe because they knew they would be disillusioned, that the place of their dreams did not exist, or couldn't possibly come up to their dreams. Some of them had gone back, been shattered by the difference between the dream and the reality, and had come away, blotting out the reality and holding fast to their dreams, which they added to and built upon so that they could have no place upon the earth.

He wouldn't be this way. He knew what to expect. He hadn't wanted to come home anyhow. He had been driven, for some strange reason. Of course there was a reason, but his mind shied away from it. He would be an alien plant in this place, he thought. He had travelled so far and experienced so much, that there would be no hope of him setting down his roots. This was sad. He had never had roots, since he left anyhow. From place to place, country to country, working until he was bored and moving on, finding it all dull after the fighting had ceased, feeling too old after a time to take any part in the unceasing small wars. This was the way some men were meant to be, wanderers, dissatisfied. This would be only another experiment. He knew what its outcome would be already. The only smidgeon of philosophy he had garnered from the years was that men were the same everywhere, whatever their colour or breed. And that wasn't a very startling revelation. He could have stayed home and sat on a rock all his life and worked that out without moving a foot.

So he allowed himself to become a little excited as he turned off on his own road. It was a very bad road. It wasn't public, so the people had to look after it themselves. Once a year they would open up the coarse gravel pit and bring out the horse and cart belonging to Jack Tumelty and throw a few loads in the pot-holes and clear the drain on each side of a year's collection of rushes and scum and silt.

It rose inexorably and it wound execrably. It had originally been a sheep track, widened by the feet of men, and when it had been made into a road, it had to follow the hard ground between the soft bogland, or it would have been swallowed up in no time.

His mind brought every inch of it back to his knowledge. Here and there on either side of the road were fertile round hills like the breasts of a woman. Here there was green grass and the very same sheep and cattle that had been there when he left seemed to be there now, raising their heads to look at him. The strange streams came tumbling down from the hills, gouging their way over the granite beds of the streams, making little impression after thousands of years, and when in a mile's time he had cleared one hill and looked down into the shallow valley he could see the water of the first small lake on his left, the first of many that ran to the sea like beads of a rosary.

One mile more and he walked the last of the hills. Here there was a gap between two giant clusters of rock – a marvellous place for an ambush, his mind told him – and from here the road descended into the Mountain.

He was breathing hard. He was sweating. He took a cigarette from his pocket and sat on his bag with his back to a rock and looked down at it.

It was a perfect saucer. The hills facing him were higher than the one he sat on. It blocked off the view of the sea. The hills rose all around the valley in an almost perfect round. The chain of lakes on his left had a river that pierced the hills in its journey to the sea, but you couldn't see it from here. He thought that if you put a bronze door in the gap where he sat you could close out the whole world for ever. The hills across from him were ten miles away. About three-quarters of the whole valley was made up of bogland, heather and sedge growing thickly, making a good bed for the grouse. The valley floor was dotted with the houses and the fields, each a sort of green fortress in the brown bogs, land that had been made green over hundreds of years by toil and sweat. He wondered how many skeletons had gone to the making of the green fields. And each green hill was crowned with a thatched cottage, its whitewash almost blinding in the April sunshine. Most of them had trees backing the house. He thought of the west wind that came sweeping down the hills in the winter-time. The road went through the valley like a white thread. He looked at the houses. There were about thirty of them, and experimentally he tried to name them. He was halting at first, but then they all came out. He had associations with every one of them.

Great God, he thought, it hasn't changed at all!

Outside, the whole world was feverishly renewing itself, tearing down, building up. He had even noticed coming in the bus that many thatched cottages had disappeared, and that tiled cottages had taken their place, with electricity poles crossing the fields with ignorant arrogance. Oh, but not here, not in the Mountain. There was absolutely no change, no change at all.

He remembered his father's boasting. Hundred of years ago, in the flight from Cromwell, Donnshleibhe had come from the north down here with all his people. By some sort of conniving he had purchased this valley, and through thick and thin had retained it for his descendants and had only lost it early in this century when cold-blooded civil servants had taken it from them at two shillings an acre and invested it in the tenants. That was when the Donnshleibhe had to become a merchant in order to survive the new order. An arrogant merchant, he thought, as a picture of his father came into his mind.

It sobered him.

I must go down, he thought, rising to his feet. He couldn't see his own house. The sight of it was blocked by the belt of trees, but he could see the fat belly of the blue lake on the edge of which it was built.

It was beginning to amaze him that he was seeing no people.

They might be on the bogs cutting turf, of course. Few of the cottages were built near the road. They were all set back from it and their neighbours, fiercely independent. He thought of Spain, where the villages were one place and the fields another place, and in the mornings you would see the people driving in the cars to the far-away fields or walking with implements on their shoulders, and coming home in the evenings tired, but with their eyes directed at the cluster of cottages where they lived. Not here! They wouldn't have anything like that. If there was a mountain for each of them they would have built on it.

The first person he saw was a girl.

At this twist of the road, there was a mountain stream on his right that came battering its way down, making white lace in a ten-foot fall before it was swallowed by a gullet under the road. On each side of the stream the grass was very green, and daisies were plentiful. Here, this girl was kneeling and collecting daisies.

He stopped to look at her.

She was splitting the stem of a daisy with a pin and then she would pull the stem of another daisy through the split. She was very intent on this and she was humming. Already she had a daisy-chain around her neck. He thought she was too big to be making daisy-chains.

'Hello,' he said.

It seemed to take a little time for his voice to penetrate to her mind. Then she looked up, and when she saw him, she stood up. She would be about fourteen or fifteen, he thought, but she was very well developed. She was in her bare feet. She wore a dress with white dots, a blue dress. Also a cardigan. Her hair was brown with golden glints in it. It was long hair falling down her back. She had regular features that were somehow hauntingly familiar.

'Who are you, now?' he asked.

She put her head on one side as if to hear better.

'I asked, who are you?' he repeated.

'Nan,' she said. 'I am Nan.'

'Yes,' he said, 'but Nan who?' – running over the features of the people in his mind. She would have been born after he had left. It was an intriguing exercise to pin a father's face on her.

She came towards him.

'You would like the flowers?' she asked. She took the chain from around her neck and held it out towards him. Now he could look into her eyes and he saw that the intelligence in them was not the intelligence of her age. This girl is afflicted, he thought, and this is a terrible tragedy. She was very handsome.

'Thank you,' he said, taking the chain.

'Will you put it on?' she asked.

'Yes,' he said. He dropped his bag on the ground and put the chain around his neck.

'I don't hurt the flowers?' she said. It was a question.

'How?' he asked.

'When I stick the pin in them?'

'No,' he said. 'You do not hurt them.'

'I do not,' she said. She shook her head in agreement. 'Are you going to see Mammy?'

'Who is Mammy?' he asked.

She laughed at his ignorance.

'Why, Nan's Mammy, of course,' she said. She laughed.

'Yes,' he said.

'I can't come now,' she said. 'I have to make the daisy-chain, of course, another one, haven't I?'

'You have,' he said.

'So I will come later on,' she said, walking back again, kneeling down and taking up her task. The waterfall was above her. The sun caught it and made a rainbow for a few seconds around the falling water. The girl seemed to be in the middle of the rainbow. She was humming again. In the sky a climbing bog-lark was singing. It was an odd scene, unreal. He shook his head, blinked his eyes. It was like being welcomed to the valley by a beautiful girl who didn't exist.

He picked up his bag and walked on. He wondered who she could be. He paused to look back once and she had raised her head. He waved at her and after a pause she raised a hand, and moved it up and down in the action of a child who waves Day-Day to you.

He went on.

Away off on his right he could see people up at the turf banks, small figures resting from their labours to look down on him. They were too far away for recognition, so he kept going. He was wondering what kind of reception he would get from the people themselves. What would the passing of the years have meant to them? Would his going the way he did have faded from memory like the ink on paper that is left out in the weather?

He shrugged. It didn't matter. He was gone long past caring what people thought.

He paused again when he turned down the road at the end of which the house lay. Behind it he could see the sheen on the water of the lake, a small tidy lake with last year's rushes rustling in the slight movement of the air. That's all it was. There was no wind.

There were some bicycles heaped up outside the wall. He wondered why this should be. It wasn't a special day.

He felt a repugnance now about going in. He had to steel himself to the effort it would require. He hadn't come this far to boggle at the last few feet. He walked towards the doorway. There was a sort of porch and inside that the two glass doors guarded by brass rails across them which would open at a push. He pushed and went in. The shop was crowded. There were many men and women there. It was hard to see their faces in the fug of tobacco smoke. They hadn't been talking loudly. This was surprising. All their eyes were turned to him at the opening of the door. He didn't look at them. There was a young man behind the counter with a white apron on him. It was dirty. Donn went to the counter, lifted the flap and walked through to the door behind. The young man was looking at him with his mouth open. He could feel the silence of the people.

Then he was in the big kitchen. There was a young girl at the big table, kneading dough. She looked up and when she saw him her mouth opened too. He could feel the heat from the big range in the great open chimney. The range was new, his mind registered, as he opened another door on the left. This went into the parlour. The last time he had seen it, he had been looking in the window from the rain outside.

It was well filled now with people, mostly old ladies, some of them running rosary beads through their fingers. They looked at him in amazement. He searched their faces. She wasn't there.

He walked past them to the door that led into the passage. This was a narrow passage on the right. He closed the door after him, shutting off the buzzing of sudden talk. There were two doors now. The first one was the big bedroom of his father, the one at the end where he used to sleep.

He opened the door on his left and went in.

The curtains were drawn. There was not much light. He looked at the big brass-railed bed. His father was lying on it, his mouth open, the breathing coming hard from his throat. The white quilt was pulled up to his chin. There were two candles burning in brass candlesticks on a small table, which held a crucifix, a white jug.

On the other side of the bed a woman was kneeling. She was praying. His abrupt entrance startled her. She raised her head, and slowly came to her feet.

Her features were shaded by the dim light, but he knew her. It was she.

They stared at one another.

She spoke first.

'Your father is dying,' she said. 'Who told you?'

'Nobody,' he said. 'Nobody at all.'

Three

HE KNEW his father was dying. He had seen a lot of dying men in his time. He noticed that his hair was still thick right down to the broad forehead. There were still a few streaks of fading brown in its whiteness. The sunken cheeks emphasized the Asiatic-looking flat cheekbones and the big jaws.

'He has cancer,' he heard her say. 'He is in a coma. He won't come out of it.'

He wondered that he had come home at this time, the compulsion that was on him each time he had resisted. But what good was it? What would they have talked about anyhow? They had never been able to talk to one another.

'He always said you would come back,' he heard her say, 'before he died.'

Her voice wasn't filled with enthusiasm. She was just passing on a message she thought he should know. He was aware of this.

'Where is my mother?' he asked.

'She died six years ago,' she said.

'Why didn't I come back before she died?' he asked.

She didn't answer him.

They heard the sound of a car coming up the road and stopping. They listened. There was silence in the room, so that the laboured breathing of the dying man was very audible. Donn thought: He is young enough to die. He is not sixty. He heard the opening of the doors and the feet in the passage and then the bedroom door opened and a young priest came in. He was a medium-sized young man with fair hair and thin features. He came over to the bed and bent over to look.

'I will give him Extreme Unction,' he said. Two ladies had come into the room after him. They knelt on the floor. As Donn turned to go out, more of them came and went into the room. They were filling the passage. He didn't look at them. He went through into the kitchen and crossed it and opened the door

27

into the big storeroom where they had celebrated his wedding. The windows were dusty, but there was good light in it. Shafts of sunlight were pitting it with a million motes. He sat on a tea-chest. He could see the rim of the hills outside stretching half-way up the window, and over them the blue sky with piercingly white clouds ambling across, like fat bubbles.

He heard her light footsteps coming in behind him, the opening and closing of the door.

'Why did you go?' he heard her asking.

'They were compelling me,' he said. 'It was nothing to do with you. I was here in this room, and I felt them squeezing me. What was love, did I know? Was I an animal? Just that. I had no practice in love. My mother was a vague pious dream. Never made contact with her. Treated like a doll for her when small, then grown-up, grown past the dolly stage for her. Too big. Too difficult. Just get rid of him like an overgrown dog, a little puppy that turns out to be an Irish wolfhound. Send him off to school. Give him goodies. Give him everything but never love. What did I know about it.'

'Your mother wasn't quite normal,' he heard her say.

'She wasn't feeble-minded,' he said.

'I wasn't asking why you went then,' she said. 'I was asking why you left your father now.'

He turned on the chest to look at her. She was over near the door. It was the first good look he got of her.

Her face had been thinner than it was now. He remembered with a catch in his stomach how in the darkness he had often traced it with his fingertips. Now her face had filled out. She had an Irish face, long and proportioned, creamy-coloured skin framed by the black hair.

Her eyes met his probing gaze indifferently.

'I got nothing from him,' he said, 'except scorn and the back of the hand across the face. Only his opinion counted: you will do this. You will do that. Even at that school, when all the others had their parents calling with parcels of food and things, did he ever come? I might have been a bastard for all I saw of him.'

'You are a grown man now,' she said. 'Why are you talking as if you were still a child?'

28

It shocked him. It was true for her, but he wanted to make it plain. He knew he wasn't a child.

'Unless I am feeble-minded too,' he said, showing his teeth. It didn't affect her. 'I have been away a long time. I have seen and done many things that should have blotted out all this, made me indifferent to it. It hasn't. The boy is father to the man. I have been asking why, why, in the strangest places. But about you and what I did to you, I am speaking. Other things I don't mind, just to try and understand. I know now after a long time, that what I felt for you was love, not lust, not romping. But they were making me do this thing, holding a false moral gun up to my head, and I couldn't do it. I had to go.'

'It's so long ago,' she said. 'It is in the past. It's what's happening now at this moment that's important. Your father is dying.'

'I feel nothing,' he said. 'I have seen many men dying. He could be just another one of them.'

'It's just in case his eyes would open, for a few seconds,' she said, 'and they would rest on you. He was a good man. It would be a joy to him to see you. He would die and say, I told you he would come back.'

He walked away to the window.

She was speaking to him as if he was a stranger, or as if she was a social worker on a visit. His eyes were caught now, by the sight of the girl on the street in front of the house. It was Nan, the daisy-chain girl. She had a chain in each hand and was hopping on the road, the hair fallen around her face. She was moving her lips.

'Come here,' he said.

He waited until he felt her standing beside him.

'Who is she?' he asked.

'She is Nan,' she said. 'She is my daughter.'

He sucked in his breath.

'So you are Nan's Mammy?' he asked.

'Yes,' she said. 'I am Nan's Mammy.'

He thought of the implications. He was shocked.

'Could I meet her?' he asked.

He felt her hesitation, or was it distaste? Then she walked away from him and opened the door out into the street. He saw her coming into the road and approaching the girl. She called. He saw the girl's head raising and looking, and saw the recognition coming into her eyes, and her face lighting up. She ran to her mother and put her arms around her neck. She was laughing. She was nearly as tall as her mother. He saw the warmth in the face of Meela, not the cold face that had been presented to himself. Nan put the two daisy-chains around her mother's neck and they walked towards the door with their arms around each other's waists.

He turned from the window and faced the door. The light was falling on him, and on the daisy-chain around his own neck. He fingered it now. Already the flowers were wilting. It's not a flower after all, he thought, only a weed.

When they came in, the girl saw him. He saw her put her head on one side, puzzled, drawing the memory of him from her mind slowly.

'Oh,' she said.

'You gave me the daisy-chain,' he said.

'Oh,' she said coming towards him. 'The flowers are dying. I will get you another.'

'Yes,' he said.

'Nan,' said her mother. 'You didn't know. This is your daddy.'

She found it hard to say that, he saw, but she said it. She had been reared in a real school, he thought.

He saw Nan struggling with the thought. What is this she said. A daddy? Eh? What's a daddy? I never saw him before. What does this mean? She was puzzled.

'You are my daddy?' she asked.

'I am,' he said, seeing himself in her face and her body. How stupid he had been not to have recognized her down the road. Hauntingly familiar. So well she might be.

He wondered how her mind would react, what she would do. She was thinking over this new thing that had been presented to her.

She held out her hand.

'I'm pleased to meet you,' she said, like a child taking refuge from puzzlement in politeness. He took her hand in his own big one.

30

'And I am very pleased to meet you,' he said. He had often wondered about this. Whether a boy; whether a girl? What resentment would have been built up over the years? How (if he ever went back, which wasn't likely) he would get on terms with his son or daughter? Well, it wouldn't be as hard as he thought. He was dealing with a child. His mind was bursting with revolt at the moment. But it was true and real, and it would have to be faced.

He looked over her head at Meela. Her eyes were inscrutable. How much she had to go through, he thought. His leaving, and this beautiful girl, watching her grow. When did she find out that she was retarded? Was it soon or over a long period? She looked after his mother, and saw her die. And she looked after his father as he was dying, and suffered his dominating personality, no doubt.

No wonder her eyes could look at him so indifferently.

'Soon you will get to know me,' he said to Nan. 'We will play, eh?'

'We will play,' she said. 'Lots of things. I never had a daddy.'

'You have one now,' he said. Then he said to Meela. 'I will go back and watch with my father.'

He left them, thinking, All right; I will sit with him until he goes. It won't do any good. His eyes won't open to light on me. Things don't happen as pat as that.

Four

YOU CAN enjoy a funeral.

People in remote places live their lives equably. Mostly it is very tranquil without being boring, but life is highlighted by incidents like a row, or a wedding, or a funeral or a lunatic going away to an asylum. So everybody downs tools and takes the day off for a funeral. They dress in their best clothes, take out the ass and cart or the bicycle and go down to the Chapel of Ease where the Dead Mass will be said.

Besides they were curious.

They had seen very little of the returned son. Long ago bodies were left in the houses for days, so that they could be waked, and many unseemly incidents had occurred. Not now. They whipped the body off to the chapel as soon as possible, and there wasn't the same zest in the waking without a body present.

Or without the son present.

As soon as his father died he took off to the hills. They had seen him go. They weren't surprised. Any man who would do what he had done on the night of his wedding in nineteen and thirty-nine would do anything. He reached the crest of the far hills where he could see the sea and he sat with his back to the valley. He had nothing in his stomach either, Bridgie in the kitchen told them.

When the hearse was pulling away from the house, he came from behind the lake and walked behind it, his hands behind his back and his face bent and stern. He'd made a fine man, they said, but odd. They were chary of approaching him. He watched impassively as the coffin was carried into the church, but he didn't go in. He turned around and he walked back again the way he had come. When the hired car with herself and the child in it caught up with him, he got in with them and they drove home.

That night when the people went to the place for a wake, they didn't see him either. He was away off somewhere. This put a bit of a damper on the proceedings, but it added a bit of food for curiosity as well and not a little resentment.

Only one incident was reported to them that gave rise to much comment afterwards even if they didn't understand it. Bridgie again overheard the conversation between the two of them.

She said: Where do you want to sleep?

He said: I'll sleep in my father's room.

They all knew that Meela herself had a room beyond the Father's and over on the other side there was a room for the child and the maid Bridgie.

She was surprised, Bridgie said. In there? she heard.

Why not? he said, what's wrong with it, I one time shared a hole with two dead men and I slept.

Now this was surprising. Would you do it? They knew that the old man and he had never got on. The proof of it was his going away like he did, but would you sleep in a bed cold from your father's corpse? Not when there's a woman like Meela around, one said salaciously, and he was hushed, because that wasn't respectable.

But he was in the church for the Mass. Without beads or book, he knelt beside Meela and watched what went on, but it was afterwards at the altar collection outside the church door that he surprised them. You know the custom. After the Mass a table and a plate is put up outside the door, before the coffin is brought out for burial, and everyone goes up and says I'm sorry for your trouble and throws a halfcrown on the plate.

Now what surprised them here was that he was glad to see them and shake their hands, and they warmed to him.

He was surprised himself. It was like as if he had been asleep and woke up. As if for many years he had been dealing with people in a dream, unreal, distant, and suddenly he was awake and looking at real people, whose faces were emerging from the past, and they were real, and he could see and recognize the colour of their eyes and the shape of their features.

'Very sorry for your trouble, Donn, and glad to see you home.'

'Thanks, Tom.' A firm handclasp from Tom McNulty, who never wore headgear, a shock of white wiry hair and a grey moustache clipped close, deep lines on his face, and many laughter wrinkles around his eyes. Always a rebel. He had fought long ago and had been in jail many times. He was a republican in the civil war and when a priest refused to give him Holy Communion he stopped going to Mass. Donn remembered this. It was the wonder of his youth, a man who wasn't going to Mass.

'Your father is a loss,' said Tom. 'We need somebody like you up there, Donn. Stop the rot.'

Donn didn't quite know what he was talking about, but his sorrow was sincere.

Like Jack Tumelty of the horse and cart.

'Sorry for your trouble. It's great to see you home again.' A burly man with a big stomach over which he couldn't button the coat of his blue suit, and his son Dino, a stocky young man with black hair, sidelocks, a big chest, flat Asiatic cheekbones and big jaws with strong white teeth.

'You were a child when I saw you,' said Donn. 'But I recognize you.' He was pleased with this recognition.

'Why not?' said his father. 'Isn't the boy father to the man?'

Mrs McNulty, a tall woman with white hair and a thin face with deep sunken eyes. Her eyes were red, he was surprised to see.

'We'll miss your father, Donn,' she said. 'He did a great deal for us. More than most people know.'

Mrs Tumelty too was red-eyed. This was surprising him. He told himself that this big fat woman was soft. She would cry over anything – but she seemed sincere.

'He's a great loss,' she said. 'He was a good man. You'll never be as good as him if you lived to be a hundred.'

Bartley Folan, dressed uncompromisingly in a black floppy hat, a bainin coat, a flannel shirt, ceann easna trousers with heavy black boots and thick hair on his cheekbones, which he did not shave.

'Only God knows,' said Bartley, 'how good he was to people. God and the books. Look at them. The whole place is glad to see you home.'

Bartley was a bachelor. He lived in a house at the extreme end of the arable land. People said, particularly the women, that he should have been dead years ago from eating his own cooking,

34

but Donn remembered having admired him when he visited. The house had two rooms, a kitchen and a bedroom, and when they were young Bartley would let them cut the tobacco from the plug and fill the pipe and light it for him. He suddenly saw the place now, with a cheerful turf fire in the open hearth and the crusted pot oven cake he had baked resting on the window near a geranium pot to cool. The women said it was a wonder that Bartley's dough didn't twist his guts, but this was probably because Bartley wouldn't let one of them into the house. He thought women were bad luck. He made poteen for the area in the holiday seasons. Donn wondered if he was still at it.

They all came and shook his hand. Their feelings of sorrow were genuine, he saw with surprise, and their handclasps were firm and welcoming. He couldn't equate their good words about his father with his own remembrance of him. If you want to know me come and live with me, he thought cynically, but this wasn't sufficient either.

It was the dawning knowledge that he belonged to a society that was making him think. He was born into it. People there remembered him as a small boy, as a youth, as a student going off to school, as a young man going to the University, as a married man, and then no more. For them the rest of his life until now was a blank.

As he walked behind the hearse to the graveyard, he thought over this. It seemed to him now that his life since was a blank too. He found it hard to cull into his memory the people with whom he had lived and loved and fought ever since. They were like cut-outs. He had worked at many jobs, in many countries. He didn't remember being nostalgic about what he had left behind, or the people, or that they had meant anything at all to him. And yet at times he would find himself thinking of little incidents that had happened at various times in connexion with them, unsophisticated things that if related would just draw blank looks from the people he was with at the time. Does a person have to belong to a community, he wondered? If you don't, are you a misfit, a wild pony, a black sheep? Is this the reason for the Irishman you would meet abroad – rebels without causes, just rebels, wandering, uneasy, nostalgic, vitriolic, because they didn't want to belong to anybody.

He was surprised to find that, the prayers over, they were filling in his father's grave. He thought he should be capable of showing some emotion, but his feelings were just normal. He wondered if he was abnormal. He tried to make himself feel young and his father was playing with him. He couldn't remember. All he remembered was gruffness, indifference and the back of the hand across the face. Why? Had he been an ugly child? Was it because his father was incapable of showing love and affection? Surely you would know then that gruffness was only a camouflage?

He saw Meela looking at him. She was on the other side. She was dressed in a black coat and hat. Her hands were clasped in front of her, holding the rosary beads from which they had recited the decade for the repose of the soul of his father. He couldn't remember if he had even moved his lips in the responses. He felt he hadn't.

Her face was pale and her eyes were red and the tip of her nose. She was a very handsome woman. He thought that she had been in his mind a lot all the time. He had never forgotten her. When she was puzzled a single crease appeared between her eyebrows. It was there now, and her head a little on one side as she looked at him. This was the way Nan looked too when she was puzzled. They were very alike, he thought, the only difference being the sharp intelligence that looked at him from Meela's eyes.

Well, he couldn't help her. He couldn't simulate what he didn't feel.

On the way out he saw this woman looking at him, a bit diffident to approach him.

He went over to her.

'Well, Jill Grealish,' he said. 'How is your leg?'

He saw her eyes widening. Then she put up her hand to cover her mouth, and she laughed.

'Imagine you remembering that!' she said.

'How are you?' shaking her hand. She was his first love. Coming back one evening over the fields she had jagged the inside of her leg above the knee on barbed wire. He had spent many fond moments repairing the small gash.

36

'Have you still got the scar?' he asked.

'I have,' she said, 'and a husband as well. Here, you know Seamus?'

He looked at the sandy-haired man with her who was grinning at him.

'Seamus Mooney!' he said, shaking hands. 'Did you get Jill?'

'I did, God help me,' said Seamus.

This amused the three of them. They laughed. And then as if simultaneously they realized that standing in the graveyard at the burial of Donn's father was not the place, they stopped laughing.

It was then the young priest came over to Donn. He was the one who had come to anoint his father.

He held out his hand.

'There's not much point in offering sympathy,' he said.

He meant it as a sort of gentle joke maybe, but it chilled Donn. He took his hand and dropped it fast. He looked at the pale-blue eyes. He felt antagonism from the young man.

'It depends on the sincerity of the offerer,' said Donn.

'I mean I didn't know you,' said the priest. 'I'm Father Murphy. I had never met you.'

'It would be hard for you,' said Donn.

There was an awkward silence.

'Well, God bless you,' the priest said then, and went on.

'We shouldn't have been laughing,' said Jill.

'There's not enough laughter,' said Donn.

'There's a time and a place for everything,' said Meela.

'Are you a prude too?' Donn asked, watching her flushing.

'Come and see us, Donn,' said Seamus. 'We'll talk of old times, eh?'

'Shows you we are getting old,' said Donn, 'when we want to talk of old times.'

'We are all glad you are home,' said Jill. 'We must go now and say a prayer for my mother.'

'She is dead?' Donn asked. Jill nodded. 'She had a lot of laughter in her,' he said then, remembering. 'She was a gay one.'

'Like the daughter,' said Seamus.

Donn left them, hurried to catch up with Meela, who had walked on. They got into the back seat of the hired car. Joe Toake was driving it. He was bunched up at the wheel. He was coughing a lot. He had a cigarette in his mouth. Never without one. The car set off. There was silence between them. She was sitting far away from him.

'You think I was disrespectful?' he asked.

'No,' she said. 'You were just yourself.'

'Do you expect me to pretend to something I do not feel?' he asked.

'I expect nothing at all from you,' she said.

After that there was just the sound of the engine, the tyres on the tarmac and Joe's coughing.

They sat in the parlour that evening. There was a turf fire burning brightly; the paraffin vapour lamp hanging from the ceiling was gently hissing.

Donn was sitting on one side and watching Meela, who was sitting opposite him stitching at something white. Her fingers were long and slender and very quick and competent with the needle. Between them Nan was sitting on the floor, her knees spread out so that her dress made a basin to hold a lot of coloured beads. She was threading these on a white string with a needle. She was concentrating very heavily on the operations, the tip of her tongue between her teeth.

He thought: Suppose you were a stranger and walked in here and were confronted with the scene, wouldn't you think you were looking at a picture of domestic bliss – husband, wife and daughter softly illuminated by the firelight. Like a set piece for a soap advertisement. He wondered how many million similar scenes were as false.

Nan was wary of him. Like a child he had to win her approval. It couldn't be gained by packets of sweets or toys. Instead of the slightly cynical teenage eyes, you were looking into the guileless eyes of a child, with all the direct perceptiveness of children, as sharp as the scalpel of a surgeon. This honesty of perception seemed to depart with puberty.

If he held her hand, she would withdraw it seconds later. She was reluctant to come too close to him.

Like her mother. If he went to her now and put his hand on her cheek, she would shrink away from him. He knew this just as if he had actually done it. He closed his eyes and thought back. She was always vivacious then. When they were at the University, he had cut her out from the herd of students when they went up the river on a picnic, six boatloads of them. She was a pious girl, rather a bit prim. She took a lot of breaking down. But that was accomplished, wasn't it, near home too, at a harvest dance in the street town below. So he knew her very well. He was familiar with her. He knew her intimately, didn't he? He had proved it. She was his lawful wife. He wondered what would happen now if he said: you are my wife, let's go to bed. Would piety make her acquiesce, or would she fight? It was difficult to read her. She had a good brain. They had many arguments long ago. Looking at her now, he felt how difficult it would be to get through the shell of indifference she seemed to have built up around herself. But she could blaze. He knew this. But he was doubtful if she would ever blaze again for him. No human being could suffer a hurt as she must have done and a humiliation such as he had presented her with, and not be changed.

To take his mind off this he looked at the pictures on the wall. There were the usual ones, prints of the Stag at Bay and the Angelus, and enlarged prints of old photographs, framed. There was his father, with the high collar and the broad shoulders and the thick hair, a fine virile-looking man, looking off to the left. Beside him a saccharine print of a picture of the Little Flower, and a picture of his mother, hair drawn tight with a split in the middle, a flowered blouse and a cameo brooch at the throat. A buxom woman, with a jolly face and sort of faded eyes. He wondered if Nan took after her, if it was from her that the weakness came. Or was it from himself? Maybe he was retarded himself?

He looked at the mantelpiece. Here there was a clutter of ornaments, Toby jugs and china dogs and small pictures in silver gilt frames, faded ones. He got up to look at them.

There was a wedding group. His mother and father in a phoney studio setting, standing up, his father's arm around her shoulders. She was slimmer then and she was smiling, and somehow she was very pretty. Even in the stiff photograph the joy shone out from her.

Suddenly to his own amazement he felt his eyelids hot, and before he could help himself he started to cry.

What's wrong with me, he wondered. I must be going mad. He couldn't stop this. He remembered warm breaths and tenderness. But when? Early. Who had withdrawn from whom? Was it she from him or he from her? Why hadn't they had any more children? Just himself. There could have been brothers, sisters. Life would have been different. He suddenly saw her the last time. He was looking in the window from the great rain, and she was sitting there, and she was pleased, with all the neighbours around her and his wife Meela. What had she felt when he had gone? He would never know. Surely he should have stopped to say goodbye. What in the name of God was wrong with him now? He was being racked with sentimentality.

He was sitting on the hard horsehair-stuffed chair and he was sobbing.

Meela was looking at him in amazement. His big hands were up clasping his face and his features were screwed up.

Nan looked up from her beads at him. There was tension in the room, the sounds he was making. Meela had never seen a man crying. She was shocked. But she couldn't do anything. Even if she had tried she couldn't have got up from the chair and gone over to him. Her mind was saying: What's this? What's he up to now? Far away the pleasure at the sound of his name, his footsteps outside her father's door, the panting heart waiting to see him come into sight from anywhere, around a corner, into a room, whistling on the road, only faint sounds now, lost in the years, wandering in the air, defying recapture.

Nan got to her knees, the beads rolling all ways over the painted floorboards. She went towards him, walking on her hands and knees. When she got close to him, she bent down under him to look up at his face. He didn't see her, so she got to her knees, and put her two hands on the hands clasping his head.

'Don't cry,' Nan said. 'Don't cry.'

He heard this. He was conscious of her soft hands on his

own. He hadn't expected it. He was bewildered. He freed his hands from his head and took her hands in his own, and she came in on her knees between his knees, close to him, and she put her head on his shoulder, her hair against his face, and she said again: 'Don't cry.'

He was looking at Meela.

'I don't know why,' he said. 'I wish I knew why. I just looked at these photographs. Can you tell me why?'

'She was your mother,' she said.

'I know that,' he said. 'We don't know ourselves at all.' He was patting Nan's hair. 'Why, after all those years? Why did I do what I did?'

'I don't know,' she said, almost shouting.

'Like cutting off lifelines,' he said. 'All you possess. People. Why? I don't know. What have I proved? Can anyone tell me that?'

'Only yourself,' she said.

'I could have fought him,' he said. 'Just hung on and fought him and we could have established a relationship. He wanted people to fight him, didn't he?'

'He liked fights,' she said.

'There were the people today,' he said, 'making you feel that you belonged. You understand? Like you said: Well now if I die there will be somebody to go to my funeral. Like they went to his.'

'They like funerals,' she said. 'It doesn't say because they go to your funeral that they love you.'

'But they go,' he said. 'There is somebody. You were somebody to them. Out there who will go to your funeral? Who will care? Sometimes in the big places men have died and haven't been found until they begin to smell. I know this is true. I have seen it happen.'

He took a handkerchief from his pocket and furiously rubbed his eyes and blew his nose. He was still amazed at this sensation that had welled up from some unknown part of him; he, a grown man, a strong man, who knew all the answers to life and death and had assessed the people of three continents.

'Maybe you are crying for yourself,' she said.

He looked at her. Nan sat now between his knees, holding

on to his hand. He looked down at her. He put his hand on her cheek. She didn't recoil from him. Her skin was soft and velvety. She was looking at him and he felt there was fondness in her eyes.

'Don't cry,' she said.

'No,' he said, 'never again. Just once in life maybe, men cry. Never again. Maybe I am crying for myself, for the lost years. What did I find to make up for the things I lost? I don't know. Experience. Yes. I killed men. That's experience. I can build sewers. I built bridges, boats. I saw the other side of the clouds from the sky, and yet nobody out there said: Glad to see you home. I am sorry for your trouble. When I had no trouble. What trouble did I have? My father died and he could have been a stranger. Was that my fault?'

'You'll have to find the answers yourself,' she said.

'Yes, but where?' he asked. 'Will you tell me where?'

'How can I?' she said. 'You'll have to find the place yourself.'

Five

IT WAS a May morning and he was walking by the side of the mountain stream that emptied the lakes at his back on its way through the gap it had worn for itself in the hills.

He had remembered this gap. He had often come here long ago and fished for the small mountain trout in the pools under the many falls. It was the easiest thing in the world to catch them. When they were too small, like sardines, he would put them back, but if they were nearly half-pound size he would bring them home and have them cooked for his supper.

He had often thought of this. It seemed the epitome of peace. In dangerous situations he had thought about it. The gap was fairly wide, with the banks rising nearly twenty feet on either side, and the floor littered with big boulders that had been gouged out of the sides when the stream was in spate. It could be dangerous then, and many sheep had been caught and drowned in its sudden rise.

Nan was walking ahead of him. She was wearing sandshoes, a cotton dress and a brown cardigan. She could still shock him. There she was now with the body and firm flesh of a full-grown woman. Sometimes he would forget and address an adult remark to her, to be met by the blank gaze and the puzzled look, and he would have to shuffle his thoughts and his speech, amazed at the flood of anger that arose in him. What was the use of anger? Who were you going to use it against? Somebody's genes were at fault. She was getting used to him. She was beginning to have confidence in him. She didn't shrink from him any more since the evening he cried.

He sat on a boulder and lighted a cigarette.

Nan was bending over a pool, fishing in the clear water with her fingers. Soon she would come to him with what she had found and he would express pleasure at whatever it was.

She came. She got on her knees in front of him.

'Look,' she said proudly.

The palm of her long, shapely hand was wet. In it rested a

white quartz pebble, a red sandstone pebble, and a long piece with bits of mica glittering in it. Soon they would dry and lose their vivid colours.

'They are beautiful,' he said.

'Will Nan get more for you?' she asked.

'Yes,' he said, thinking, some day I must bring her to the sea and she can pick shells. She would like all the different shells.

'You mind them,' she said.

'Right,' he said, and took them from her. She went back to the pool. She is part of me, he thought, whatever the circumstances, she is part of me; savouring this intangible relationship.

He smelled smoke, suddenly. Not cigarette smoke, but turf smoke. He wondered about it. Up here they were away from the bogs, where the men would have turf fires lighted to make their tea in the black kettles.

He stood up. The smell of it was coming from his right, he thought. He walked to the butt and climbed the rough wall. At the top he pulled himself over by clutching the tough tufts of heather. He stood on the top and looked. They were high in the hills. The plain stretched away for miles, scooping down to the village, a carpet of heather and bright green sedge. The morning mists still hadn't burned out of some of the hollows. To his left there was a cleft that ran into the gap. It was heavy with mist, but as he looked he thought some of the mist was suspiciously blue. He walked in that direction. There wasn't much wind, but what was blowing was sending the blue smoke in his direction and it became stronger as he approached the cleft. When he reached the lip of it, he stretched himself on the heather and looked over.

It was deep, like a place that had been quarried. The floor was very green and the grass was good in it, obviously a place where sheep sheltered from the west winds and fertilized it in their resting. He looked closely and finally spotted the smoke coming from the far side, rising miraculously from the heather. So he examined the face of the cleft and finally saw what he was looking for, the three big carelessly-laid stones that hid an opening into the side. He remembered it well. It was a cave made by nature out of the place where two great granite rocks had rested against one another, and when flood rain had wiped out the soil in between them, a comfortably large cavern had been left. He had often sheltered in it himself. Now it was being used for more serious business, he saw, grinning. He burrowed down in the heather and waited patiently.

He heard the bog-lark singing. He tried to spot him sheltering in the misty blue sky. He could barely see him, rising and falling, but suddenly up above him again he saw another bird, seeming to be standing still in the air. It was a sparrow-hawk. Oh, you silly lark, he thought, why didn't you look about before you took wing?

At the same time from the gap on his left he heard Nan calling. She was saying 'Shoo! Shoo! Go away! Go away!' and then she had scrambled over the top and stood there waving her arms, shouting: 'Go away! Go away!' She started to run, and she came very near where the smoke was emerging from the ground, calling and shouting. It didn't save the lark, he saw, whose song had ended and who was flying for cover when the hawk dropped. Nan ran forward waving her arms and still calling. He wondered at the perception she had shown, in seeing the lark and the hawk at all.

Her calling had done one thing. It had brought Bartley Folan from inside the cave. The top rock of the three fell and he came out of there and stood on the floor of the cleft looking upwards towards the sound of the girl's voice.

'Hello, Bartley,' said Donn, and he saw his back stiffening as if he had received a blow between the shoulders. Then he slowly turned. It was a little while before he could see Donn's face in the midst of the heather. When he saw and recognized his grinning face, he took the black hat from his head and threw it on the ground and said between his teeth: 'Oh, you brown bastard! May your eyes fall out!'

Donn rose to his knees.

'Why are you cursing me, old man?' he asked. 'I only bid you the time of the day.'

'How did you get here? What are you doing?' Bartley asked, bending down for his hat.

'My daughter and I just came for a walk after breakfast,'

said Donn. 'Presumably you did the same.'

'I wouldn't have come out but I heard the girl's voice,' said Bartley. 'Is she all right?'

'She is,' said Donn. 'She was trying to frighten a hawk.'

'I don't know what she did to the hawk,' said Bartley, 'but she frightened the guts out of me.'

'After all those years?' Donn asked sarcastically.

Bartley climbed slowly up to him and sat beside him on the heather.

'Do you know how many times I have changed my burrows?' he asked.

'No,' said Donn, 'how many?'

'Twenty-two times,' said Bartley, reaching for his pipe. It was a clay pipe. You didn't see many clay pipes nowadays, Donn thought.

'But nobody in the valley would inform on you,' said Donn.

'They would inform on their own mothers,' said Bartley. 'All it wants is a little note without a signature sent to the police station.'

'They wouldn't do that to you,' said Donn.

'Yerra, have sense,' said Bartley. 'Do you think the whole world is saints? People in high places would betray you if you look crooked to them.'

'I smelled the smoke,' said Donn.

'Ah,' said Bartley. 'I was going to move out of here anyhow.'

'There's no need for smoke,' said Donn.

'No need?' said Bartley, 'where there's fire, there's smoke.'

'Have you ever heard of bottled gas?' Donn asked.

Bartley considered this.

'It comes in cylinders,' said Donn. 'Easy enough to transport in the turf basket on a donkey's pannier. Just light it under the still. No smoke.'

Bartley considered this.

'No smoke,' he said. 'But the old ways are the best ways. Would the right tang be left on the drink?'

'It isn't the heat that makes the tang,' said Donn, 'but the ingredients. Right? What goes to make it?'

Bartley considered this.

'I think that's true,' he said. 'But no smoke. The smoke has been the curse of centuries. To be without smoke.'

'I see them cooking on a turf stove below,' said Donn. 'I am going to suggest that they cook on a gas stove. We get bottled gas brought in for the stove. And there you are, bottled gas and no smoke.'

'Ah, well, I never thought of that,' said Bartley. 'It took you to think of a tricky thing like that.'

'If there is no smoke how would you be tracked?' Donn asked.

'You have a bit of the divil in you,' said Bartley. 'It will cost more of course.'

'Prices are going up all the time,' said Donn. 'Sixpence extra on the bottle of stuff and you cover your costs.'

Suddenly Nan was standing on the bank opposite them. She was holding a dead lark in the palm of her hand. She was crying.

'Look,' she said, holding out the dead bird. 'He killed him. I screamed at him. He dropped him. The poor little bird is dead.' She stroked him with her other hand.

They stood looking at her.

'Which is the biggest thing?' Bartley asked. 'A small bird killed by a hawk, or gas for making raw whiskey, good raw whiskey?'

'Gas,' said Donn.

'Do you mean that now?' Bartley asked.

Donn went down and climbed up the other side. He put his arm around Nan. 'He was a bird of the heather,' he said. 'So we will dig a hole in the heather, and line it with moss. What do you think?'

She thought it over. She rubbed the tears from her face with the back of her hand. 'Yes,' she said. She held out the bird to him. He took it. It was still warm, the small head lolling. 'I will get moss.' She walked away from him and went down the incline towards the river. He stroked the still-warm feathers of the bird.

'Gas!' said Bartley sneering.

'It's what is important to a person,' said Donn. 'That is what is most important. For you, gas; for Nan, a dead lark. Have you a knife?'

Bartley felt in his pockets. He pulled out a large jackknife, threw it across the gap. Donn caught it deftly. He got on one knee, left the bird on the ground, and opening the biggest blade of the knife he cut a rectangular clump from the soft ground.

'Did you learn a lot all the time you were abroad?' Bartley asked.

'I did,' said Donn, thinking. 'I learned how much I don't know.'

'And will you go off again to learn more?' asked Bartley. 'Now that your father is buried, what stop is on you?' He was probing.

'I don't know,' said Donn. He heard Nan coming back. She had to climb with one hand, since her other held a bunch of soft damp moss. She got on her knees beside her father. She looked at the hole. Then she squeezed around it with her fingers to make it smooth. Then she lined the bottom and the sides with the moss. It was an inviting bed. She placed the bird on this gently. The green colour of the moss gave the drab plumage of the bird a sort of glow. She looked and then she covered the body of the bird with moss too. Only then did she look up.

'Now,' she said. Donn placed the tuft he had cut over the moss and pressed it down with his fingers.

Nan blessed herself. She looked up at the sky. 'God,' she said, 'please watch over the little lark. Let him fly.' She sat back on her heels. She looked at the grave and she looked at the sky, then she looked at her father and said: 'Nan is hungry.'

'We will go home now,' said Donn, rising to his feet, wondering at the quick change her mind could make, the sort of ruthlessness of the young. No sentimentality, in a way. Don't cry over spilt milk.

'Bejay,' said Bartley, 'there for a minute I thought the bird would fly out of the grave. I'd say her like would have a clear line to Heaven like a telephone.'

'She'd be better off without it,' said Donn. 'It was in the beginning she needed it. People afflict themselves and their children. These things are man-made.' He spoke very bitterly. Bartley looked at him in surprise. He now saw that the face of Donn was not as smooth as he had thought. There were a lot of bitter lines near the mouth. One minute he could be cheerful and the next like this. A stormy face, Bartley thought, one to be afraid of.

'Are you coming down, Bartley?' he asked.

'Yes, yes,' said Bartley, 'there's feic-all I can do here now. I'll go down with ye.'

'Off you go, Nan,' said Donn.

She got down into the cleft and scrambled up the other side and started to run down the hill, her arms spread out. After a short run she stopped and turned back to them. 'Look! Look!' she said and spread her arms again and ran once more. Bartley thought that in the distance like that when you couldn't see her eyes, she was a beautiful young girl, and if she wasn't as she was all the young men of the seven valleys would be going mad after her. He didn't say this as they set off down.

It was beautiful now. The sun was warm. The shadows of the soft white clouds chased one another slowly across the hills, revealing the emerald colour of the fields one minute and dimming their brilliance the next. About three hundred yards down they came on a flat granite rock, with a top as smooth as a table. Donn rested his elbows on this, looking down at the valley, all the houses spread out on the green hillocks, the walls white, some of the thatches coloured yellow from fresh straw, others grey with their thatch of sedge, the white roads like a lace tracery.

'It's a brave sight,' said Bartley, leaning beside him.

'It looks good,' said Donn.

'It's false,' said Bartley. 'It's bleeding to death.'

'Is it?' asked Donn.

Bartley pointed out six houses, naming their people. 'These are all shut up,' he said. 'The latch is on them. They are gone, all gone.'

'Where?' Donn asked.

'Where?' he asked. 'I don't know. The world. They are gone. Lost for ever. Not a house of the others that hasn't a boy or girl who is gone and going too. You take blood from your veins often enough and there will be no blood left, and sure if there is no blood for the body, won't it die?'

'It will,' said Donn.

'It's too good to die,' said Bartley. 'Won't somebody do something to save it?'

'Is it worth saving?' Donn asked.

'It's a way of life,' said Bartley. 'A good way. Is it worse than all the ways you have seen?'

'It is,' said Donn. 'It's acceptable. It's unambitious. Sit by a lake or snug in the heather on the fine days and dream your life away looking at the sky. Spit in the ashes of a fire of winter and listen to the wind. If you don't want to do anything. If you don't want to be anybody. If you want to be a vegetable.'

'Not so,' said Bartley. 'It still has the people, and as long as it has those it has the seven deadly sins. It has the valley of tears. You know that. What has the others but big buildings and lights and lots more of people.'

'What are you getting at?' Donn asked.

'I'm trying to get at you,' said Bartley. 'Your people always advised the other people. You don't know that. It comes from way back when there was a headman that people could go and talk to when they were in trouble. Your father was like that. He listened to enough trouble to burn his ears, and did a lot to ease the pain.'

'What,' Donn sneered, 'do you want me to become Lord of the Mountain?'

'I don't know what I want,' said Bartley. 'You have a way of settling things. You settled me with the gas and you settled Nan with the bird. You could settle a lot of things if you would think over them. You could be a help. You could try and put a stop to the withering.'

'Me?' Donn asked. He thought. He laughed at the thought.

'What did you do but sow your wild oats,' said Bartley. 'You were brought back. I don't know what brought you back, but if it was strong enough to bring you back it might be strong enough to make you stay for a while.'

'You know nothing about me,' said Donn. 'You don't know the torrents at war inside me. Do you know me?'

'I think you could be a dangerous man,' said Bartley, 'but it takes soda to kill the blight.'

Donn looked at the figure of Nan, getting smaller and smaller as she raced down the hillside, a quickly-moving splash of colour. 'At the moment,' he said, 'there is one string holding me and that's like a silken thread that could snap in a second.' He suddenly realized how painful it would be if it did snap. 'While I'm here,' he went on, 'if anybody wants my advice they are sure to get it. There's nothing easier than giving advice.'

'It'll take more than that,' said Bartley. 'You'll have to put your mind working on it.'

'No,' said Donn. 'I don't want to become involved.'

'I hope you have to,' said Bartley, 'some way. Now I leave you.' He went away from the stone and swung off to the left. Donn looked after him, the sturdy sure-footed stock of a man, an isolationist if ever he saw one, he thought, and had to laugh at the idea of Bartley urging him to become involved with people he himself avoided.

But Bartley was sincere, if inconsistent, and the valley did look beautiful under the sun, with no sign at all of cancer.

We'll see, he thought, as he made his way down the hill.

Six

WHEN THE postman had left and she had looked at the bulky letters, Meela suddenly became determined. She went looking for him. He wasn't in the house. Nan was in the storeroom on her knees with a piece of paper on which she was trying to draw birds with coloured crayons. Her attempts were quite good if you knew her. Why didn't I think of that, Meela wondered.

'Where's your daddy?' she asked, wondering at how slow the word 'Daddy' was on her tongue.

'Nice bird,' said Nan, holding up the paper. It had no relation to a bird, just a mess of colour out of which one dot for an eye made the whole vaguely discernible. 'Daddy out,' she said and went back to her work. She was always with him.

Meela went into the shop.

'Where's himself?' she asked Paud. Paud was in his early twenties. He had sandy-coloured hair standing up on his head and big teeth. He always said 'Hah?' when you asked him a question. He said 'Hah?' now.

'Did you see him going anywhere?' she asked.

'Oh? Ah!' he said, scratching his head. He was very slow. You could nearly see the words forming in his mind. But he was honest and she was glad to have him. 'Think he went off down by the lake,' he said.

She went out. It was cold enough. There was an east wind blowing. When the sun came out of the clouds it warmed things up. She wondered if she would get her coat, and then decided against it. She buttoned up her cardigan and set off down towards the lake. Down at the rough pier, she looked but could see no sign of him. It seemed she was always looking for him. He is not doing anything, she thought angrily. She knew of a place he might be, where the river left the lake in three big falls. Somewhere like that he would be out of the wind. They had spent many hours together there, long ago, out of the shelter of the wind, when they were on vacation from the University. She thought of it with a sort of cold wonder as she made her way along by the shore of the lake. The land was divided by stone walls, but the lake was low and you could pass the ends of the walls by stepping on the foreshore. Places it was sandy, other places it was rocky, and other places still there were boggy streams running into it, which she had to jump. Once her foot went deep into the slime and she felt the coldness of it as it covered her shoe. 'Damn!' she said, and plucked some grass to get the worst of it off.

It didn't endear her to her dear husband. That was the way she thought of him: my dear husband, with an excellent ingredient of bitterness. She often thought it might be better if she could curse him, or hit him with a pickaxe handle. She knew this would be no good. He would let her batter away at his handsome head.

She came to the river. Here it was quite broad and flowed slowly. She walked along the bank, until it suddenly turned left and fell. She had to go right to scramble around the big rocks there, and then left again to come out on the lower bank under the fall. There was a round sheltered place here, near the fall, which made a loud noise as it threw itself over recklessly. She looked for him here, and only when she lowered her eyes saw that he was swimming in the pool under the fall. His hair was plastered to his head, she could see his arms a yellow colour in the brown bog water. She called. She was angry. She didn't really know why.

'Come here!' she called. He didn't hear her.

'Donn!' she shouted. That got his attention. He turned towards her. He smiled. His eyebrows lifted.

'Come here!' she called. He said 'Hah?' like Paud, put one hand to his ear.

'Come here!' she said.

'All right,' he shouted, reached an arm to a rock, pulled himself up and came out of the pool. He was naked. She knew he had done this deliberately. What did he expect her to do? Turn away in maidenly confusion. She didn't. She just kept her eyes on his eyes. She couldn't stop the colour that rose in her face, but that was mostly anger.

'You want me?' he asked, reaching for his shirt and holding

it in front of him. She knew what he meant with 'you want me'. He had a way of saying those things that could anger her.

'Will you please come up to the house and talk business,' she said.

'What kind of business?' he asked. 'Nice business or business business?'

'It's your business,' she said hotly. 'Your father left it to you, you know.'

'I don't want it,' he said. 'You can have it.'

'I don't want it,' she said. 'It's nothing to do with me.'

'Why are you getting so fussed so?' he asked.

'Lots of people have been working to make it all clear,' she said. 'The least you can do is come and look at their work, and then you can do what the hell you like.'

'Bad language,' said Donn shaking his head. She just tightened her lips. 'Do you want me to come as I am, or will you give me time to dress myself?'

'As long as you come,' she said, 'you can come walking on your hands.'

'We are a bit angry today,' said Donn. He saw her hands clenching, her breast rising. He thought she might bend down and pick up a stone and throw it at him. 'You look very desirable today,' he said. This was the truth, but he knew it would anger her even more. It did. She turned and walked away from him. He laughed. His laughter brought her halfway around the lake, before she relaxed. She knew he said those things deliberately to annoy her. She tried to remain calm, but he nearly always succeeded in rousing her feelings.

When he came to the parlour she had all the papers and books spread over the table. He was carrying a coat over his arm. She could see damp patches on his shirt. She was going to say: you'll get a cold doing things like that, but then she knew it was what he would expect her to say, so she didn't say it. He sat down opposite her.

'Well, let's have all the dirt,' he said.

She didn't rise to that either.

'Things haven't been easy,' she said. 'I have had to look after things for the last five years, since your father got sick. I tried to do it as well as I could, but I'm not very good.'

54

He glanced at the neat figures and the neat writing. He leafed through the big books.

'Do I have to look at all those?' he asked.

'You should,' she said. 'They are yours.'

'Isn't there a summary or something?' he asked.

'Here,' she said. 'I got an accountant to do it all. You won't have to pay death duties. There isn't enough left.'

He bent closely over the papers. She watched him. He could be serious enough when he wanted to, she knew. She saw the strong handsome features, the muscular neck, the big sensitive hands. They meant nothing to her, she thought, and tried to think back to the time when they had meant everything to her.

'Haven't any young men been chasing you at all?' he asked suddenly, looking up at her.

'Leave me alone,' she said. 'Please look at the accounts.'

'I've looked at them,' he said. 'We make about £800 a year. We are owed about £900. There isn't what you would call a fortune in the business. We have about £3,800 in the bank. Is this a fair summary?'

'It is,' she said.

'I could make more than that digging sewers in New York,' he said. 'You have done a good job. Why did you do it? Why didn't you pull out years ago? You could have made a living. You could teach, couldn't you?'

'Yes,' she said. 'I could teach if I wasn't a girl who had been deserted by her husband on the day of the wedding and left with a child whom people said might have the wrong father.'

'Who said that?'

'It doesn't matter,' she shouted. 'We are talking business.'

'All right,' he said. 'Why has business dropped £250 over the last three years?'

'That's because a travelling van has taken to coming in. He is from away off. He brings in things, and goes to the houses. It saves people walking all the way to us.'

'They give him the cash and give us the credit. Is that it?'

'That's about it,' she said.

'Why didn't my father stop him?' he asked.

'He was sick when he started to come in,' she said.

'And what day does he come in, then?' he asked.

'On Thursday,' she said. 'Every Thursday.'

'What a coincidence,' he said. 'Today is Thursday.'

He got to his feet. He put his coat over his shoulder. He looked at her.

'You are a great woman,' he said. 'I don't know of anybody in the world who would have done what you have done. I'll look after your travelling van for you anyhow.'

'Not mine, yours,' she said.

'All right, mine then,' he said, and walked to the door. He turned there and smiled at her. 'Don't go away,' he said. This only angered her. He went into the shop. He went behind the counter. He got a small brown paper bag used for holding a pound of sugar. He went to the place that held the hardware, filled the bag, went out of the shop and headed down the road to the entrance of the valley.

Coley Collery was a bachelor. He had all the appearances of it. He was fat, with three rolls of chins and a big stomach over which a buttoned waistcoat was sadly creased and soiled from all the cigarette ash that fell from a cigarette which never seemed to be out of his mouth. Once he lit a cigarette he kept it in his mouth. He talked through it, coughed through it, and would at times even eat through it. He seldom managed to shave himself successfully and the collar of his shirt was always crumpled and held by a tarnished tie-pin.

He worked like a slave for long hours. He never read anything outside the racing page in the newspapers; and his account books, which were written up in indelible pencil, intelligible only to himself, would baffle a professor of Sanskrit.

He had bought an old lorry, and built a body on it himself from bits of timber and plywood, and then painted it a horrible green. It was shelved. It contained a bit of everything. The only thing it didn't hold was a coffin. Also strong drink, for which he hadn't a licence, but he was not above exchanging edibles for a few bottles of the strong stuff they made in the mountains. He could find a market for it. He could find a market for anything.

He covered four villages a day over a very wide area, five

and a half days a week. The half-day he used for restocking, and took a dim view of God for having rested on the Sabbath.

His makeshift van was held together by bits of wire. He knew enough about engines to keep this one going. In order to do so he had cannibalized every bit of crashed or worn-out machinery over a hundred square miles. Men said he would have cannibalized his own mother if he needed her for a carburettor.

As he made his way up towards the Mountain this morning, he was thinking of nothing at all. When he thought he thought in percentages. He just drove along slowly, because the van couldn't go quickly, and listened to the sound of the engine finding the hill hard. He knew every wheeze and grunt of her. The front wheels bouncing in the pot-holes gave him a good shaking. He was well-cushioned and adjusted himself to the bumps. As he rounded a hill and came to the place where the road ran through the gap that led down into the village, he noticed a man in a white shirt sitting on a huge stone on his right. He didn't wonder about this. If a man chose to sit on a stone on his head it would have been no cause for wonder to him either. There were no people in the world for him, only customers and percentages.

He had driven about twenty yards into the gap when the van started to behave very curiously. It no longer seemed cushioned by anything at all. One time in his life he had driven a steamroller, and that is just what it felt like now, a steamroller going over rough stones.

I must have a puncture, he thought, puzzled that a puncture should be so bad. The wheel rattled in his hands. He put his foot down on the brake, which wasn't a very good brake, and he put his hand down and pulled up the handbrake, which wasn't very good either, but the van slithered to a stop, square-ways on the road. She shuddered. He wondered if he would switch off the engine. Sometimes it took him a long time to get her started, but if he left the engine on she would be using petrol, and this wouldn't be so good. He switched her off and opened the door. He had to let down the glass to open the door from outside because the handle was broken inside.

He eased himself out, grunting. It was a bit of a squeeze to get himself out, but finally he did. He walked to the front and looked at the tyre there. Ah, it was flat. Well, that wasn't so bad. He had a spare, a very worn one, at the back. He walked around. He was then shocked to see that the twin tyres on the back were also flat. He scratched his head of thick, greying hair, that was liberally sprinkled with bran and chicken-mash and flour. He walked to the other side of the van and there were the other two wheels also flat.

He got down and examined them. There were several felt nails stuck in them. He looked at the others. They were also decorated with felt nails, their flat galvanized heads winking at him.

He then looked around him on the road. He walked back a bit and saw all the felt nails scattered on the road, hundreds of them. They had been in a belt across the road. The wheels couldn't miss them.

'Well, shag me!' he said, not being able to think of anything else.

Then this fellow standing on the rock spoke to him.

'Are you in trouble?' he called.

'Am I in trouble?' asked Coley. 'Well, shag me! Who did this?' He was holding up a few nails he had picked from the road.

He watched the man. He came down from the rock. He leaped down and walked on the slope of heather and grass towards the road. As he came nearer he seemed to get bigger and bigger.

'Are you in trouble?' he asked again.

'Am I in trouble?' Coley repeated himself. 'Look at this!' He held out the nails. The man moved them on his palm with his fingers.

'Ah, felt nails,' he said. 'Somebody must have dropped them.'

'How could anybody have dropped them, for God's sake?' Coley asked. The butt was burning his lips. He caught it and threw it away.

'Coming home in the evening,' the man said. 'They probably fell out of the back of the ass cart. The bad road, you know.'

'They'd fall in a lump,' said Coley. 'How could they spread themselves across the road so neat, eh? How about that?'

Coley took a cigarette. The man had a match lighted and held it to the cigarette. Coley sucked. He looked at the man suspiciously. He always suspected free gifts. He wouldn't give you a cigarette himself if your tongue was hanging out for one.

'We mustn't leave all those nails about,' the man said, bending down and picking them up. 'The same thing might happen to somebody else.'

'But how did the nails get scattered?' Coley asked.

'Cattle,' said the man, bending and picking. 'All that is commonage. They're all over the place.' He had a handful. He threw them away to the right towards the stream by the side of the road.

'Who are you?' Coley asekd.

'My name is Donnshleibhe,' said Donn.

Coley thought over this.

'Oh,' he said. 'Are you the one that came home when the old fella died?'

'I am,' said Donn.

'I heard of you,' said Coley. 'You have the shop above now so?'

'That's right,' said Donn.

'Somebody scattered the nails,' said Coley.

'The cattle,' said Donn.

'Do you think I'm an eejit?' Coley asked.

'No,' said Donn. 'Why have you such a poor opinion of yourself?'

'Your father didn't like me coming into the valley. I heard that,' said Coley. 'I have to make a living too. It's a free country.'

'That's right,' said Donn. 'You don't pay rates or taxes, or labour, like other people. Come and go when you like. A nice life. I don't think there's enough room in this place for two of us, do you?'

'You scattered those nails,' said Coley.

'It's a good job,' said Donn, 'we haven't a witness, or I'd have to sue you for slander. That's a terrible thing to say.'

'I've a mind to hit you,' said Coley. He looked like it too.

'I wouldn't,' said Donn, 'because I'm much bigger than

you and I know dirtier fighting tricks.'

'What am I going to do?' asked Coley. 'There's no justice.'

'All you have to do is walk two miles to the post office, where they have a phone, and phone for a breakdown truck to come and help you. You should be out of here then before nightfall, and once out, you don't have to come back.'

'I know it was you did it,' said Coley. 'You won't get away with it. It will cost me a lot of money. Think of the wasted time. Who will pay me back?'

All the time Donn was collecting nails from the road and throwing them into the stream.

'Well, that's the lot, I think,' he said, dusting off his hands. 'There's nothing more I can do for you, so I better be going, and you better be going.'

'But you can't do things like this!' Coley shouted. 'These are new times. Men died for freedom. Nobody can do things like this. All my tyres are flat!'

'It's a tough life,' said Donn. 'Goodbye now. I'll be seeing you.' He turned and walked away towards the valley.

Coley followed after him.

'You'll be seeing me all right! You'll be seeing me all right! I'll be up there the first minute I can and I'll have the police with me. You can't get away with things like that, do you hear? I'll fix you, do you hear? You just wait, you big bog-trotter. I'll be back. You watch out. Nobody can do a thing like that to Coley Collery and get away with it.'

Donn had walked a good quarter of a mile before the sound of Coley's outraged voice was killed by distance.

They were sitting eating their lunch in the kitchen when he came in. He sat at the table.

Meela looked at him.

'Coley won't be coming into the valley any more,' he said.

'What did you do?' she asked. She was ever suspicious. He wondered how long it would be before she lost that.

'I just talked to him,' he said. He laughed. 'I just talked to him.'

She frowned.

Seven

MEELA WAS brushing her hair at the mirror of her dressing-table when the door opened. She saw him in the mirror. He saw her face. Her eyes were startled. It was the first time he had come into her room like that. He leaned against the lintel. He was grinning. He reflected on the difference there was seeing a person's face in a mirror and looking at them directly.

'Don't be frightened,' he said.

He watched her mouth tightening on the clip she held between her teeth.

'Put on a pretty dress,' he said. 'The sun is shining. I have sent for Joe Toake. You and Nan and myself are going away for the day.'

'Where?' she asked.

'A surprise,' he said.

'Who will do everything?' she said. 'Friday is a busy day.'

'Paud and Bridgie,' he said. 'That's what they are here for. In their freetime they can play slap-and-tickle in the kitchen. It is only the English who could invent an action phrase like that.'

'But where are you going?' she asked.

'Let it be a surprise,' he said.

'Your surprises could be unpleasant,' she said.

'Not this time,' he said, looking around the room. She had made a refuge, he saw. It was a pleasant room. There was bright wallpaper on the walls. It bulged a little where the walls themselves bulged. Bright cretonne curtains. A basket chair, painted white with coloured cloth on the back and the cushion to match the curtains. The bed was neatly made and covered. All the bits and pieces were neatly arrayed on the dressing-table. There was an open bookcase, with little gew-gaws on top of it. A room that would resent a man, he thought.

'All right,' she said.

'Make up your mind to enjoy it,' he said. 'Don't start off

resenting it, or there will be no pleasure in it.'

'I'll try to enjoy it,' she said, loudly. 'It would be easier without the lectures.'

He refrained from answering her. He looked once more at her angry eyes and then closed the door. He found Nan in the kitchen. Bridgie was fixing her hair. She was jigging up and down, Bridgie saying: 'Ah, Nan, keep quiet until I do you!' 'Surprise! Surprise! Surprise!' Nan was saying. 'Where are we going, Daddy?'

'You'll see,' Donn said. 'Are you right now? Joe will soon be here.'

'Is Mammy coming?' she asked.

'Yes,' said Donn. 'She's coming. Come on. We'll go outside and wait for Joe.'

She took his hand and hauled him. He had to exert his strength in order not to be made to trot after her. They arrived outside laughing. The June sun was hot. It had been hot now for a few days. There was a heat haze all over the valley.

'He's not here,' Nan said. 'Will I go and look for him?'

'Do,' said Donn, 'but don't get dirty. You are grand and clean now. You hear?'

'Oh, no,' she said. 'I won't leave the road.' She ran away from the house along the verge of the road, keeping her black patent-leather shoes from the dust. When she reached the fork, where the road met the main road into the valley, she stood on a rock and shaded her eyes with her hand. Then she turned and made signals with her arms. So he knew that Joe was coming.

Meela joined him. He looked at her critically. She was dressed in a light summer frock. She carried a headscarf and a handbag.

'You weren't long,' he said.

'It's not as if I was going on a date,' she said.

'We'll go up to Nan,' he said. 'Joe is coming. He can turn up there.'

They walked towards Nan.

'She is very excited,' he said. 'Did she ever get taken out of here at all?'

'She went with me when I went to the town,' she said. 'But

she darts around. It's hard to look after her if you have things to do. I'd always be afraid she would get lost.'

'He's coming! He's coming! He's coming!' Nan was shouting. They looked. Joe was making a lot of dust, coming into the valley. In the distance they could hear the sound of Jack Tumelty's horse-drawn mowing-machine, cutting a meadow. Donn thought what a pleasant sound it was. Even though they couldn't see where he was working, they could smell the new-mown hay.

'Try and be happy, Meela,' he said.

'I'm happy,' she said.

'Like hell,' he said. 'Just for the day. Think of me as your brother.'

'Oh, brother,' she said, and he laughed.

Joe's eyes were red.

'It's an early call,' he said. 'There was a wake over the way last night. I was hardly in bed when you had me out of it. Where do you want to go?'

'Into the big town,' said Donn, opening the back door for Meela. Nan was already sitting in beside Joe, bouncing up and down on the springs.

'I'll be able to get a cure there so,' said Joe, starting off. 'Drink should be abolished, eh, Donn?'

'Think of all the people you'd throw out of work,' said Donn.

'Bygob, that's right,' said Joe. 'Amn't I keeping the country going? I'll have to stop in the small place below for petrol.'

It was hot in the car. They let down the windows. It was an old car, but it was roomy and well-sprung and hitting the pot-holes didn't knock too much out of them. Only Nan talked. She would say: 'Look at this! Look at that!' odd things that took her fancy and they would be past them before Donn knew what she meant.

At the petrol pump in the street town, Joe was out when this man pushed his head in the open window. It took Donn a little while to answer when he said: 'Hello, Meela. Hello Donn. Glad to see you home.' He raised his arms and Donn saw the stripes on his sleeve.

'Oh, hello, Sergeant, I had almost forgotten your face. You were a tall thin young man when I saw you last.'

'Ah, we all grow up,' he said. 'That fella Coley was talking to me.'

'Oh,' said Donn.

'A very bitter man,' said the Sergeant. 'He wouldn't buy a Mountain man for twopence ha'penny now, if they were selling them.'

'A foreigner,' said Donn.

'That's true,' he said. 'But even though it's hard to see through his disguise he's a human being, and he has rights.'

'So have other people,' said Donn.

'What I'm saying,' said the Sergeant. 'He had a queer tale about yourself. I thought it was tripe or I'd have been up.'

'Some people,' said Donn, 'are inclined to blame their troubles on other people.'

'What I told him,' said the Sergeant. 'It's a pity you didn't have a witness, Coley, I said. You know what his answer to that was? Can cows talk? he asked. Can you serve a subpoena on the birds?'

Donn laughed. 'I'm glad to hear he has a sense of humour.'

'He hasn't,' said the Sergeant. 'He was serious.'

'That makes it funnier,' said Donn.

'I won't be keeping ye,' said the Sergeant. Joe was back in his seat. 'It's nice to see ye all together again, thank God.' He stepped back and waved, and Joe drove off. Donn was humming.

Meela couldn't keep quiet.

'There were other ways of dealing with Coley,' she said.

'There is only one way of dealing with parasites,' he said.

'There was the right way,' she said firmly. 'We could have competed with him, reduced our prices, or something.'

'Trade war in the Mountain!' Donn scoffed.

'Your way is always the right way, isn't it?' she asked.

He thought over this.

'Can't we drop it?' he said. 'Let us not darken the day.'

She was going to continue, but she decided against it. It was hot. They welcomed the breeze the opened windows made. The cattle in the fields were under trees, seeking shade wherever they could find it. Near a small lake on the left-hand side of the road they were standing in the water up to their bellies, chewing the cud, but turning their heads to watch the traffic on the road.

It was stifling in the town. People were dressed in summer clothes. Everyone seemed to be listless in the unaccustomed heat. Shirt-sleeved car drivers were honking their horns impatiently.

Donn directed Joe.

They stopped at this garage on the far side of the town. 'All right Joe,' Donn said, when they got out, 'you can go and get your cure now,' handing him his money.

'What time will I be back?' Joe asked. 'Where will I meet ye?'

'No time, nowhere,' said Donn. 'We will get home again under our own steam.'

'All right,' said Joe, letting in the clutch, 'don't say I didn't warn ye.'

'What are we doing here, Daddy?' Nan asked. 'Where are we going?'

'Right in here,' said Donn, taking her hand. A grey-haired man had been watching them through the window. He came out now.

'All set?' Donn asked him.

'All set,' the man said, smiling, holding out keys. 'There she is.'

They walked over to a black car, shining new, with red upholstery. 'There you are, Nan,' he said. 'All for you.'

'Is it ours?' she asked. 'This car is ours?' Her eyes were wide. He opened the door for her. 'All ours,' he said. He turned to Meela. 'Do you like it?' he asked.

'How can we afford it?' she asked. He laughed. Nan was already sitting in it, testing the springs of the seat, looking around it.

'Funny smell,' she said. 'Funny smell.'

'Are we going to get in?' he asked Meela. She got in beside Nan, cautiously. It was a wide front seat. The three of them could fit on it.

'Good luck, now, Donn,' the man said, as Donn got in. 'Well wear.'

'Well wear, soon tear,' said Donn remembering, long ago when you got something new, this was the cant. He drove away from the garage.

'This was the surprise?' Meela asked.

'Isn't it?' he asked.

'A bit frightening,' she said.

'You have been keeping the accounts for too long,' he said. 'If you want to make money you have to spend it. The day is not over.'

'More surprises?' she asked.

'Nan likes the new car,' Nan said. 'Nice Daddy.'

'This is not the way home,' Meela said.

'We are going the long way home,' he said. He stopped the car outside this shop. 'I won't be long,' he said. He left them.

'Funny smell,' Nan said.

'It's the new things,' said Meela. 'New paint, new upholstery.'

'What is that?' she asked.

'The covers,' said Meela, thinking it will be a great convenience to have a car. It will save such a lot of time and walking, at the same time thinking of all the pinching and scraping she herself had done over the years, so that if one day Donn came home everything would be in order and the place wouldn't be bankrupt. The people must have thought she was very mean. She had wanted to account for every halfpenny. There was very little discount. She would never have bought a car.

She saw him coming out of the shop. He had a box in his arms. He lifted the lid of the boot and put in the box. Then he went away again and came with another box. He closed the boot and sat in beside them again.

'Would you like to go to the seashore, Nan?' he asked.

'The sea?' she said. 'The sea?'

'Yes,' he said. 'Sand and sunshine and green water and shells and cockles and mussels and little fish and seaweed.'

'Oh,' she said. 'Oh.'

'I knew you'd like it,' he said. 'Here we go. Would your Mammy like to see the sea?'

'Blue water, green water,' said Meela.

* * *

It was a peninsula far out along the coast road. It was shaped like an apple that had been eaten into on two sides. A long curving beach, nearly a mile long, that looked golden in the distance. You walked on sand dunes covered with coarse green grass and came to another curving beach on the other side. The long headland at the sea end of the beaches consisted of solid great rocks that had resisted the pounding of the centuries. It was scarred and battered but it had proudly protected its sand beaches.

Donn watched Nan as they walked the dunes to the beach on the other side. They went to this beach because there were people, not many, sunbathing, swimming and picknicking on the other one. Nan would run forward and then turn back to them and clap her hands and say 'Oh! Oh! Oh!' She took off her shoes and stockings and came back to her mother, handed them to her. She was breathless, her eyes shining, and then she ran ahead of them, her arms spread, her hair flying, and Donn said: 'It is a blow to the heart to look at her and see a grown young woman, and then you see her acting like a child.'

Meela said: 'I have had a long time to get used to it. I am used to it.' She spoke grimly.

When they came to the beach, he threw down the boxes he was carrying. He opened one of them and threw a bathing-togs to Meela. It lay on the sand at her feet. She looked down at it.

'Nan! Nan!' he called. 'Come here!' She was walking in the water, looking at her feet. She came to his call, running. 'You would like to go in the water?' he asked, holding out another bathing-togs.

'Yes! Yes! Yes!' she said, catching the end of her frock and going to pull it over her head.

'No! No!' Meela said. 'Come and change here behind the rocks.'

'There's nobody to see,' Donn protested.

'Come on, Nan,' Meela said firmly, and took her by the arm and walked her towards the rocks.

Donn looked after them, then shrugged and took off his own clothes and pulled on a swimming-trunks and ran into the sea. It was cool enough, but he swam out into the deep. When he turned back after a time, he saw Nan waiting at the edge of the sea. She was waving to him. Meela was still dressed, he saw. She had just taken off her shoes and stockings and was paddling.

'Daddy, mind me! Mind me!' Nan was calling as he came towards her.

'Come on,' he said, holding out his hand to her, waist-deep in the water. She came to him with all the trepidation of a child in the water for the first time. He had to coax her, saying 'Come on! Come on!' like you would with a child. He saw the anxiety in her eyes and the anticipation, the sense of adventure and the joy when his hand finally caught hers. 'Now,' he said, 'swim, like this,' showing her, but she shook her head. So he went back to her, as you would with a child, and he told her how to bend forwards and lift her legs and he held her waist, while she screwed up her face and thrashed away with her arms and legs, screaming when her face went under the water, so he kept one hand under her chin and the other around her waist, seeing her as the finely-built young lady she was, and groaning at the same time.

He played with her at this for some time, until she became bolder. Then he showed her how to look for cockles in the shallow water, finding six for her before she herself could see the tell-tale holes and dig her fingers into the sand, shouting with joy the first time she found one on her own. He left her there and went in to Meela, who was sitting on the sand.

'You wouldn't swim,' he said, lying down near her.

'No,' she said.

'You don't want to expose yourself to the public gaze?' he asked.

'I don't like sea-water,' she said.

'Is there nothing at all can be done for Nan?' he asked. 'No brain operation, nothing at all?'

'Nothing at all,' she said. 'Don't you think I have tried?'

He thought over this. 'I'm sure you have tried,' he said.

'Don't you think that I love her more than if she was normal?'

He thought over this too. He thought of his own feelings towards her, a sort of outraged protective feeling. So what must Meela feel?

'I do,' he said.

'You have to live with it,' she said. 'Accept it.'

'We better eat,' he said, pulling the box towards him. He put out a sheet of paper on the sand and put the cooked chickens and packets of crackers, bottles of beer and lemonade, cheese, fruit, and chocolate, all over the paper.

He called: 'Nan! Nan! Come on here. Eat. Look!' holding up the chicken, which he had broken into portions. 'Here you are!' handing some to Meela.

'It's Friday,' said Meela.

'So what?' he asked.

'We don't eat meat on Friday,' she said.

'Are you crazy?' he asked her. 'Oh, God, eat fish on Friday or you'll go to hell for all eternity!'

'It isn't the fish, it's the principle,' she said.

'Do you really believe that you'd go to hell for eating a bit of chicken on a picnic?' he asked.

'We live on principles,' said Meela. 'Some people do, some people don't.'

'Well, I think it's all bloody nonsense,' he said.

'And I don't,' she said. 'Do you want to force me to your way of thinking?'

'That'd be the day,' he said grimly. 'Do you think I would send Nan to hell by giving her a piece of chicken?'

'Do what you like,' she said. 'I'll eat the cheese.'

'Here, Nan,' he said. She took the chicken and bit into it joyfully with her small even teeth. He bit into his own piece of chicken. 'M'm, scrumptious,' he said, looking at Meela.

Nan didn't eat so much, as she was anxious to get back to the sea. He went with her and showed her the odd-looking shells that she could pick above the water-mark. She got on to this soon, and picked ones he would never choose. She came back to where they were several times to show them, and a pile of odd-looking shells began to build up at their feet. Meela cleaned up and packed the remains in the box, and then lay on the sand beside him again.

'I read a book once,' he said, his arms over his eyes. 'A man was chatting with an angel on a beach like this, and as they talked the angel with his fingers would make a city out of the sand, and then he would make people, all running around the city under his thumb. Now and again he would follow one of them with his thumb and when he got him would crunch him under his thumb, pulp him so that the blood spattered on to the sand. Then he would cover him and follow another little man to crush him idly too.'

'That's horrible philosophy,' she said.

'I saw it happening like that,' he said. 'People crushed to bloody pulp by the hands of angels. They used shells or bombs or grenades, or mines, but it was the same thing. Done idly, you would say. Why the other fellow, why not me? It was all chance.'

'It was not,' she said.

'So people are important to people only, this is what I believe. You love people because they are people and this thumb is hovering over them. But it is better to love people who are yours, who have a claim on you or who belong to you by companionship or association or because they are the fruit of your seed.' Suddenly he turned on his side and reached and took her hand into his. He felt it tightening. 'All the time I thought of you. I would say, Meela belongs to me, because I possessed her. You will find this hard to believe, but I thought of you belonging to me, but when I catch your hand like this and see the muscles on the jaw tightening, that you turn your eyes away from me, or when you turn them towards me angrily and you look at me, and I see no affection, no love in them for me. What do you feel for me? Nothing at all?'

'What do you expect?' she asked him.

He dropped her hand, and fell on his back again.

'I don't know,' he said. 'I think you have built yourself into an unreal world. I think you have been hurt so much that you have erected almost impenetrable barricades between yourself and everyone else. You are not going to be hurt any more. Nobody on God's earth is going to hurt you any more. Is this it?'

'Nobody is going to get the chance,' she said. 'What you did today, you would do again tomorrow.'

'Love your enemy,' he said. 'Forgive those who persecute and calumniate you. Do you swear to love, honour and obey, in sickness or in health, richer or poorer, till death us do part. I do. What about all that? Isn't it more important than eating fish on Friday?'

'That's perfection,' she said.

'Well, you are a believer in it,' he said. 'Is it easier to practise the small things that don't matter, and harden your soul against the things that do matter. I will obey, Lord, but not today.'

She laughed.

'Talk about the devil preaching scripture,' she said.

'Maybe even the devil could be converted,' he said, 'if he saw even one person trying to practise what they are supposed to believe. Even I could be. I have never met one.'

'What are you trying to do?' she asked.

'I want you to take another look at me,' he said. 'I want you eventually to forgive me, and, forgiving me, get to love me.'

She sat up.

'How can you light a fire that's stamped out?' she asked loudly. 'Can you even begin to imagine what you did to me?'

'I can,' he said. 'I have thought over it a lot.'

'I want to go home, now,' she said, getting to her feet.

He thought for a while. 'All right,' he said. He called: 'Nan! Come here, my love. We are going home.'

He stopped the car in the gap leading down to the valley.

'You see that?' he asked. 'Well, I am going to change it. I am going to get it done over. It is not going to die.'

'What,' she said, 'are you going to be Lord of the Mountain?'

'If necessary,' he said.

'It might be dangerous,' she said. 'Did you think of that?'

'Not dangerous,' he said, 'but exciting.'

'You are going to stay, so,' she said.

'I am,' he said, 'doesn't that make you happy?' He was grinning at her.

'I don't know,' she said. 'I don't know.'

Eight

HOW DO you start to change the mind of a valley?

Here you have the old thatched cottage with a front door and a back door. The front door is never closed, winter or summer, only when you go to bed. You put a half-door there to keep out the rain and the chickens use it as a perch and your floor as a convenience and you have to shush them off with a broom umpteen times a day. There are cold stone flags as a floor or maybe mass concrete that never gets warm no matter how many carts of turf you burn in the great open fireplace. There is a dresser loaded with delf that you never use unless somebody dies or gets married, a wooden table that has to be scrubbed to its present whiteness every day, or covered with gay printed oilcloth.

You have the churn in which you put the cream from your milk to churn to butter. That must always be cleaned and scalded. There is a table where you have water buckets which must be brought from the lake below, a hard haul, and not easy as you get older. There is the pot oven, in which you do your cooking. Irons swing out and over the fire. You must bend down every time. You know that the food that comes out of the pot oven is luscious, the stews, and the big brown crusted cakes resting on the window stool to cool would melt in your mouth, if Granny taught you to mix the dough the right way. Some ladies didn't. Their cakes would fall into your stomach like globs of cement falling from a height. No wonder all the middle-aged ladies go around holding their backs.

Then there are those cursed oil lamps. If the paraffin is good, it burns away all right, but if the paraffin is bad, the thing is always smoking, and you have to douse it and trim the wick, and clean the globe. If you want bright light you turn up the wick and it burns, and so you have to keep it so low that it's only a glimmer, and just when you might be at an interesting part of a paper or a book, what happens but the bloody thing goes out and you have to get up and take it off the nail, and burn your hands on the hot globe, and you curse and suck your hand, and then you have to fill it up again and be careful about what height you turn it. In fact this lamp is only one stage removed from the grease lamps of a hundred years ago.

Candle grease? Everywhere. On the furniture, on the bed-clothes, on your polished Sunday boots, on your suits. You have to get a bit of brown paper and heat a knife blade in the fire, put the paper over the spots and rub them with the hot knife to transfer the melted grease from your clothes to the brown paper.

Two bedrooms or maybe four, small, two off the kitchen on one side and two off the other. Only the ones near the fireplace will be warm. The other two would freeze you even though you are sunk in a feather mattress.

Look at the beautiful whitewashed cottages, shining in the sun, and the straw thatch or the sedge thatch of various colours, a fit setting, waiting for the brush of an artist or a photographer of quaint scenes. The artist or the photographer can come and go back to his house with a flush toilet. He doesn't have to be getting up in the middle of a cold night to go out and manure the haggard, or have pisspots all over the place which must be hidden when callers come.

And thatches must be thatched. How, nowadays? Most men get the thrasher to thrash their oats or their bits of barley or wheat. What happens then but the thrasher breaks up all the straw, so that it is useless for thatching. So if you want straw, unbroken straw, you must cut a field with a hand sickle or a scythe, and thrash it with a flail, like the old days, in order to have your straw good enough. All this costs time and money and it must be renewed every five or ten years, so however much you sneer at the houses below with the tiles and the slates on them, sometimes you must wish that you had them over your head. And if you were a careful person and liked your house to look white, didn't you have to be buying a penny packet of blue to mix with your lime to whitewash twice a year: and you got lime on your clothes and in your hair and on your skin.

There are lots of things crying for changing, but there's old Momo sitting on the hob, smoking her pipe, or Daddo on the

73

other hob chewing his tobacco and throwing sizzling spits at the flames, talking about how easy the young ones (maybe young sixty or seventy) have it nowadays; how they lost the use of their spade hands or feet, or the scythe and how many carts of turf they cut in a day, and the young women didn't know how to collect roots to make good dye for the homespun cloth. They didn't know how to spin or weave, and wasn't the whole countryside ruined since they invented the knitting-needle and they bought their balls of wool ready and dyed from shops, if you please. How many hours did Momo spend over the big three-legged pot stirring the clothes in the dye with a stick, while all her man could earn was eightpence a day for cutting turf from daylight till darkness? By God, but they had it easy with their doles and their grants and the devil knows what, and not one of them as good a man or woman as their fathers and mothers who wore shoes going to Mass only on a Sunday and ate meat twice a year at Christmas and Easter. No wonder they were debilitated nowadays, stuffing themselves with pig-meat and mutton that one time would have to go to pay the rent. No wonder they were constipated, and had bottles of pills and yokes all over the house that nobody ever heard of. If it happened to them Momo would go up on the hill and pluck a herb and boil it and squeeze the juice out of it and there they were. All their troubles were over.

At least this was the way Donn looked at it as he thought it over and he wondered what was the first thing they required; and it didn't take him long to think of that one. Light. Let the light in first.

Why was the light in the next place below and not in theirs? Because the electricity men went around collecting signatures to find how many would take the electricity, and in the whole place there were only two would do so. Seamus Mooney and Jack Tumelty. His own father was against it on aesthetic grounds, he had been told. What? Let them dirty black poles with the bits of string on them crawl all over the place. Look at the ugliness of them. Weren't they an insult to the sky? And not only that, they would kill half the wild fowl flying into them and breaking their necks.

Besides it cost money, two or three shillings a *week*. Wasn't it worse than the rack-renting landlords? Devil chase them, where did they think a man could find nearly twelve pounds a *year* for the sake of a bit of light on a wire. Wasn't paraffin good enough for them? Wasn't it ahead of fat grease? Where did they think poor men like them would get money like that!

It was a coincidence when all the lamps in the place suddenly went bad. Donn didn't do it deliberately. It was just that the 600-gallon tank in the yard went low because fresh stuff wasn't ordered; and what was in the bottom of the tank but mainly water that had condensed from the cold steel. Of course he refunded all the bad stuff and gave them new stuff, but that took a while, so he paid a visit to all the ladies, and encouraged them to curse the lamps, since they were the ones who had most to do with them, and he planted in their mind's eye the glory of the little switch, and the bulb, light at all times at the flick of a finger. He let it simmer, and then decided to strike the next time the Station came into the valley.

This happened twice a year, in the spring and the autumn, when the priest would come to a house in rotation, and hear confessions and say Mass and preach a homily. It was a relic of the days when the priests were hunted in the same way as wolves and Mass had to be said secretly; also for the old people who couldn't travel the long way to the church, and looked forward to the Station with all their hearts and their vivid faith.

Again it was a coincidence that this year in October the Station was to be said in Donn's house. This he found unpleasant, but at the same time he decided to make use of it.

The altar was set up in the parlour. This consisted of a table raised waist-high on wooden blocks and covered with sheets and a white tablecloth, with silver candlesticks and vases of nice flowers. It was mild weather and Meela always kept a small flower garden out at the back near the vegetable plot, so there were still flowers of some kind around the house: even in the shop, at the pub end, she had small pewter vases in front of the mirror that advertised a certain whiskey, and although the flowers didn't last long there before wilting, they looked good even to the boozers.

He got pleasure out of welcoming the people as they came. He met them at the door of the shop and said 'You're welcome' and showed them into the parlour from the kitchen. Mrs McNulty, but not Tom. 'He will be along later,' she said, shaking her head, since she deplored his religious rebellion. Jill Grealish-now-Mooney, but not Seamus since somebody had to stay home and mind the house and the children; Mrs Tumelty and Jack, since Dino had to stay at home; Bartley Folan with a new bainin coat on him and the black hat that he kept for big occasions, Mick and Mary Curran, the parents of Bridgie. There were a few very young children since the bigger children were at school, about forty people in all, so that they filled the parlour.

When they got there, the sight of the prepared altar silenced them. Some got on their knees, the few older people with their lined faces, sat on chairs, and let the beads slip through their fingers: Ned Molloy, who was near the hundred mark, a wisp of a man with heavy veins on his big hands and dark sort of spots on his forehead under the white silky hair: Sarah Magee, the Momo of the Magees with the fourteen children, a belligerent old lady who wore round spectacles when she thought nobody was looking at her, because she was proud of her age, near ninety, and always boasted that her eyes were as good as ever they were.

They all sat there, thinking or praying, until the priest's car drew up outside the door. Meela went there to welcome him, and he came in the parlour way with a small altar boy carrying a case that was nearly as big as himself.

When the priest came in, Donn discreetly withdrew himself, but he knew what went on from long ago, how the priest would put on the thin purple stole and go into the bedroom and sit on a chair and one by one the people would come in, and as he bent away from them tell him their sins and be absolved and go back again and the next one would come in. Donn remembered well. It had always embarrassed him to go to confession in the open like that. It seemed much different from the church where you went into the box and told your sins through a hole in the wall, and all you heard was a voice whispering at you, or admonishing you, giving you the penance you would have to say. Somehow in the dark you could feel that you were confessing to someone apart from the priest, but out in the open at a

76

Station, he remembered how the effort of open confession had brought sweat to his upper lip.

Afterwards the priest went into the altar and vested himself and offered up the Mass, and walked amongst the kneeling people to give them Holy Communion.

Donn, who was resting his elbows on the counter in the shop, traced it all from the tinkle of the altar boy's little bell. After Mass the priest recited the Rosary, and he could hear the murmur of the voices answering him. He wondered a little why it all left him feeling cold. He could hear the voice of the priest then talking, and afterwards reading all the names from his book, and as he called the family name the man or his deputy went up and placed a halfcrown or two halfcrowns on the plate, and it would all be over.

He was ready when they came. He had filled about twenty pint glasses of porter from the barrel with Paud's help so that when the men came through the kitchen the glasses of black stuff with the inviting froth on top were there waiting for them and they went for them like thirsty men going to a well. Most of the ladies went home to get the breakfasts ready, but Sarah Magee stayed to have a glass of port wine and a few other older grandmothers stayed for a drop, and Donn, reminding the men that he would be seeing them in an hour or so, went back again to the parlour to sit at breakfast with the priest and Meela.

When he opened the door they were standing talking to one another behind the table, which had now been removed from the window back to the centre of the floor and was laid for breakfast.

They were laughing. They didn't hear the opening of the door. He stood a minute to watch them. Meela was smiling. He noticed laughter wrinkles, fine ones, at the sides of her eyes, that her teeth were strong and even, and that when she was smiling like this she had a slight double chin, that became her since it gave her face fullness. But, he thought, I never see her smiling like that for me, and this annoyed him. The young priest had a strong face, a long nose and fair hair that was inclined to be curly.

He closed the door sharply behind him. He saw the two faces

turning towards him, and almost simultaneously the smiles departed.

'It was just the same,' he said, 'as the blinds coming down over your faces.'

They were puzzled.

'When you saw who it was,' he explained, 'your faces closed up like somebody snapping closed an open book.'

'We were talking about Nan,' the priest said, as if that answered anything. 'Your wife tells me that she can write a few sentences, and that she can ever read a few lines. This is great, thanks be to God.'

'This is great, thanks be to Meela and myself,' said Donn, coming over to them. 'Mainly Meela, because she has the patience, which she has learned in a hard school.'

'Please sit down, Father,' said Meela. 'I'll go and get the breakfast.' She went out to the kitchen.

'Thank you,' said the priest, sitting. Donn sat opposite him.

'Does it embarrass a young man like you to be called "Father"?' Donn asked.

'It takes a bit of getting used to at first,' the priest said, 'but after a while you don't even notice it.'

'What is your first name?' Donn asked.

'Bernard,' the priest said, a bit warily.

'Does anybody call you by your first name?'

'Yes,' he said, after thought, 'my parents and my brothers and sisters, other priests who knew me at the College.'

'How long are you ordained now?'

'Five years,' the priest said.

'That would make you about twenty-nine,' said Donn.

'About that,' he said.

'Do you feel you have a lot to learn?' he was asked.

'Haven't we all?' said the priest.

'Some people more than others,' said Donn, leaning back in the chair and playing with the fork. 'I wish you knew as much as I do, for example, about people.'

'You have met many more than I have,' the priest said.

'I have,' said Donn. 'Living and dying. Have you ever been at the deathbed of an atheist?'

'No,' said the priest, 'only saints.'

78

'All of them?' Donn asked.

'As far as I could see,' he said, stirring uneasily. 'After all I am not God. He is the one Who decides.'

'Have you been converted?' Donn asked.

'What do you mean by that?'

'Every man, no matter who he is,' said Donn, 'in his time has to be converted. He has to make a choice for or against these beliefs of yours.'

'Well, looking at me,' said the priest, fingering his collar, 'wouldn't you hazard a guess that I have made a decision?'

'How do I know?' said Donn. 'You might be just a conformist.'

He thought for a moment he had made him lose his temper. He saw the well-shaped hands on the table clenching a little on one another.

'I hope to God I'm not,' he said. 'Don't you think we ought to change the subject?'

'Why?' Donn asked. 'Are you running away?'

'Running away from what?' he asked angrily.

'From discussion,' said Donn. 'Are you not willing to discuss? Do you want everyone you meet to agree with everything you think is right?'

Father Murphy thought over this.

'I don't think so,' he said earnestly.

Meela came in then, carrying a tray, followed by Bridgie with the teapot and a plateful of bread.

'I'm sorry it took so long, Father,' said Meela. 'You must be hungry.'

'To tell you the truth I am,' said the priest, smiling. It was amazing how young-looking the smile made him appear.

'Well,' said Meela, 'tuck in so.'

It was a good meal, home-made brown and white bread, and bacon and eggs, with currant cake, and jam, and plates of fresh fruit.

Before he began the priest looked at Donn. Then he carefully blessed himself, Meela also, and he said grace in Latin, blessed himself again and took up his knife and fork and started to eat.

'Wouldn't God understand all that if it wasn't said in Latin?' Donn asked.

The priest chewed and swallowed and then said: 'It isn't words but what's in the heart that counts. What on earth does it matter what words are?'

'I just wanted to know,' said Donn. Meela was frowning at him.

The words of the parish priest were in the mind of the priest. There's that fella up there that came back after deserting his wife and child almost on the altar, and what is he now but a shocking bad example to the whole place. He'll have the lot of them corrupted up there, not that a lot of them weren't ripe for corruption anyhow. What a bodac like that fella needs is a good rise in the arse and when you go up there next time see that he gets it.

The parish priest was an old blunt man. He wouldn't understand the mind of a man like Donn, the priest thought. He looked across at the handsome face bent over his food. Then the blue, terribly intelligent eyes were suddenly looking into his own, challenging him, slightly mocking. How in the name of God do you tackle a fellow like that, he wondered? Certainly the ways of the parish priest wouldn't do. Yet he couldn't go back and report that he had said nothing at all. So he said it.

'Why don't you go to Mass?' he asked. 'Even in your own home?'

Donn left down his knife and fork. 'I'm glad you asked me that,' he said.

There, said the priest's mind, I knew it was a mistake.

'Are you asking me why I don't go to Mass, because I am a bad example, or are you interested in me personally?'

'Could it be both?' the priest asked.

'Why do you answer one question with another?' Donn asked. 'I don't go to Mass because I don't believe in it. Does that answer your question?'

'It does,' said the priest gently.

'And it's your fault that I don't,' said Donn.

'This is the second time I have met you,' said the priest.

'Please eat your breakfast, Father Murphy,' said Meela.

'I met you since I was a child,' said Donn, 'and your failure is my disbelief, from the penny catechism up. Who was there to say to me: Look, we are all Catholics but none of us are Christians. What was religion but being bored every Sunday morning, counting the marbles in your pocket, or later looking at the thighs and breasts of the girls in their summer frocks, or gawping with your mouth open and your thoughts not even interrupted by the bells? When you asked yourself: What am I doing here, what's it all about, there was nobody to answer. At school even, dragged out of a warm bed for Mass every morning and forced to go to this empty mummery, there was nobody to say that it wasn't mummery, to tell you what it was all about, just dull books written by dimwitted clerics loaded with clichés.'

'I am sorry for you,' said the priest.

'Don't be,' said Donn. 'I found out the hard way. What is the most important thing in the world?'

'God,' said the priest.

'No,' said Donn, 'but man. You can see him. You can hate him or you can love him. You can help him or you can injure him. That is what the world is all about; that it is peopled with men and women and children. They are God. I saw. There would be a hundred of us. Did God aim the mortar-bomb or the shell or the bullet, so that such a one would be crunched out here, another there. Do you want to tell me that God was the trigger finger of the men that fired them? Do you want to tell me that God has the least interest when you can look at an area filled with blood and guts and limbs, sprawling, unrecognizable, not even as neat as a slaughterhouse. Who cared if you didn't, because you had borrowed a cigarette from one or you had got drunk with another. What did it matter whether they were Catholics or Protestants or Jews or Mohammedans or Buddhists. What did it matter? It came to them, purely by chance, by where they happened to be at a certain time. That was all. The important thing was who they were and who would by crying for them, and what you had done for them or to them before they became bloody splotches. There are moments in everyone's life when he must choose. I know that. I made my choice. I chose the human race.'

The priest was disturbed, he saw.

'I would like to help you,' he said.

'You can't,' said Donn. 'If I saw you down washing out Sarah Magee's sheets, or digging Tom McNulty's spuds, you might be able to help me, but until I see you doing that, I see no future for you in my world.'

'Will you try and convert other people to your world?' the priest asked.

'No,' said Donn. 'That is freedom, to think as you will without other people trying to force you to their way of thinking.'

'What do words like faith and grace mean to you?' the priest asked.

'They are words of five letters,' said Donn.

'How can we ever get to understand one another so?' he asked.

'I don't know,' said Donn, 'unless you want to join me in helping the people. You look at this valley and all you see are the number who go to Mass. You don't seem to see the young ones who are going away, or the old ones who are decaying. You don't seem to see the day when this will be a deserted village. You don't seem to be doing anything about it, except saying your Masses and collecting your dues and preaching things they don't understand.'

'Being with them when they are dying,' said the priest, 'listening to their sins and having the power to forgive them. Are these not important?'

'If they believe it is a help to them it is important,' said Donn. 'But it is more important to be a help when they are alive and living and vibrant with life, not when they are dead and dying and decaying.'

'Long ago,' said the priest, 'if you said all this to a priest, he would have turned you into a drake.'

He laughed. This annoyed Donn.

'It's not a laughing matter,' he said.

'Why not?' the priest asked. 'You are not looking for anything from me except that I become a sort of saint of the washtub. You have spoken what you feel. I don't want to laugh, but when one is helpless, all one can indulge in is helpless laughter.'

'Well, I'm off now,' said Donn. 'You know where I stand.' He rose to his feet. 'The air is clear between us. I'm sure nobody will want to ask me again why I don't go to Mass.

And you can tell all that to the old man below so that he won't be trying his hand either.'

He went out and closed the door after him.

The priest toyed with his food.

'Is he really serious?' he asked.

'I think he is,' she said.

'Why do you say "think"?' he asked.

'I don't know him very well,' she said. 'The last time I met him was sixteen years ago and he hadn't left a favourable impression on me.'

'Oh,' he said. 'I see. I'm sorry. Not for you, but for myself, because I like him. I could get to like him very much. But now?'

'That's what I'm afraid of,' she said, 'that I would get to like him myself. So there are two of us.'

The priest looked at her.

'There should only be one of us,' he said.

'Oh, no,' she said, buttering a piece of bread vigorously, 'I'm not going to the stake again.'

Nine

IT WASN'T easy.

Men who chose to live in lonely places, almost completely cut off from what other men regard as civilization, educated painfully up to the age of fourteen, who only get to read books by chance, who have to travel many miles if they want to see films in a cinema, whose knowledge comes from their witness of the things and people around them, and argumentative discussions over turf fires when they have gathered in the kitchen of a man who has a battery radio set where they listen to the news – such men cannot be converted overnight to new ways.

They have lived in the lonely places because they are independent, not because they are like their own sheep. What they have is not a lot but it belongs to them and they have to thank no other man for it. It reared their fathers and grandfathers and great-grandfathers and all their generations and they see nothing wrong with it. They have enough to eat. They have enough cattle or sheep to sell as meat or wool to provide the necessary money for clothes.

They have become used to seeing their children emigrate. After all, a small farm can only support one family, and the eldest son will take over when the mother and father are old, but all the others must be provided for in some way. If they can't afford to send them to be educated after the seventh book, and if there is no work for them within cycling or walking distance of their own place, what else can they do but set off to places where they can become the hewers of wood, the drawers of water, the builders of railways and roads and tall blocks, or mercenary soldiers in other people's wars?

Donn was aware of all this because he had given it a lot of thought. It was only when the young people themselves said: we don't want to go away, and made demands, that something would have to be done about it. It needed a revolt from the young, but he'd see if conditions couldn't in the meantime be made more favourable for their staying.

He was looking at a lot of hard men, sitting around on tea-chests or bags of meal or on forms, with pint glasses in their hands, their faces seamed by the weather, all individuals, independents. No inroads had been made among those people by farmers' organizations, or the potent People of the Land. Agricultural advisers knew more than to come into the valley, since they knew that the whole few hundred acres of the valley wasn't the equal of one good midland farm.

'What's got under the women?' Tom McNulty was asking testily. 'I'm hearing nothing from morning to night but switches and bulbs, switches and bulbs. Didn't we settle all this years ago when we told them to go to hell with their poles and their follies?'

'I'm surprised at you, Tom,' said Donn. 'You were the one of us here that fought for freedom. What was that all about? Was it just so that we'd stay as we are for ever?'

'That's the size of it,' said McNulty.

'What does your son Sean think of it?' Donn asked.

'That fella!' said McNulty. His son was a sad blow to him. He had managed to get the money to send him to a boarding-school to be educated to go on to something good, and what did he do but renegue on him, and decide to become a priest. He had now been in a seminary for two years. It was very ironic. 'Young people are always wanting something new,' he said testily. 'They see all those things in other places, and nothing will do them but to have them at home. Where's the money going to come from?'

'Where did it ever come from?' Donn asked.

'You tell me something, Donn,' said Mick Dunn, a huge ruddy man who was known as Bailiff Dunn, because he got something like four pounds a year from the riparian owners to keep an eye on the salmon that came up to the lakes in the big flood. 'What are you doing all this for? What are you getting out of it?'

'And how do we know,' squeaked Mick Curran, 'that you won't be haring off again on us like you did once before and we are back again where we started?'

'That's a fair question,' said Seamus Mooney, taking the pipe from his mouth and laughing.

'All right,' said Donn. 'First because I want the electricity in my own place. That's selfish. And I won't get it unless at least seventy-five per cent of the people in the valley sign up for it. I was talking to them. They don't like coming back. We gave ye a chance before, they said, and you wouldn't take it. There's thousands of people all over the country dying for it. Why should we bother our heads about the people of Mountain?'

That stirred McNulty.

'Who the hell do they think they are?' he asked. 'Aren't they our servants? If we say: We want light, they better come running with light or we'll talk a different language to them. Not,' he went on hastily, 'that I'm for the light. I'm just saying that if we want it we'll get it and to hell with them!'

That was a good start, thought Donn, as he saw the twinkling eyes of Seamus Mooney regarding him.

'Once the light is with me,' said Donn, 'I can do other things to make money. I have to make money too. For example, going over all the books, I find that there are people in this valley who owe my business about £600.'

He paused. He didn't look at anyone, but he thought they got the message.

'I want to do something so that all of those people will make more money from the things they have at the moment, and when all of you make more money, then I make more money. If you get the light, won't you need wires, bulbs, switches? You will buy them from me if I have them. Who knows that you'll throw out the pot oven some time and put in electric cookers? And where will you get them? From me if I have them. You will want radio sets that run on electricity, not to be having the batteries running out at the most interesting part of a programme. Who knows, but the day will come when Tom McNulty will be sitting up in bed waiting for his wife to bring him his tea and toast that she has just popped out of an electric toaster?'

They started to laugh at that, a low rumble. Even McNulty had to hide a smile with a cough and a quick pull from his pint glass.

'As long as you are out in the open like that,' said Mick Dunn, 'we know where we stand, don't we? You want to make money. That's fair enough. I can't stand these feckin' fellas that go around wanting to do you good for the love of the saints or somethin'. I'm for it so. You can sign me up, and anyhow the children are playing hell with me over in the house.'

'Well, that's four of us,' said Donn. 'Myself and Seamus Mooney and Jack Tumelty and Mick Dunn.' He looked at the faces in front of him. They were far from conquered. Corney Kelly with the pure white hair and the young face sitting on the floor under a window; Tim Woods with the thick-lensed glasses, bad eyes but a great worker, all his farm and buildings neat and well-kept.

'Well, you can count me out,' said Bartley Folan. 'You hear that? The paraffin is good enough for me. It'll see me out with a few candles. You hear that?'

'It's easy known he hasn't a wife,' said Seamus Mooney.

'You were the one,' said Donn, 'who talked to me about the decay in the valley, and here's the first chance you get and you're against the light.'

'Other things, other things,' said Bartley, 'but not that. It's against nature. I would be afraid of my life of it.'

Just then the door opened and Father Murphy came in. They craned their necks at the opening of the door and as they saw him, some of them rose and touched their hats to him.

'Don't get up,' he said, 'I only came to say goodbye. I am off now.' He walked up to Donn. 'Thank you for the Station,' he said, holding out his hand. Donn took it and dropped it again.

'Won't you have a drink?' he asked.

The priest touched the Pioneer pin in his lapel. 'Not with this,' he said. 'Thank you.'

'It's a pity you can't have a pint with the people,' said Donn.

'We were talking about the electricity, Father,' said Seamus Mooney. 'Whether we should have it or not. What do you think?'

'You should have it,' he said straight away.

'What about the money then?' Mick Dunn asked.

'It will only cost two pints a week, or a packet of cigarettes.'

'Or maybe they could deduct it from the Easter dues, hah,' said Tom McNulty.

'There's that in it,' said Father Murphy. 'You could do that, Tom, if you ever gave an Easter due.'

Corney Kelly laughed.

'The bitterness! The bitterness!' said Tom McNulty, because he couldn't think of anything else to say.

Father Murphy walked to the door that led to the street.

He looked back at Donn from there. 'Thank you,' he said, and went out.

'There's a lot in what he says,' said Tim Woods.

And Donn felt frustrated. He was sorry the priest came in. He had wanted to persuade them himself. Now he knew they were persuaded just because the Church walked in and threw away a couple of sentences.

'Well, I'm for it anyhow,' said Corney Kelly. 'Let's get it signed up.'

'See what I mean?' said Donn's mind.

When they were gone, some of them home to their breakfasts, some of them reluctantly back to their work, some of them into the pub where they would spend the rest of the day trying to hold on to the holiday, Seamus Mooney sat watching Donn, who was sitting on a tea chest, a half-emptied pint glass drooping in his hand.

'What are you sad about?' he asked. 'You got what you wanted.'

'I'm not sad,' said Donn. 'I'm looking at the floor.'

'What's wrong with it?' Seamus asked.

'It's as rough as a cobbled yard,' said Donn, kicking at it. It was made of wide boards, well worn, with the knotty parts making hillocks, and the nailheads shining.

'Isn't it good enough for its purpose?' Seamus asked.

'You know what I see here?' Donn asked.

'No,' said Seamus.

'We knock out that back wall,' said Donn, 'and we make it half as long again as it is. We rip out the floor and put down narrow boards of good pine, that shine, and that people can dance on.'

'The Lord save us,' said Seamus.

'We have to think of the young people too,' said Donn. 'You

88

see? We will have a place for dancing. We'll get bands in for them. The old half set is dead. You see the shifts they go to travel away to modern dances. Well, we'll give them somewhere to dance. Maybe once a week when we have the light we'll show films. What do you think of that?'

'That's sound,' said Seamus.

'Come on out here,' said Donn, going into the kitchen and opening the door into the yard. Seamus followed him. 'You will cover that space there,' he said. 'You will erect a storehouse here, a good sound building between the long room and the vegetable garden. Also off it we will put up toilets for the ladies and gentlemen. You get it?'

'I will do this?' Seamus asked.

'Aren't you the only man that knows about proper building in the place?' Donn asked.

'I worked at it a bit in England, hodding bricks,' said Seamus. 'I put up an extra room for Jill's mother at the side of the house. I'm a gobaun. You know that.'

'You could work from plans, couldn't you?' Donn asked. 'Come on back in.' Seamus followed him. 'You could knock out the end wall and build on, couldn't you, if you were put to it?'

'If I had a proper carpenter,' said Seamus.

'Can't you get one?' Donn asked.

'Corney Kelly's son is a trained man,' said Seamus. 'He is working in the town.'

'Bring him back,' said Donn. 'He can start in here. By the time we get going there'll be enough work to keep him here for the rest of his life.'

'You mean this?' Seamus asked.

'I'm not joking,' said Donn. 'Somebody has to make a start. I will be first and then you come after.'

'I do?' asked Seamus.

'Daddy! Daddy!' said Nan, coming in then from the front door. 'Look what I have done! Look!'

'Show me,' said Donn, sitting on the form and holding out his hand.

She came to him. She sat on his knee. She was holding a jotter in her hand and a pencil.

'See,' she said. 'The writing.'

He looked at it. The letters were badly drawn. They were big, but they were distinguishable. *I saw cat*, they said.

'Did you do this all by yourself?' he asked.

'All by myself,' she said. He looked at her. Her eyes were shining. There were pencil marks on her red lips, strokes of it on her cheeks.

'It's marvellous,' he said. 'All by yourself.'

'It's right?' she asked. 'Is it right?'

'Just a little wrong,' he said. 'See. I write it now. *I saw the cat*. You see? *T-H-E*. You left that out. *I saw* the *cat*. Now you put in *the*, and you will have a perfect sentence.' He rubbed his palm on her hair.

Seamus felt embarrassed, but surprised at the look in Donn's eyes, a mixture of sadness and love. He thought of his own healthy extravert children, and he was suddenly sorry for the big man. He had become very attached to Nan in a short time, he saw. The people knew that Meela and himself were still apart. Pity, they said. God knows it's the easiest and most pleasant thing in the world to make children. Why can't they come together and do just that, and Nan wouldn't then be such a lonely tragedy?

'I'll go so,' she said. 'I'll do that. I will show you then.'

'That's right,' said Donn. 'Come and show me then.'

He watched her all the way out until the door closed after her.

'Why are you doing all those things, Donn?' Seamus asked.

'What things?' Donn asked.

'All this,' said Seamus. 'Light and building, the people. What are you doing here at all if it goes to that? You could be doing anything you like, anywhere you like.'

'That's the word, "like",' said Donn. 'That's the trouble. I would be digging a ditch. They would say, That's no place for a man like you. Come up to the office. So I would be an overseer, and they would say, That's no place for a man like you: Come into the building. Later they would say, This is no job for a man like you, come higher up; and I would quit, and go and start digging a ditch somewhere else. You see?'

'Didn't you want to get on?' Seamus asked.

'What's "get on"?' Donn asked. 'What are you doing? Where are you going? Who are you helping? What's it all about? The only thing I know about life now is that you must leave things better than you found them, but for somebody you know, not for a lot of impersonal people you will never see or meet.'

'Do you think too much about things?' Seamus asked.

'I don't think enough about them,' said Donn. 'Listen, here we have a dream. We can make it come to pass, if we want to. We can take this valley by the neck and shake it and make it come alive, not like a caricature of a village from Somerville and Ross.'

'What did they do?' asked Seamus. 'Who the hell were they?'

Donn laughed.

'It's just as well you didn't know them,' he said. 'Don't you want a new house?'

'I do,' said Seamus, 'but in my own time.'

'Everybody wants new houses,' said Donn. 'But who is going to be the first man to put one up? You should be. Listen, I have been talking and reading, and you can put up a new house, with your own labour and the help of a carpenter, for the amount of the grants you can get from the Government, for building septic tanks, water, bathroom, toilet. You will be paid for your own labour. The people will watch you and when you succeed, they will all be stirred into activity.'

'You haven't been talking to Jill?' Seamus asked suspiciously.

'Of course I have been talking to Jill,' said Donn. 'You have a dream and it will never come true unless you share it.'

'I was wondering where all the talk was coming from,' said Seamus.

Donn went over to him and took his arm.

'Come on out here,' he said, bringing him to the door and out into the street in front of the shop. In the pub the men were singing.

'Look at it,' said Donn.

There was pale sunshine on the houses scattered round the great valley. The hills were covered with the fading heather, turning brown, and the patches of sedge were golden.

'It looks all right to me,' said Seamus.

'It's something out of the past,' said Donn. 'It's like something they would put up in a museum so that people would come to look at the way men lived a hundred years ago. Now close your eyes and think of it with tiled roofs of different colours, solid houses, warm and comfortable and convenient, with fields four times greener from the lavish spreading of artificial manure, four animals cropping where there are now three, a thousand sheep where there are six hundred, men with money in the bank, and their children not so eager to take the boat at the first chance they get. Look, if even half the people survive in better places isn't that a cure? Isn't it better to see that than to wait until one by one the latch is put on the doors, and the whitewash becomes green and the thatch falls in and the whole place is left a valley of desolate ruins?'

'Oh God,' said Seamus. 'I can see that you are going to talk me into building a new house.'

Donn clapped him on the back and laughed.

Ten

BRIDGIE CURRAN and Paud McNally were married in February when there was heavy frost on the ground. They were married on a Sunday so that they could be back at work on the Monday. No announcements in the paper about Mister and Mrs McNally going to Italy for the honeymoon. Paud would just shift his belongings into Bridgie's home, since she was the only child and there was a spare room. If they went to live in McNallys' they would have had to sleep in the loft, because they had eight children. The Currans were pleased with this. They were glad Bridgie was getting married, and that there would be a young man in the house, since they were married late themselves and were getting old.

So Mick took a lot of his savings out of the mattress, the price of a three-year-old bullock, men thought, and did some lavish spending on food and drink, borrowed half the crockery and cutlery in the place, cleaned out the barn and the cowshed, which had a fairly smooth concrete floor, installed the half-barrels on tap in there, did a deal with Bartley Folan as well as Donn, got out his hard hat and brushed the green mould off it, invited half the country to the wedding, polished his leather boots, cried like a woman down in the church when the priest said the fatal words over his daughter, and afterwards came back home determined to have the father and mother of a time for himself. It could only happen once to him, he told everyone, and it was going to be memorable.

It was memorable too – for Donn as well. It was only long afterwards that he saw the way it fitted into the pattern of their lives, when he was old enough to see that life has a pattern, somewhat like a jigsaw puzzle. The pieces are all provided. It is for you yourself to fit them into the picture.

He was waiting for Meela outside. It was a night of glittering stars, like most frosty nights. The moon was on its way down towards the western sea and was reflecting itself in the waters of the lake. He walked around to where Seamus Mooney and

Cooper Kelly, the carpenter, were extending the long room. The building blocks were up and the pale roof timber ready for the insulating felt and the matching slates. The ground was littered with sand and empty torn cement bags and pieces of scaffolding, all the inevitable flotsam of builders.

'Are we going?' the voice of Meela asked behind him. 'Will you never be done looking at the building? Looking at it won't make it go any faster.'

He laughed and went up to her.

'No matter where you go in the world,' he said, 'men are always fascinated watching new buildings. In America they call them sidewalk superintendents, and leave glass holes for them to peer through. You are looking well tonight. Any man's fancy.'

'Oh,' she said, 'I am going to have a good time for myself. I am going to enjoy this hooley even if it kills me.'

'I hope it doesn't do that,' he said. 'Is Nan all right?'

'The Mooney children are with her,' she said. 'They are kind. They don't tease her.'

They started to walk up the road. She wore silk stockings and high-heeled shoes. Nice legs Meela has, he thought. She always had nice legs. He smelled her perfume too, a gentle sort, like orchards in the springtime.

'You always had nice legs anyhow,' he said out loud.

'You are full of compliments,' she said. 'What has got into you?'

'I am always paying you compliments,' he said, 'but you don't listen to them. Are you afraid?'

'No,' she said. 'I just have to protect myself.'

'Don't you think I am sincere?' he asked.

'I thought you were sincere once before, too,' she said.

'Will this go on for ever?' he asked.

'I don't know,' she said. 'You are sincere about the things you are going to do, aren't you?'

'I am,' he said, 'I am as sincere about them as I am about you.'

'That makes me wonder,' she said.

'Don't you trust anybody at all any more?' he asked.

'Myself,' she said. 'That's all.'

You couldn't miss Curran's house. There were lamp lights all over it. Out in the street before it there were several cars. As they came closer to it, they could hear the sound of lively music. It was a still night and sound travelled far, two melodeons he would say, and a frantic fiddle. Voices hurrooing, and laughter. Laughter is such a good thing, he thought. The barn sloped away from the house. They went to it and stepped in the open door. It was filled with people, mostly the older people. The big open fireplace held an enormous fire and was almost covered with kettles and pots, and the hearth all around it held covered dishes.

Mary welcomed them. She was a large woman. Bridgie had taken after her. Her face was flushed. She wore a blouse and a dark skirt, and she was stretching them well. She was sober.

'We thought you mightn't come,' she said. 'We are so pleased to see you. It would never be the same without you. Come on back to the room. The couple are there with Mick and the holy Father. You are looking like a girl, Meela, God bless you, and Donn looks like a lord, on me oath he does. Make room there now for them.'

They followed her to the open door of the room opposite the fireplace, saying, Hello Ned. How are you Sarah? Goodmorra Jack. They were all a bit bleary-eyed. Donn wondered at this because they all seemed to be drinking orange juice.

At the door Mary Curran said: 'Here they are at last, and nobody is more welcome.'

It was a small room with a big table. It held as well a sideboard of veneered wood, the top of it decorated with china dogs and marriage pictures of obviously American relatives. The other people were sitting at the table. It was a very tight fit, but there was a white cloth on the table, and it was well set.

'Mick,' she said, 'what are you doing? Won't you make them known to each other, since I have to get back to the goose?' She left them. Mick helped himself to his feet with the assistance of the chair.

'You are as welcome as good weather,' he said. 'Here, let ye come up and sit down next to me and the holy priest. Father, you know Donn and Meela. Good decent people. He made the young ones a present of a half-barrel and an elastic bed. There's goodness for you.'

'What in the name of God is an elastic bed?' the priest asked.

It wasn't Father Murphy, Donn saw, but the old man himself, a white-haired spare man, with thick hair that made his old lined face look all the older, sunken brown eyes, darting around, and a heavy chin.

'He means a foam-rubber mattress,' said Donn, squeezing himself into the chair at the priest's left hand.

'Isn't that what I said?' said Mick. 'And there's me brother Martin from over the other side of the hill, and his missis, Josey. Shake hands with the best people in the valley now, let ye.'

They did so.

'What'll they be thinking of next?' the priest wanted to know. 'Is it comfortable sleeping on elastic?'

'They say it is,' said Donn.

'You are looking very well, Bridgie,' said Meela.

She was too. And so was Paud. You would hardly recognize him in his Sunday clothes, and his hair slicked back with oil. A sort of a dazed look in his eye. Bridgie had this light in her eye too, and when she laughed, her face shone. Donn looked at them. He thought of this special moment in the lives of two people who are just married, no matter where you are, it is the same. The glow and the separateness of them from the people and the goings-on around them. It is something special. If it could be held on to for always it would mean that there would never be unhappiness in the world, but as it is, he thought, it is just a feeling that can be frantically held on to for such a short time, maybe twenty-four hours, before reality and life start robbing it of its wonder.

He looked at Meela. She had been looking at them too, and now she looked at him. Her eyes were sad, he thought. Well, ours didn't even last for twenty-four hours, I saw to that. And for a moment he felt pain.

'You'll have a glass of the hard stuff,' said Mick filling his glass.

'I will,' he said. 'Long life to you, Bridgie, and happiness and peace.'

'And a kish of children, don't forget that,' said the priest.

'And a kish of children,' Donn said.

'Here it is now,' said Mary, coming up with a steaming dish, followed by some of her girl assistants with more dishes.

'The Lord save us,' said the priest. 'Isn't it a pity I'm not younger, and have a shrunken stomach?'

It was an awesome sight, brownly roasted goose and smoked ham, chicken, sausages, roast duck, mutton and beef, enough to feed an army, but there was an army there to finish it when the people at the table had their pick of it.

Donn was hungry and he ate heartily. He was conscious of the priest beside him eating very little, and pretending to eat a lot. He was also conscious that the priest was interested in him, and kept watching him covertly, as if he wanted afterwards to write a paper on him and give a lecture on Behaviourism. So he drank most of the glass of whiskey and felt a comforting glow of recklessness creeping over his mind.

'Is it true you are going to build a dance-hall?' he heard the priest say.

'That's right,' said Donn.

'You know I'll have to oppose that,' the priest said.

'Why?' Donn asked.

'Dammit,' said the priest. 'Haven't the young people enough occasions of sin without adding to them?'

'They would be better off in a hall,' said Donn, 'than out in the haysheds.'

Oddly, the priest laughed. It was a sort of chortle between closed teeth.

'Not just dancing,' said Donn. 'Films too.'

'That's as bad,' said the priest. 'Showing them foolish life that they'll be bulling to follow, not knowing it's not for real at all, but only a shadow.'

'Do you want them all to be put into monasteries?' Donn asked.

'The monks have enough trouble,' said the priest.

'You have to allow them some freedom. If they don't get a few of the little pleasures here they'll go somewhere else and find them.'

'You don't look like the devil,' said the priest. 'Although he's a smooth operator too. And always has sound arguments.'

'Isn't this a time for joy?' Donn asked.

'I can't understand,' said the priest. 'All your people were such good Catholics.'

'Everything changes,' said Donn.

'Not that,' said the priest.

'That too,' said Donn, 'or are you going to lose more than me?'

This conversation took place under the table, as it were. Mick was in great form, shouting at Meela. He told his brother and his wife that the McGerrs always had good-looking women in their loins, complimenting Meela who was laughing at him, and that Bridgie and Paud would produce the finest children seen in Ireland since the days of the Fianna.

'I'll have to go now,' the priest said, standing up. 'I didn't have time to say the Office all day.'

'It was gracious of you to come, Father,' said Mick, 'and we'll remember it to our dying day.'

'God bless ye! God bless ye!' the priest said. 'Will you come out to the car with me?' he asked Donn.

Donn rose and followed him into the kitchen. 'I'll see you outside,' he said to Meela.

The priest made it a procession. He knew all the people in the kitchen by name, Donn saw, and asked after all their families, whom he also knew by name. They were fond of him, Donn knew. When anyone was sick or dying he was the first man they sent for, but to Donn he was a tired, old and ineffectual man.

It was good to get into the cold air. Donn walked with him towards his car. They paused there.

'Look,' the priest said, 'I'm an old man. I'll soon be gone. I'll have to go up there and they'll open the books and they'll ask me about every soul that was in my care and what I did to save them. Whether you understand that or not is immaterial. I believe it, and that's what counts. In the name of God, leave the young people alone. Don't pervert them with your own ideas.'

'You have judged me now,' said Donn grimly, 'even though you don't know me at all.'

'God forbid,' said the priest. 'I just wanted to say that.'

'Every man makes his own judgements,' said Donn.

'Isn't it grand,' said the priest, getting into his car, 'the way they are all drinking orange juice? Thank God the great drunken times are gone anyhow. It's getting too expensive, I suppose. Goodbye Donn, and I'll pray for you.'

He drove away. Donn stood looking after him.

'I heard that,' said a young man, coming up to Donn with a glass in his hand. He was Josie McNally, Paud's next brother, a fair-haired good-looking young man. 'The poor old man. Here, have a glass of orange juice, Donn.'

Donn took and smelled it. He had to draw back his face from it, it was so pungent. 'I have heard of gin and orange and gin and lime,' said Donn, 'but this is the first time I heard of poteen and orange.'

'The poor man,' said Josie, 'we didn't like to hurt his feelings.'

'No wonder everyone is half-scuttled,' said Donn.

'Are you coming dancing?' Josie asked.

'By God I am,' said Donn taking a slug of the concoction, and shrinking. 'Lead me to the barn.'

It was a gay place now, well-lighted with lamps, borrowed ones and yard lanterns. It was a cold night, so people more or less had to dance to keep themselves warm. The girls and women were well-dressed, in colourful clothes. The music was lively and in tune. He emptied his glass and he took the floor himself with one of the McNally girls. She was young and lively, and he noticed that he hadn't forgotten the steps of the dance. He talked with everyone. They were all there to enjoy themselves and in between dances he drank what was offered to him: a terrible mixture of porter, whiskey and the raw poteen. It was a mistake, he knew, because when he drank a certain amount he always became melancholy. When he felt this descending on him he pulled away into a corner where the light did not penetrate and a ladder led up to the loft above and he sat there and just looked for a while.

The gaiety was unending. This was because all the people came to enjoy themselves, as he saw, and indeed as they told him. He noticed his wife Meela. She was a favourite with all the young men, and her energy seemed inexhaustible. She was laughing with them too. He saw the way she would throw back her head and he could see the muscles moving in her throat. This is what I missed, he thought, when I walked out, a right good hell of a party like this.

He thought of parties he had attended, the cocktail parties with the women beautifully attired, no room to move. Talk, talk, talk, like here, wasn't it? Much the same talk: about neighbours, about people. But the young ones didn't care. They didn't know when the next wedding would be so they were going to make the most of it.

Mick Curran took the floor and did a step dance for them. It was amazing how good he was, if he wasn't so drunk, and kept himself upright with waving of his arms and his body. Men sang and women sang. Even Meela sang a song in Irish in a sweet faint soprano voice, like it was coming from a great distance.

He remembered then how sometimes in the summer when they would be lying out in the sun, joined only by their holding hands, she would sing a little song like that, out of the blue, from nowhere.

Later, it was some time before he saw the young man beside him.

'I was saying your wife is a wonder, Donn.'

Donn had to close one eye to focus on him. No more drinking, he said to himself then.

'It's you, Dino,' he said. 'I thought you were away in England.'

'No,' said Dino, 'I didn't go back after the Christmas.'

'Didn't you like it?' Donn asked.

'Like it or lump it,' he said, 'I'll have to go back again soon.'

'Don't go,' said Donn. 'There are things to do here.'

'Fed up,' said Dino. 'Fed up.'

He had curly hair, dark and broad Asiatic cheeks, flared nostrils, thick lips and good, even teeth. He was well-built with heavy shoulders.

'Your wife Meela is very good-looking,' he said.

'All the girls are good-looking,' said Donn.

'Nice stuff! Nice stuff!' said Dino, grinning.

'Are you fond of the girls, Dino?' he asked.

'Take 'm or leave 'm,' said Dino. 'Girls are nice. They are all right. You travelled far. You saw many girls, I bet, eh? Tickled a lot of them too, eh?'

'They are all the same in the dark,' said Donn.

This amused Dino. He laughed, slapping his hand on his leg. 'All the same in the dark, man! That's it, eh, Donn? You don't look at the mantelpiece when you are stirring the fire. You saw them all over, eh?'

'Yes,' said Donn. 'They say such girls are the most beautiful girls in the world. You see beautiful girls everywhere. That's true, Dino, but it doesn't matter a damn how beautiful they are until you find out what's inside their heads. You see?'

'It isn't their heads I want to be looking in,' said Dino.

'You are young. You'll learn,' said Donn.

'I hope I'm a long time young, then,' said Dino.

'What were you doing in England?' Donn asked.

'Driving a tractor,' said Dino. 'Come the winter the work died out. There will be more in the spring.' He was impatient now. His eyes were darting from person to person, mostly the girls, Donn saw with some amusement. He was tapping his right foot to the sound of the music.

'Why don't you get a tractor and work here at home?' said Donn.

'Man,' said Dino, 'that Woods girl has marvellous stuff in her. Look at her from behind. How could I get a tractor here?'

'Buy it,' said Donn, 'on the instalment system. Men want their fields tractor-ploughed, their hay tractor-cut. You would pay it back in two years.'

'How about my father?' Dino asked.

'There are places a horse can go that even a tractor can't, said Donn. 'There will be room for two of you.'

'You are exciting me,' said Dino. 'If only I could raise the deposit. I have only about thirty pounds.'

'I'll loan you the rest of the deposit,' said Donn. 'So go and get yourself a tractor.'

'You're fooling me. Are you fooling me?' he asked. He was so excited that he was gripping the lapel of Donn's coat.

'No, I'm not,' said Donn. 'The more of you that stay at home the better this place will be. We have at least five fields that haven't been touched with a plough for ten years. You could start on those.'

'I could contract out and about, all over the place,' said Dino.

'I will want lots of things and goods brought from the Town. You get a trailer and you can do that for me, building materials, bags of manure, other things. You will be kept busy.'

'You'll start me!' Dino said. 'You mean it! You are not drunk and be forgetting again in the morning?'

'No,' said Donn, amused. 'If I say a thing I mean it.'

'God,' said Dino. 'This is great. I never wanted to go back again. You are a stranger. You don't know where to turn. You are like an African the way they give you the back of the hand. It's still there, you know. No Irishmen need apply.'

'To hell with them,' said Donn, pleased at Dino's enthusiasm.

'Listen, you're my man,' said Dino. 'You want to do a thing, you do it. No arsing around. You will never regret this, you hear. Can I tell my father?'

'You can tell anyone you like,' said Donn.

'Whoo!' said Dino, letting a shout out of him and leaping into the air. It wasn't even noticed in the middle of the noise that was going on. 'God help the girl I grab tonight,' said Dino then and burst his way into the packed floor.

Donn laughed. A cheap way to incite enthusiasm. He would lose nothing, but Dino would gain something and there would be another young man staying at home who would be open to suggestion. All this must be for the future, he thought. It must be for the young people who come after.

He didn't drink any more.

He danced with the young girls. It was nice to feel them in his arms and that their eyes were warm to him. And the young married women. They all knew where the light was coming from, the black poles approaching inexorably over the hills which would reach them by May or June. You are a great one, they told him, sharing a secret with him, as if they were in a conspiracy against their own husbands.

He saw Meela dancing with the other young men. Now and again their eyes met. He didn't know if it was the effect of the drink, but it seemed to him that her eyes were a bit warmer. She didn't seem to like him dancing with the young ones, no more than he liked her in the arms of the virile, laughing young men.

It seemed to him in a hazy way as if they were not at the wedding of Bridgie at all, but as if they were at the tail-end of their own. The one that had never been finished. And that they were finishing it now. He had to shake his head several times to get that notion out of it. But it persisted, as if they were being polite and keeping separated until the last moment before they would be able to come together again.

This was a travesty, he thought. It has no basis.

But when the dawn came, and the jaded listlessness of the last drop being extracted from a rare festive occasion, and Meela came to him in a lull and said: 'We will go home, now, Donn,' and when he went with her after bidding goodbye all around, and they went into the cold air, on their road home, he found that he was holding her hand.

Eleven

HE WAS surprised when she didn't take her hand away.

It was cold. Over in the east there was a faint streak of approaching dawn over the hills. The moon had gone. It felt as if they were walking in a pool, a saucer of darkness. There was still light from the stars.

Suddenly Meela slipped and stumbled. He put his arm around her. Her coat was hanging loosely open. He felt the warmth of her body through the thin stuff of the dress. Like long ago.

'I must be squiffy,' she said, as she recovered and pulled away from his arm. 'I drank some of that orange juice that wasn't orange juice at all.' She shook her head. The dark hair fell about her face and she pushed it back with her free hand. 'Do you feel as if we were in a sort of nightmarish dream?'

They were walking on, more carefully now.

'I do,' he said. 'It is strange you should feel it too. Like we were taking part in something that was never finished.'

'Weddings are always that way,' she said. 'People who are married keep thinking of all the troubles that are facing the young couple. People who are not married are envying them, because they don't know what the reality will be like. Isn't this it?'

'It's a fair summation,' he said. 'If somebody told them what is facing them, they wouldn't believe it.'

'Why did you run away?' she asked. 'Why did you really run away?'

'I tried to tell you,' he said.

'It's too vague,' she said. 'Did you think of what you were doing to me? Did you think of what you were leaving me to face?'

'It is easy to be wise many years later,' he said.

'If it was now,' she persisted, 'if we had just been married now, would you do the same thing?'

'I might,' he said.

'I thought that you were sure,' she said. 'It never entered my head that you would do what you did. It took me months to realize that you had actually walked out on me on our wedding night. Did you hate me then? Because I was pregnant? Was I ugly? All the things you said to me in the years before. All the dreams. Was it because I was promiscuous?'

'I wanted to know about myself,' he said, talking carefully. 'I would never know then. Smothered in that house, bad enough as it was, but with you and a child as well. How would I ever escape to find out what I was? I thought it was the only way. I couldn't face it.'

'And did you find out what you are?' she asked.

'You shouldn't say you were promiscuous,' he said. 'That wasn't true.'

'I loved you,' she said. 'Whatever you did or said was right.'

'Is that being promiscuous?' he asked.

'Nobody should ever surrender that much of themselves to somebody else,' she said.

'So you learned a lesson,' he said. 'You got something out of it.'

'Oh, I got more than that out of it,' she said bitterly. 'I had to face it all on my own. Salacious pity. You would never know what that is because you could never be a pregnant girl. I couldn't run away. Your father and mother were too strong for me. My own father needed me. And then Nan needed me. And then your mother needed me. And then your father needed me. Other people's need. That is all the use I have been. Supplying other people's need. And supplying yours was the first one that led to all the others.'

'It was more than that,' he said. 'You know it was more than that.'

'How do I know?' she said. 'When you were gone, I said: He will be here soon. He is only gone somewhere short. I watched at the window until it was dawn. I couldn't believe that you had gone away. I couldn't believe it during that day or the next day. You were seen going on the train. But I couldn't believe that either. Trains run in two directions, don't they? Then they said: Oh, he will write. And that absorbed a few years. But you never wrote, did you?'

'No,' he said. 'I never thought I would come back. I wanted all of you to forget me, to forget that I ever existed.'

'But you came back?' she said. 'Why did you come back?

'I wish I knew,' he said. 'Did you think I had forgotten you?'

'You must have,' she said.

'I did not,' he said. 'It is the only thing left to believe in, the tie, between two people. Because it must be mystic as well as physical.'

'Are you trying to tell me that you remembered me?' she asked. 'Do you really expect me to believe that?'

'I don't expect you to,' he said. 'I am only telling you about the fact of it. I met many girls on the way, and many women, but always they fell short of you. I don't care whether you believe this or not. When they talk in the sagas about love potion, an actual drink, this is what they are really talking about. Two people meet, and for ever afterwards, no matter how hard they try to break away their destinies are bound together for good or ill.'

'That sounds good,' she said. 'But what truth is in it?'

'You ought to know,' he said. 'Did you make no effort at all to break away from my hold on you?'

'Where?' she asked. 'In a small village community, with one shop?'

'I bet you got invitations,' he said.

'Oh, yes,' she said. 'Men look at someone like me, a pregnant girl left at the altar practically, and they say: Oh, there's a one, she should be easy meat. Because you don't have to marry her. On the rare occasions we went to the big town, you would meet those men, who can spot people like me a mile away, people like me and young widow-women. Their hands are always stretched out for us, under the table at a dinner, whereever the vultures gather. So all I did was to tear up your photographs.'

'That did something towards destroying the image?' he said.

'Not much,' she said. 'Because I looked at them so long before I destroyed them. You and I in the hayfields on a summer day with pitchforks in our hands. The one taken at the dress dance in the hotel. The one in the boat on the river. The one of you in the river with your rod bending, and the salmon leaping. You had no picture at all of me to destroy?'

'No,' he said, 'I left them all after me.'

'I found them,' she said. 'I burned them too.'

'It was small satisfaction you got out of that,' he said. 'I had you in my mind. I couldn't get you out of it. Can't you think of that as being worse in its way than destroying a few photographs?'

'A just punishment?' she asked.

'I don't know,' he said. 'I don't believe in this punishment. Men do things. They turn out right or wrong. They are happy or they are sad. Now that I am walking this frosty road with you, and I feel your hand in mine, I realize that I am sad, that the action I took must have been wrong, but that there was no other action I could have taken. It is useless going back. That is history. What is important is the here and now.'

'That's what I am afraid of,' she said. 'I was wrong then and how do I know that I am not wrong now?'

They walked on in silence. He could hear the crunch of their shoes on the frozen dirt of the road. He thought over what she had just said: How do I know that I am not wrong now? He took up this sentence as a hungry man would take up the crusty end of a loaf and chew it. It had a meaning, but he would have to savour it and taste it with his tongue, find out if the meaning he hoped was in it was real or imaginary.

They came to the house, and stood at the front door that led into the parlour. They stood looking at it as if they had never seen it before, for quite a while. He was conscious of the warmth of the palm of her hand, and her breath visible on the cold air. Her palm wasn't smooth and powdery to the touch as it had been long ago. He could feel a roughness and a callous or two at the base of her fingers, but in some odd way this seemed to make her more real.

It made him sad. It seemed to symbolize all she had done over the years, looking after the needs of other people as she had said; working, keeping a place together, holding on, so that she could hand over to the heir something he wasn't really interested in, only now as a sort of chess game, using the pieces for an obscure objective.

He moved and opened the door. He dropped her hand. He

went ahead of her. The light was dim. The lamp was turned low. He turned it up. Their other two lamps were on the table ready for them.

'It will be a great thing,' he said, 'when the switches are in, and the bulbs.'

She closed the door.

He took up the two lamps.

'Here,' he said, handing hers to her. 'We will go to bed. I don't really know how you could ever bear to talk to me. I must fill you with revulsion.' He walked ahead of her, when he had blown out the parlour lamp. Her light threw a huge shadow of him on the wall in the hallway, three times his size, making him look like a great ape.

He stood at his own door, his hand on the knob.

'Goodnight Meela,' he said. 'I am sorry.'

He went into his room, walking towards the table beside the bed to leave the lamp on it.

He was surprised when he saw that his great shadow went before him. He turned.

'I hadn't finished what I set out to say,' said Meela. She was standing looking at him. Her eyes were bright. He thought there was a flush on her face. But that might be the after-effects of the orange juice.

'Oh,' he said, leaving down the lamp and sitting on the bed.

'I didn't like to see you dancing with the young girls,' she said. 'When you looked at me over their heads, I felt like long ago at dances when you would look at me over the heads of the duty-dancing girls.'

'How did you feel?' he asked.

'I tried to tell myself that it was only secondary stimulation, just that because there would be a wedding night for Bridgie and Paud, every person there thought of this and remembered their own or imagined their own of the future. That sort of thing.'

'I see,' he said. 'Most people feel that at weddings.'

'And then there was the orange juice as well,' she said. 'That is supposed to be a stimulant too, isn't it?'

'So they say,' said Donn gravely.

'This lamp is heavy on my hand,' she said. 'I will leave it beside yours. Do you mind?'

'No,' he said.

'Do you mind if I sit beside you on the bed?' she asked.

'No,' he said.

She sat beside him. Their combined weight brought their bodies close together.

'Why did you sit down on the bed?' she asked.

'My legs were shaking,' he said.

'You see what I mean,' she said. 'You too. Maybe it's all just physical, do you think?'

'If you wish now,' he said, 'you can stand up and go into your own room and I will do nothing to stop you.'

'Once,' she said, 'you lectured me about the duty of Christianity and charity, to forgive. You remember that?'

'I said so many things,' he said.

'I remembered,' she said. 'I think I have been in love with you all the time. I don't know. That's why I'm afraid. Maybe I am wrong. If I am right, and I say that I love you, having tried hard to hate you, and we love, maybe you will go away again.'

'Meela,' he said, rubbing the palms of his hands together, 'I will never go away from you again. You know what they say about the man who looked at his own face in the mirror and then went away and forgot what he looked like. I looked and I went away. But the mirror is not a mirror as such. It is like the love potion. This time the mirror must be the eyes of somebody you love. This is where you must always see yourself, and then you will know when you are right and when you are wrong.'

She stopped his rubbing palms with one of her hands. She had her other hand on his shoulder.

'All right,' she said. 'I love you. Doesn't that bring us back where we were before?'

'Are you sure of this, Meela?' he asked.

'No,' she said. 'You will have to make me sure of it.'

'I will,' he said, raising his hands to her.

Twelve

THE LIVES of people are as closely bound as the weave of a tapestry. There is really no such thing as a casual meeting. No man can be an island. True, he doesn't understand himself, but he cannot shut himself away from the people around him. The hermits tried to do that in the desert and they were sought out, and forced to set up communities. Even there they are not without temptations – like the story of the two hermits who lived in amity in side-by-side cells until one succeeded in making a wooden spoon from the branch of a thorn tree and excited envy in his companion.

Sean McNulty came intimately into Donn's life on a day in late June. There had been much rain, as a foreign tourist said, and the river was in full spate and falling and a few salmon had managed to make the long journey from the faraway sea, jumping rockfalls, avoiding lures, and enticing flies, determined to get to the high lakes where they would jump and fall on their sides to get rid of the irritating sea lice that moved in their own jellies all over their bodies.

So Donn was fishing.

Sean McNulty cycled home from the church below where he had been attending morning Mass. He was a tall young man, taking his height from his mother and his thick hair from his father. He was dressed in the black suit of a seminarian with a white shirt and a black tie. He was nineteen years of age. He was handsome and the girls at Mass on Sunday admired his long eyelashes. They regarded his embryonic vows of eternal chastity as a waste of a nice marriageable young man. They sighed that all the good-looking eligible ones either went into the Church or emigrated.

Sean was unhappy, even though the morning was sparkling after the rain and the sun was reflecting a millionfold from even the blades of new green grass, and the tumbling waters of the overblown streams. He had an unenviable task in front of him. He could procrastinate. He didn't have to go back to the seminary until October. He could put it off until then. He had served Mass in the Church. He had been conscious of the presence of God and dismayed at the lack of response in himself.

So he would have to go home to his mother and say to her: Mother I am very sorry but I have not got a vocation. I do not want to be a priest. Not, I do not *think* I want to be a priest, but I do not want to be. There was no thinking in it. He knew. Besides, when he had talked over his doubts, they had confirmed them for him. As far as they knew, and they were experienced men, he had no vocation for the priesthood after two years trying.

He walked the bicycle to the gap and stood there for a few moments before mounting and freewheeling down. For a time he didn't know what disturbed him about the look of it and then his eyes focused on the line of black poles carrying the electricity into the valley. Nobody could say they were beautiful. He wondered what the birds thought of them, particularly the ones who hit them in the dusk in flight and broke themselves on them, so that you often found them on the road dead or dying. But it was progress and the light from the switch was comforting.

His mother had his breakfast ready, as usual, fried bacon and eggs and brown bread and butter. She was a thin woman, very active. Her eyes were always alive and filled with questions. She took great pride out of the fact that he was supposed to have a vocation. She treated him differently from the rest of the family. This made him uneasy.

'And who said the Mass this morning?' she asked.

'Father Murphy,' he said.

'He's an active young man,' she said. 'He gets around. He takes an interest. Not like some of them. If that young man had been around at the time of the trouble, your father wouldn't feel the way he does.'

'No,' said Sean. 'Father Murphy would probably have been out with a gun himself. Times have changed anyhow. How can we throw our minds back and see what way it was then? Maybe the priests were right to try and stop the fighting the only way they knew.'

'They should have been Irishmen first,' she said.

'A lot of them were,' he said. 'They were killed for it.'

'One swallow doesn't make a summer,' she said. 'Aren't you hungry? You are not eating.'

'I'm not very hungry,' he said, wondering if he would tell her now or if he would let the months go by before he told her.

His father came in.

'I'll have a cup of tea,' he said, sitting down at the table, pushing the hat back from his forehead. 'I'm not as young as I was. But I can still get a good edge on the scythe.'

'Why on earth don't you let Dino cut your hay?' said Sean. 'It would only cost a few shillings. You could be doing other things then.'

'Lazy ways,' his father said, buttering a piece of bread. 'You fellows would be better off if they taught you how to dig and mow instead of stuffing your heads with a lot of bloody nonsense. When it's all over isn't it only experience that counts.'

'It does good to know first,' said Sean.

'It galls me to think of a young man like you becoming a priest in a few years' time. What will you be? Twenty-five, twenty-six. You'll come out of there and you'll be expected to advise men twice as old as yourself about things. How? Won't they know more than you? Won't they all be near dead by the time you have enough experience to know what they are talking about?'

'Knowledge is a short way to experience,' Sean said. 'What you are doing is studying and gaining the benefits of other men's minds. Great minds.'

'I don't see it,' his father said. 'So you get old and encrusted in your ways like a lot of them. Dug-in positions. No forward march. All separated from real living.'

'We were over all this before,' said Sean. 'We are tramping old ground.'

'Well, plough it! Plough it!' his father said, laughing. 'That is what you are supposed to be, a holy ploughman. Put your hand to the plough and don't turn back.'

Sean's heart sank. He looked at his father. He was a good man. He worked hard. He had big hands, broad shoulders.

Long ago he had executed two men with a .45 revolver. He had told them about this. They were proved informers. They had been court-martialled by the Volunteers. Afterwards he had fought against the free-staters until he was taken up and interned. It was during that time, when he was on the run and had gone to Mass and went to the altar rails for Holy Communion, that the priest had passed him by and left him with his tongue out and his eyes closed. The republicans were under an interdict at the time. When it dawned on him that he had been passed by, he stayed at the rails, alone, his face pale, but the priest had gone back to the altar and left him there. So he got up and walked down the aisle with the eyes of the people on him, and he had walked out the door of the church and had never gone back.

Sean wondered if it was his father's complete antipathy to the Church that had turned his own thoughts to it. Very few sons liked to be the same as their fathers. They wanted to be different. All these things had happened to his father over thirty years ago, but they were the highlights of his life, the dramatic moments that he had known. Very few dramatic things happen to men in the course of their lives, and the ones that do, they nurse them. He knew his father had been mortified by his decision, that it gave an opportunity for ironic laughter in the valley. All he said, because he was a just enough man in his way, was: well I hope you make a better one than the fellows I knew.

And now he would never know whether he would or not.

'Do you want my help in the field?' he asked.

'No,' his father said. 'Later will do. Patsy and Jane are there. Go off for yourself. You want to get some of that book-larnin' blown out of your brain. Take a rod, there are a few salmon up. But don't let Mick Dunn the bailiff catch you. We will need a hand at the hay in a few days. Off with you.'

'You didn't eat much,' his mother said to him.

'I ate plenty,' he said. 'I'm going down to the river.'

'Bring a coat. It might rain,' she said.

'It won't,' he said. 'Rain won't hurt me.'

'You are not used to the open now,' she said.

'Please, Mother,' he said.

'All right, all right,' she said, 'but don't say I didn't warn you.'

He got away from her. He couldn't tell her now. He was impatient with her fussing. He knew she was deeply pleased that he had chosen to be a priest. She had probably prayed hard for it and was still at it. She was a sincerely Christian woman. It would mean a lot to her spiritually to have a son a priest. Now she wouldn't. The thought made him squirm, but he would have to postpone the telling of it.

He took the greenheart rod from the pegs in the barn. It was mounted, with an odd-looking fly that his father had made himself, a regular killer, his father said. He put it on his shoulder and set off for the river.

He came down the hill road, and then broke from it and set off across the fields. He heard the sound of the tractor on his right and veered that way. He had to go over a short hill before he could see the red machine in the field. It was a two-acre field and most of it was laid low in neat swathes. There was a girl following the tractor, clearing the blades at the corners with a rake. He stopped at the stone wall that ended the field, rested his arms on it and watched them. Dino was a good man. He had proved that. He was looking back. When he came near the end of the side he was cutting he saw Sean and waved his arm and shouted. Sean waved back. He turned off the engine, swung his leg over the iron seat and came towards him.

'Hello, Sean,' he said. 'I haven't seen you since you came back. How are you?'

'Don't let me keep you from your work,' said Sean.

'Ach,' said Dino, sitting on the wall, 'I can do more in an hour than the oul' fella can do in two days. How are you? You're looking great. A bit pasty maybe, like a bad apple tart.'

'I'm fine,' he said. Dino was sunburnt. His shirt-sleeves were rolled, his arms bursting with muscle. He was a vibrant person.

'Quit it up for a minute, Susan,' he said. 'Come and talk to Sean.'

The girl smiled. She threw down the rake and came towards them. She was about seventeen, a fair-haired girl. The sun tanning suited her. She was wearing a light dress. As she came towards them the wind of her walking pressed the dress to her body. She was well-built. Sean was watching this. Suddenly he saw Dino's eyes on him – he couldn't help himself – he flushed.

'Hello, Sean,' Susan McNally said, holding out her hand. 'Glad to see you home.' Her hand was hard to his fingers but the back of her hand soft to his thumb. He dropped it quickly.

'You go to work on Sean, Susan,' said Dino, 'and he'll never go back to the monastery.'

'It's not a monastery,' said Sean.

'Whatever it is,' said Dino. 'One coort with Susan would be better than three years there.'

'It's something you'll never get anyway, Dino,' she said.

'Wait'll you see,' he said. 'When the hay is saved we'll christen it.'

'Not while I have a pitchfork,' she said. 'Will you be home long, Sean?'

'Until October,' he said.

'You have three months to work on him,' said Dino. 'You mean to say you never see any girls at all in there, Sean?'

'Very rarely,' said Sean. Susan was leaning on her elbow beside him. He noticed the soft roundness of her arm, the way her breast swelled the stuff of her dress.

'I must be going,' he said.

'Urgent appointment?' asked Dino sardonically.

'I don't want to be interrupting your labours,' said Sean.

'We'll be seeing you, Sean,' said Susan.

He waved a hand at them and walked off.

'How would you like him in the haggard, Susan?' Dino asked.

'He has lovely eyes,' she said. 'It's a pity. All the good-looking ones want to become priests.'

'What about me?' he asked.

'You'll never have a vow of chastity anyhow,' she said. 'No more than a stallion.'

'With me the girls know what they want,' he said, getting off the wall.

'With you they know what they don't want,' Susan said, walking back towards the tractor. She paused to look after the departing Sean. She liked his gentleness. She was conscious of his looking at her and not looking at her.

Sean veered his way to the right, where he knew a pool from which he would not be visible from the houses. Mick Dunn as a bailiff was a bit of a joke, but if he saw you he would have to do something. When he didn't see you, he could do nothing.

He came over the crest and looked down at the pool. There was a man fishing there, throwing a fly expertly from a long rod, a man with a sensitive ear too. He heard Sean's movements over the sound of the swollen river and looked up. He drew in his line carefully.

'Hello, Sean,' he said. 'Are you the new bailiff?'

Sean laughed. He helped himself down the slope with his free hand.

'No,' he said. 'Just a would-be poacher like yourself.'

They shook hands.

'I haven't seen you since you came home,' said Donn.

'I hear you have been doing great things,' said Sean.

'Don't believe it,' said Donn. 'Just jizzing up the natives, mainly by blackmail, in order to serve my own needs.'

'I don't believe that,' said Sean. 'Are there any salmon in the pool?'

'There are three,' said Donn. 'Come and look at them.' He got down on his belly with his head over the water. Sean got down beside him. 'Now see,' said Donn. 'Watch the one white stone.' Sean did so. After a few seconds he could make out the waving body of a salmon.

'Wow,' he said.

'He must be eight to ten pounds,' said Donn. 'The others are small. This is the fellow we want. He wouldn't take my fly. Drift yours down over him. Get well back from the water.'

Sean went back from the water and freed his line. He gauged his distance and placed the fly gently at the head of the race so that it would sweep down over the fish and then travel up against the stream at the pull of the line. He wondered at his excitement. But it was always that way, even shooting a rabbit with a .22, you got this excitement. He thought of his father lying in the heather with a rifle ready to shoot men. What feelings would you have then?

'A little higher at the stream and more in the middle,' Donn called to him.

He adjusted his cast.

'That was right over him,' said Donn. 'He won't take. But try again.'

Sean tried again and again and again.

He lay down beside Donn. The salmon was in the same place.

'I tried every fly in the box,' said Donn, 'except one. Will I get him?'

'How can you get him?' Sean asked.

'Ah,' said Donn. 'We tried all the fair means. Now we will have to try other means.'

He untied his blue-coloured fly from the line, and took a dun-coloured one from an envelope. 'What do you think of that?' he asked. It was a big awkward-looking fly.

'It doesn't look like anything at all,' said Sean. 'Like a piece of driftwood, that's all.'

Donn laughed. He tied it to the gut. 'Now watch,' he said, as he stood up. He didn't go back far. He stayed where he could cast and see the salmon at the same time. Sean watched the fly land. It was hard to see it in the boggy water. He saw it taken down by the stream and sinking, and being carried towards the weaving body of the salmon. Then he saw Donn jerking the rod and immediately the pool was a flurry of action.

'Here,' said Donn, handing him the rod. Sean thought what a generous gesture this was. He wondered, if he himself had a salmon on a rod, if he would pass the fight, and all its pleasure, to somebody else. Then he had to concentrate on holding the salmon, which was going mad. The tackle was strong, so he could hold him from going upstream. He managed to keep him in the pool, with all his leaping and straining. Out of the water in the sunlight he was a gleaming silver colour, sparkling and beautiful, curving and falling.

In twenty minutes he was lying on the bank. Donn hit him on the head with a stick and he quivered and died, and almost immediately it seemed the silver glints started to leave him.

'But the hook is not in his mouth,' said Sean, looking down

at him. The hook was buried near his gill.

'That's why he fought so hard,' said Donn. 'He was foul-hooked.' He was freeing the hook from the fish. It took him quite a time. It was bloodied. He reached into the water and cleaned it. He handed it to Sean.

'It's very heavy,' said Sean, surprised.

'Of course it is,' said Donn. 'It's leaded. If you can see a fish, a stubborn fish who doesn't answer to sporting rules, you can always hook him with that. Do you want it?'

Sean hesitated. Donn laughed.

'Are they teaching you to be a fishing gentleman as well?' he asked.

'Not that,' said Sean. 'I always thought there was only one way to catch fish.'

'We learn something every day,' said Donn.

Sean laughed.

'I've been hearing a lot about you,' he said. 'It is all true. You are livening up the valley at a great rate. Thank you for the fly. I'll keep him.'

'He'll keep you going,' said Donn, 'until you go back.'

'I am not going back,' said Sean.

'You said you are not going back?' said Donn, surprised.

'That right,' said Sean. He was sitting, arms on his knees, smoothing the strange fly with his fingers. 'I haven't told anybody yet, but you now.'

'Why me?' Donn asked.

'I don't know,' said Sean, honestly. 'Why would I tell you?'

'I'm damned if I know,' said Donn. 'I'm the last person you should tell. Why don't you want to go back?'

'I know now it's not for me,' said Sean. 'I don't mind being poor and I don't mind being obedient, but I don't want to be chaste. I like looking at girls. Girls are very beautiful. How can I feel like that and not know? So you find a peg. I find Latin. I say: I am very thick, I just cannot learn Latin, so I don't; but it's not Latin you see, at all. That's just a peg. I have no vocation to be a priest.'

'Whew,' said Donn.

'I'm finding it hard to tell my mother,' said Sean.

'You told me,' said Donn. 'That's practice. Tell a few more and it will come easy on you.'

'No,' said Sean. 'I told you. I don't know why. You don't believe in anything at all, they say.'

'I believe in you,' said Donn, 'and me, and all the people.'

'Thanks for listening,' said Sean. 'After all, one time you were the Lords of the Mountain and people went to you with their troubles.'

'That's dead,' said Donn. 'I'll tell you. We will fish up the stream and soon Meela will come with lunch in a basket and we will sit and eat it. I will think. After that you should go home and tell your mother. If you have a bad tooth what use is waiting to get it pulled? Come on, rise up and we will go fishing.'

So they rose up and went fishing.

Thirteen

THEY FISHED for about another hour, but all they caught were a dozen small brown trout, some of them so small you would wonder how on earth they got their mouths open widely enough to take the big flies.

They worked the pools back to where they had caught the salmon, then Donn said: 'That's enough for now, we will wait for the lunch to come.'

'Why didn't you bring it yourself in the bag?' Sean asked him.

Donn smiled. He didn't want to say: Because Meela will bring it and I like to see her and I am looking forward to her coming. So he said: 'Women's work,' imitating Tom McNulty, who wouldn't peel a potato.

Donn liked Sean. He was a gentle young man. He had a slow probing mind. He didn't know it yet himself, but his studies had left a mark on his mind, trained it.

'What did you find worst there?' he asked, 'apart from the longing for the pretty girls?'

They were lying down. The sun was warm. They were sheltered from the wind.

'The bell,' said Sean. 'Everything is done by the bell. It is the hallmark of obedience. You must answer it fleetly, and at once. This is to train you to obedience, to discipline your body and your mind. If you are going to revolt you will revolt against the bell.'

'It seems sensible enough,' said Donn. 'When you are freed from the bell will you find liberty?'

'I don't know,' said Sean. 'You rage against something and then when it's taken away you feel lost without it.'

'Are you going to stay here?'

He shifted uncomfortably.

'I don't know,' he said. 'This spoiled priest thing people have.'

'That's nonsense,' said Donn. 'Years ago it might have mattered. Things have changed. Besides, two years in a seminary doesn't make anyone even a half-spoiled priest. Do you want to go away? Do you want to go out and see the world?'

'No,' said Sean, 'I like it here. I like what we are doing now. I like the water and the hills and the hay and the oats and the big fires in the winter, and the frost on the road and roast goose at Christmas time. I am not made for adventures. You had many of them. What did it do for you?'

'I don't know,' said Donn. 'I am thinking over all that. One day you can hear all about it. Unless you settle somewhere and start crying into your green beer on St Patrick's Day, you are like fluff carried on the wind. It took me a long time to come home. Now I am home, I like it very much. I keep waiting for something to happen to break up this feeling of contentment. Holding my breath. You say; it cannot last. Something has to happen. Where is happiness? You only ever catch on to the tail of it for fleeting seconds. You are pursuing it all the time. I think that is what life is all about; this pursuit of happiness. What is it? If you got it would you know what to do with it? Do you feel free now?'

'When I have told my mother,' said Sean, 'then I think that I will feel free.'

'We need young men in the valley,' said Donn. 'Think over that. Look at Dino. He is making a good living. This was always a fit place to live but a hard place to make a living. If we can make that part easier we would have everything. I will make you a proposition when we go down below. You can see what you think of it.' He was standing looking down. 'Ah, here they come at last,' he said. Sean stood beside him. He could see the two figures passing the lake and walking beside the river. That is the mother, Sean thought, looking at the one in the coloured dress, then he saw the sun glinting on her hair and had to change his mind. That is the daughter. He knew her, but he hadn't seen much of her for years. His mind registered the fact that she had grown so that you could only tell the difference between the mother and the daughter by the colour of their hair.

He looked at Donn. He had a strong face with lines etched at the mouth and the eyes, but it was a soft face now. He was smiling. He was a tall man, and broad. The top of Sean's head would be only up to his chin. Sean felt affection for him. He had been kind to him. He had listened to his talk. He could not imagine talking to his own father in this way. His father was always inclined to refute everything you said whether he meant it or not.

'There are many pretty girls in the valley, Sean,' Donn said. 'You find the right one and marry her.'

'I didn't learn anything about that in the seminary,' said Sean. 'They didn't even teach you the rudiments of coorting.'

Donn laughed.

'That's instinctive,' he said. 'Like never forgetting how to swim when you have learned, or to drive a car or a bicycle. You don't have to have book-learning for that, I can tell you.' He waved his hand and then walked out to meet the two coming towards them.

Nan was ahead carrying the basket with the white cloth covering the food.

'I beat Mammy,' she said.

'You bet she did,' said Meela, her hand on her heart. 'Mammy is not as young as she used to be.'

Sean noticed that she was looking at Donn with very bright eyes. Donn went to her and took her hand and walked back with her.

'Sean has been fishing with me,' he said. 'I hope you brought enough food.'

'Hello, Sean,' Meela said, holding out her hand. 'You are welcome home. And did you catch any fish?'

'We caught a salmon,' said Sean. 'He's a big one.'

'You killed the fish?' said Nan.

'Yes,' said Sean. 'Come and look at him.' He walked to the bank where they had laid him under the shelter of a stone, covered with green ferns.

'No, no,' said Nan pulling away. He looked at her in surprise. She is the most beautiful girl I ever saw, his mind said. Why didn't I notice that before?

'She doesn't like to see things killed,' said Donn.

Sean covered the dead salmon again.

'Oh,' he said. 'I'm sorry.'

'Nan,' said Meela, 'don't you remember Sean?'

She looked at him. She considered him. She came over towards him, holding out her hand.

'Hello, Father,' she said.

'I'm not a "Father",' he said, shocked at the childlike eyes in the almost perfectly featured face.

'It's the black clothes,' said Donn.

'No Father?' Nan asked.

'Only Sean,' he said. 'Just Sean, Nan.'

'Oh,' she said, considering him, her eyes not leaving him, moving up and down. 'Hello, Sean.' She looked at Donn for approval.

'That's it,' said Donn. 'Great girl. Now open up the basket. I'm hungry.'

They sat down and Meela opened the basket. She spread the white cloth and took out the food, buttered brown cake and meat which she sliced with a knife, bottles of stout and minerals.

'Do you often have picnics like this?' Sean asked.

'Oh, yes,' said Meela, laughing. 'We are very high-class people. We tour a lot, ever since my husband came back from foreign parts with all his high-class notions.'

'And Paud and Bridgie look after the store,' said Donn.

'I heard about that wedding,' said Sean. 'I believe it lasted for a week.'

'It was a memorable wedding,' said Donn, chewing, and meeting Meela's eyes. She blushed. Sean wondered at this.

Donn held out a bottle of stout to him.

'Oh, no,' said Sean, pointing to his Pioneer badge in the lapel of his coat.

'Oh,' said Donn. 'Do you mean to say you have never had a drink in your life?'

'Not an alcoholic one,' said Sean.

'Explain it to me again,' said Donn.

'Well,' said Sean. 'You make a heroic offering, see. You sacrifice yourself for the sake of all men who are alcoholics.'

'And what does this do for them?' Donn asked. 'As far as I can see it just leaves more booze to go around.'

'I don't know what it does,' said Sean. 'Just by you making

a sacrifice maybe it saves somebody else. I don't know.'

'But what sacrifice are you making?' Donn asked, 'if you don't know what you are sacrificing about?'

'Hah?' said Sean, like Paud.

'You take a drink or two,' said Donn. 'You find out what it is like. It's very nice. Men have always liked it. But what is the point? Sacrifice means giving up something you like for the sake of other people. How the hell do you know what you are giving up if you never tasted it?'

'Don't mind him, Sean,' said Meela.

'I never thought of it that way,' said Sean. 'You just think of the badge as a protection. People see you wear the badge and they don't press you to take a drink.'

'That's all cod,' said Donn. 'Now if you were a terrible boozer and took the pledge and wore the badge there'd be some sense in it. Besides it's like wearing virtue on your sleeve. The sacrifice would be harder if you had no badge and you had to resist temptation without its help.'

'Can't you leave him alone, Donn?' said Meela. 'Don't tangle with him, Sean. He'll leave you so that you won't know where you are.'

'Have a bottle of stout,' said Donn, holding one out to him.

Sean looked at it. 'No, thanks,' he said, 'but I'll think about it.'

They laughed.

'When we leave here,' said Donn, 'I want you to come with us. I want to show you a few things.'

'All right,' said Sean, thinking how pleasant it was to be with them in the sunshine, eating from a basket. He tried not to look at Nan too much, but he was fascinated by her. She had the body of a grown girl and yet she sat like a child, with sprawling limbs. She ate her food heartily, but she did not talk at all, unless suddenly to point her finger and say: 'Look!' at a bird maybe, or a gull, or a feather floating on the river. When she finished eating she leaned her hands in the river and dried them on the grass and then wandered away from them by the water, throwing in pieces of stick and following their progress along the bank.

'Sean is not going back to the seminary,' said Donn.

'Oh,' said Meela. 'Maybe you shouldn't have told me that.'

'It doesn't matter,' said Sean, 'everybody will know it soon.'

'Are you sad?' she asked.

'I am a bit,' he said. 'Nobody wants to fail at anything I suppose. But then I am glad because I have made the decision.'

'I hope everything works out well for you,' she said.

'Well, we need somebody to keep the books below,' said Donn. 'Isn't Sean the man for us?'

'There will soon be no work left for us at all,' she said.

'That'll be the day,' he said. 'Don't you know that the essence of genius is delegation? Would you like to work with us, Sean?'

'You mean for pay?' Sean asked.

'Yes, that's right,' said Donn. 'Real money. Not much. But if we prosper you will also prosper.'

'Are you doing this because you are sorry for me?' he asked.

'Like hell,' said Donn. 'You have a good education. We will need somebody like you as things become more complicated. I'll show you.'

'Bejay, I'd be delighted,' said Sean.

'We'll go down,' said Donn, rising. 'Better put the salmon in the basket, Meela. We don't want to make life hard for Mick Dunn. We'll carve up the fish below, Sean, and you can bring home a share, just to show you weren't wasting your time.'

'That's good,' said Sean.

'Go down the river and collect Nan,' Donn said, 'and you can follow us down. She might wander for miles.'

'I'll do that,' said Sean, taking his rod and going down the river after the girl.

'Why did you do that?' Meela asked as they walked the other way.

'I wanted just you and myself walking home,' said Donn. 'How are you?'

'I'm well,' she said. 'Too well.'

'What do you mean by that?' he asked.

'Why amn't I pregnant?' she asked.

He laughed, a loud long laugh.

'You are rich,' he said. 'What does that matter?'

'It was easy enough when we didn't want it,' she said. 'That's all. How do you arrange these things? Isn't it strange?'

'It doesn't matter,' he said. 'It's just us. What does it matter?'

'But it's very strange,' she said. 'Don't you want a son to carry on with all those big things you are doing?'

'Or to dissipate it all afterwards. I don't care. Maybe I am too selfish. You alone suit me fine.'

'Still, it's disturbing,' she said.

Around the bend Sean stopped at a pool. He knelt there and looked at himself in the flowing water. Near the bank the water was smooth. He could see his face. Too long and too serious, he thought. He saw the black tie and the white shirt. He left down the rod and unknotted the tie. He looked at it. It was well worn and creased where the knot had been. He held it in the air and dropped it into the water. It floated on the current and then started to sink. He took the pin from his lapel and looked at it. There was something taken without thought, a badge worn without reason. He flipped it and watched it sink into the dark-brown water of the pool. Maybe it would catch a salmon. He opened the button at the neck of his shirt and looked in the water again. Without the tie and with the shirt collar opened he looked different. Was it as easy as all that to change your personality?

'What are you doing?' Nan asked.

He looked up. She was standing beside him with her hands behind her back.

'Looking at myself,' he said.

She got on her knees beside him.

'In there,' she said. 'I see me. I see you.' She hit the water with her hand. 'Now we are broken,' she said. 'Nan is broken and Sean is broken.'

'Only in the water,' he said. 'Your father told me to tell you he is going home.'

'All right,' she said, getting to her feet abruptly. 'We will go home. Come on.'

She held out her hand. He took it. Her hand was soft and wet from the water. He didn't know it was a privilege to hold her hand. She was very shy with strange people, as Donn could have told him. As they walked he felt as if it was a fantasy, walking with a beautiful girl, holding her hand, sensing her nearness, and answering lots and lots of questions as with his own sister when she was small. What's that? Where's he going? Why is the moss green? Why is it grey? What kind of flower is that? Pick that flower for me. Pick many flowers for me. Now I have a bunch of flowers. I will put them in my room in a jar.

Donn was waiting for him outside the house.

'Come and see,' he said.

He showed him the hall they had made. It was now shut off from the shop and the pub and had its own entrance where one of the windows had been. It was nice inside. There was a floor of narrow pine boards, and the walls were panelled and there were lights all around the walls. There were benches and folding seats.

'You can learn how to show pictures,' said Donn. 'We will have pictures on Friday nights. And we will have dances. We get the bands and the people will come from all over. Do you think this is a good idea?'

'It will wake the place up,' said Sean.

He showed him outside. They had made the old kitchen an extension of the shop and built a new kitchen into the extension they had built in the yard. It was a neat kitchen with a lot of things in it like a cooker and a refrigerator, a big white one. He showed him the new bathroom and the toilets, everything as yet smelling of drying plaster and newness.

'Now,' he said, 'we will go and see Seamus Mooney, and then I will show you the books and the plans we have. I want you to see Seamus because he is building a new house as you see, and in ten years' time everyone will have a new house, and we must be prepared for that. We must be able to supply the timber and the pipes and the cement and the fittings and the fixtures. Now you see why I want somebody like you, so it was just as well you decided to come home.'

He clapped him on the back.

Seamus Mooney was glad to see them. His new house was ready to be roofed. It was a cavity-wall house, the first that anyone had seen in the valley, and it was exciting a lot of comment. He was tapping the water from the roof into a large concrete tank which he had built in to the ground, and he was using a small electric pump to get the water to a storage tank under the roof trees.

'That's what I wanted to see you about,' said Donn. 'Listen, how could we get water to this whole place?'

'We could pump it from the lake,' said Seamus, 'if we had a big pump, and we could build a reservoir, if we had the money, and then let it run all over the place, if we had the pipes and the money for the pipes.'

'Come out here,' said Donn. They followed him. 'Look up the hill.' They looked. 'What is the highest glint you see up there?' he asked.

'That's the water of the river Dearg that comes down from the lake above,' Seamus said.

'How many yards away is it?' Donn asked.

'About two thousand,' said Seamus screwing up his eyes.

'What's to stop us building a big concrete reservoir up there?' asked Donn, 'and sinking plastic pipes under the ground right down to here and let whoever wanted to tap it, tap it. Wouldn't it be gravity feed? What need would there be of expensive pumps?'

'By God,' said Seamus.

'Wouldn't it cost a lot of money?' Sean asked.

'There are grants and things,' said Donn.

'Not enough,' said Seamus.

'There are other ways of getting the money,' said Donn.

'Oh,' said Sean. 'Have you thought of a few?'

'Dances, raffles,' said Donn. 'These are ways; but a few other ways too. Let us collect a certain amount and then we can call on the rest of them for their labour. No labour – no water.'

'You'll have this place like a suburb of New York one of these days,' said Sean, laughing.

'Now you see why I want you,' said Donn to Sean. 'You can become part of this too.'

'Yes, yes,' said Sean. ' I can see that. It is something to work for.'

'That's right,' said Donn.

'I'm your man,' said Sean.

Fourteen

MICK DUNN crouched under an overhang of the bank near the river below the waterfall, but it provided no protection at all from the rain. It fell in slanted sheets blown by a south-west wind. He was wearing oilskins and rubber boots and the rain was making a tattooing sound on his oilskin hat, almost deafening him. He tried several times to get his pipe lighting, but it was impossible, so he put it away and hunched miserably. It was July and the clouds were smothering the hills and it was very dark.

This was a consolation in a way. If anybody wanted to get salmon out of the pool they would have to have lights. He could hardly see his hand in front of his face.

He was very miserable. The few pounds he got for watching the whole length of the river and the lakes in the valley was scarcely enough to provide him with tobacco for a few months. The rain which had fallen incessantly for the last two days had sent the river spating and raging towards the distant sea. So he knew that the salmon and sea trout were running. He wasn't interested in this heroic dash of theirs from the sea. He wasn't really interested in the saga of their return after years to the ground where they had been originally spawned. All he knew was that they were running. While it was still bright he had seen them, hundreds of them, making their way up. The only thing that had impressed him about them was the immense power they showed swimming a four-foot fall of angry water.

He was sure that the night was too bad to bring anyone out after them. All the same, you couldn't be sure. It was few years that there had been such a run. A run like that would tempt the devil himself, Mick thought, as long as he was well rigged out against the rain. He wondered if he would go home to hell out of it. What did it matter if people took a salmon or two from the river? All the same, if he went home it would be known that he went home and letters would be sent to his employers saying, what kind of bailiff have ye there at all, at home in bed with the wife nice and snug and the salmon running and being poached wholesale.

So he sighed and hunched himself into his clothes. All he could see was a dull gleam, slightly whitened where the river ran over the fall into the pool. He had no watch. He knew he would have to stay there until the sky lightened, rush home and get a mug of tea and then get back again and try to keep his eyes open for the rest of the day, snooze a bit in the afternoon when people were abroad and then get back again the following night. He would have to keep up this watch until the waters subsided, the salmon stopped running, and reached their gravel beds where they would spawn. Soon their silver colour would be dark red; they would not be good to eat, and he could let it lie.

He stiffened when he heard the sound of walking, the swishing of wet boots in the heather over his head. Then he heard the voice calling: 'Mick! Mick Dunn! Do you hear me, Mick Dunn?' He recognized the voice, and after thinking over it, he rose and shouted: 'Here, I am, Bartley.'

'Where the hell is here?' he heard Bartley asking over his head.

'Under your feet, man,' he said. 'What are you after?'

'After you, you amadan,' said Bartley. 'I wouldn't believe that you would be out on a night like this. Are you off your head? What madness is on you?'

'Don't I have to do it?' Mick asked indignantly.

'You do not,' said Bartley. 'Where do you think the men are who pay you? They're in some hotel or other spending more money on a round of drinks than they give you for the whole year. Come on up to the house man and have a sup of hot tea, and if you are wild enough after you can come back again.'

'Ah, I couldn't do that,' said Mick.

'God give me patience with you,' said Bartley. 'Amn't I only over the hill? Won't you be there and back in half an hour if that's what you want? Come on or we'll be going to your funeral. Seven doctors wouldn't save you after being out on a night like this.'

'Well,' said Mick.

'Give me your hand and I'll give you a haul.'

Mick saw the hand reaching down, was tempted and fell. He caught the hand and wondered at the strength that was in it as he scrambled up the slippery slope. He could barely see Bartley. He would hardly have seen him at all but for the white bainin coat. Bartley was wearing no rain clothes. The black hat brim, sodden, was falling around his head. 'Come on,' said Bartley. 'Keep your eye on me, or you'll end up in the bog.'

Mick followed him. The walking was hard and dangerous, but by swinging his arms he managed to keep his footing.

He thought he never saw anything as beautiful as the glow of light coming from the small window of Bartley's house. When they went in and shut out the rain and wind, and he looked at the turf fire blazing and the sitting stools on each side of the hearth, he said, 'Sure Lord God, man, not even a dog should be out on a night like this.'

'What I told you,' said Bartley, just taking off his wet hat and shaking it heartily a few times to get most of the wet out of it, and putting it back on his head again. 'You'd get your death out there. Look, isn't the kettle boiling. Take off your garments and sit down and I'll make the tea.'

Mick did so.

'Have a sup of this first,' said Bartley then, handing him a glass of what looked like water.

'Is that the hard stuff?' Mick asked doubtfully.

'It's not water,' said Bartley.

'Sure, I rarely touch it,' said Mick.

'All right,' said Bartley, 'put it in your belly or in your boots. It's one and the same thing. But it's better in the belly.'

Mick took it and gulped a little. It was like drinking living fire. He opened his mouth and breathed. Then he took another sup. He could feel it warming his belly, burning his belly. He wasn't a drinking man really, a few pints on a Saturday night and a bit drunk on a fair-day. 'Man, that puts the life back into you,' he said, and drank the rest of it.

'Well, now I'll make the tea,' said Bartley, thinking: that's you off the river for the rest of the night, boyo, and I've done my bit.

* * *

While Dino turned the tractor outside McNulty's house, Donn got down and ran to the door. He could see the sheets of rain against the bright light from the window. He lifted the latch on the front door and went in. Tom McNulty was reading a newspaper, sitting at the fire. He was in his shirt sleeves. He was wearing his hat. He always wore his hat. Some time Donn meant to ask him if he wore his hat in bed too.

'Bad night, Tom,' he said. 'We are looking for Sean.'

Tom looked at him over his glasses, then took them off and shoved them into his waistcoat pocket. He was annoyed that Donn had seen him wearing glasses. He was proud of his sight.

'He's back in the room,' he said. 'What devil's work are ye up to?'

'Social service,' Donn said, grinning, and walking over to stand with his back to the fire. He looked at the bulb hanging from the roof. 'Do you find the electric light better?' he asked.

'Dangerous thing,' said Tom. 'Man has to be careful with it. You could be killed with it.'

'You could be killed tripping over a stone too,' said Donn.

'Tell me something,' said Tom. 'The day the boy came home and told his mother about staying at home, had he talked to you?'

'He had,' said Donn.

'And you offered him the job?' said Tom.

'That's right,' said Donn.

'I hope you had no hand in turning him from his persuasion,' said Tom.

'Why would I do that?' Donn asked.

'I don't know. Did you? I wouldn't like to think you did.'

Donn thought.

'You have believed a certain way of life all your life,' he said. 'Would a few minutes' conversation from me or anyone else change your way of thinking?'

'No,' said McNulty, 'but he's only a boy. His mother is hurt.'

'Were you much more than a boy when you made your decisions?' Donn asked.

'No,' said McNulty. 'You have a very persuasive way with you, haven't you?'

'I believe in man's liberty,' said Donn, 'to believe whatever the hell he likes. I wouldn't interfere with anybody.'

'I would make a bad enemy, Donn,' said McNulty, his jaw tight.

'Look, Tom,' said Donn. 'Aren't you pleased that Sean is working at home? He is very good at what he is doing for me. I wouldn't like to lose him. But say the word and I will let him go if this is what you want. I thought you would like to have him working at home instead of going away.'

'So do I,' said McNulty. 'But his mother is in an awful taking. Maybe she is using you for her disappointment. All the changes that are happening so fast. Maybe that's it.'

'If Sean wanted to be a priest,' said Donn, 'there's no power on earth could stop him. Is this true?'

'I suppose so,' said McNulty, 'but his mother says the devil strews the path with temptations. You are one of them.'

'I don't want her to feel that way. Would I find her and talk to her?'

'No,' said McNulty, rising. 'Leave her be. She'll grow out of it. You went out with a vocation, she told him, and came back with a bit of salmon. The loss was greater than the gain. Hey, Sean! Sean!' he called, walking up to the door of the room beside the fireplace. 'Don't tell me where ye are going. I don't want to know. What's this talk of a reservoir up on the Red River?'

'It's only talk,' said Donn. 'We'll see what happens by next winter. What do you think of it? Water coming out of a tap there next the window, clean mountain water, hah?'

'Spoiled, this generation will be,' said McNulty. 'They will lose the use of their limbs. There won't be a muscle left on them. Tractors now doing the work of men. They'll have to have a glass case with a spade in it so that people will ponder at how they used to work one time.'

Sean came down from the room.

'Didn't I fall asleep on the bed,' he said. He went over where the oilskins were hanging behind the door and started to pull them on, rubber boots and pants and coat.

'Mick Dunn will be abroad tonight,' said McNulty.

'I hope it keeps fine for him,' said Donn, laughing.

'I'm right,' said Sean.

'Well, let's go,' said Donn. 'You wouldn't like to come, Tom?'

'Too much of that I did in the old days,' he said, sitting down in his chair and settling himself into it. 'Wet heather, and slack stomachs, that's what leaves me now with the aches in the bones. Good luck to ye!' He took up the paper again, so they left and went into the rain. They got on each side of Dino in the tractor. He had a kind of a hood over it. There was a trailer on the back of the tractor with wet sacks in it.

'Right, Dino,' said Donn. 'Off we go.'

'Hang on,' said Dino. 'It's going to be rough getting there.'

'Turn out your lights when you get off the road,' said Donn.

'The Lord save us,' said Dino. 'I haven't cat's eyes.'

All the lights were doing anyhow was showing the rain to them as if it was a shimmering sparkling curtain.

They waited above the waterfall while Donn went away from them. They didn't talk. Several times on the rough track they thought that the tractor would tumble over and fall into the river.

'This Donn,' said Dino, whispering, 'brings you to the most queer places, and makes you do queer things.'

'He did all right by you, Dino,' said Sean.

'Help me, help himself,' said Dino. 'That's the way, isn't it.'

'I don't think it's all that with him,' said Sean.

'Don't tell me,' said Dino. 'He did well out of me. All he did was invest. That's the way it goes. If you have money, you make money. He'll get value out of you too, don't fret.'

'It's no use talking to you,' said Sean. 'You don't read enough to know enough about anything except the obvious.'

'Here,' said Dino, 'don't be giving me the big words. Facts is facts. Nobody does anything for anybody without getting something out of it. But he makes for fun, Donn does. I'll say that for him.'

'It's all right,' said Donn, appearing beside them as if by magic. 'Mick is not about. Bartley must have enticed him away. Let's hope he can keep him out of circulation.

They got out of the tractor and went to the trailer.

'Get the net and the sacks down by the water,' said Donn. 'I'll have to leave my clothes in the tractor. They'll stay dry there.'

While they went to the trailer he took off his oilskins and then, pausing, he took off his coat and his shirt and trousers and stood in the rain. It was shocking at first but he got used to it. He pulled on light shoes and went down to the pool. They were there. They could see his pale body in the darkness.

'God,' said Dino, 'you make me cold looking at you.'

'Hurry,' said Donn. 'Where's my side of the net?'

'Here,' said Sean, who was holding it.

Donn took it. He looked at the boiling river. They could hear it thundering over the fall.

'There are bound to be a lot of them,' he said. 'Pay out the net as I go. I'll cross with it and get under the fall. When you hear me shouting, start hauling, slowly. All right?'

'It's your funeral,' said Dino.

Donn laughed and went into the river.

He was amazed at the power of it. For a few yards he could walk, spreading his legs, bracing his chest against the brown flow. Then it got very deep and his head went under and he had to swim with his right arm. As the net came behind him it started to hold and he had to drag it. His right hand found rocks then where the river went out of the pool. He wrapped an arm around one of them and rested. He wondered: will someone tell me why I am doing this? For whom am I doing this, when I could be at home in bed with Meela and we could be talking about all the things we haven't caught up with talking about yet? He laughed.

'He's crazy,' said Sean, grinning. They could see him only vaguely.

Donn ploughed on across the pool, sometimes under, sometimes over, the water. I'm doing all this, he thought, because I like it. All people have to have drama in their lives, big or small. If they don't meet with it, they have to make it. His shoulders were clear of the water and he could haul the net with both hands. Then when he found he could travel a bit more freely, he pulled himself and the net along by the far side of the

135

pool with one arm, until he was almost under the fall, and he could feel it thumping down on his head.

He paused here for a moment. He knew the ground was deep right under the fall, but it couldn't be very wide. He could be swept down, thus losing all the ground he had gained, and the net would catch nothing. But he was strong, he knew, and three strokes should get him out of danger. He let go and swam, using the hand holding the net as well, although the drag on it was terrible. He was tumbled in the smothering white water but he kept reaching his hand until he found something to grasp and hold on to, and rested there while the force of the current pulled at him. The great power of water, he thought, thinking what a pity it was all wasted and running to the sea.

Then he rose and it was only reaching his chest, so he fought it, scrambling and pulling at anything within reach, and he came to the bank and hauled himself up, and after panting there for a time, he shouted: 'Right! Haul!' and started to pull at his end of the net and went sidestep by sidestep down to where the other two were. Soon they stood side by side, hauling away. The net was heavy.

'Maybe,' said Dino panting, 'there isn't a fish at all in it.'

'There has to be,' said Donn. 'I saw a lot of them in the pool today.'

'I wouldn't do what you did,' said Sean, 'for all the fish in the world.'

They kept hauling.

They knew that it was successful when they saw the silver flashing even in the dark in the bag of the net. The strands of the net seemed to come alive in their hands, taut and almost twanging.

'Look at them!' Dino shouted. 'For God's sake look at them!'

It took the combined strength of the three of them to get the bag on the bank. They threw the rest of the net over the struggling and leaping fish, and started hitting at them with the priests. They took a lot of killing.

'How many?' Dino asked. 'How many is there?'

'Twenty, thirty,' said Donn.

'Jay, is that all?' he asked.

'It's very good,' said Donn. 'Untangle the net. There are more of them. We'll have time for three hauls.'

'You wouldn't go back in there again,' said Sean.

'Why wouldn't I?' Donn asked. 'We want about a hundred. Then they can be bagged and Dino on his way with them before dawn.'

'You'll murder yourself,' said Sean.

'Isn't it a good cause?' asked Donn. 'What other reservoir in the world will have been founded on fish?'

He laughed. Sean wondered how he could laugh, but then found himself laughing with him.

'If we ever get this cursed net untangled,' said Dino.

They bent over the net.

Fifteen

FATHER MURPHY drove towards the Mountain in a reflective mood. Ever since Donn had come into the valley, he thought, the changes he had brought about had affected nearly everybody, including himself.

He was used to townspeople, because he was one himself. They were more or less predictable. He remembered when he was young, that if you walked a mile outside the environs of the town you thought you were venturing into a strange world which made you uneasy. It was the eternal misunderstanding between the people who chose to live in communities and the men who chose the freedom of the fields and the loneliness.

He had spent a few years teaching in a college after his ordination and then he had been appointed a curate out here. He was finding it very difficult to adjust to the change. The people treated a priest with respect, but it was a distant respect. Even when he went into their homes and talked to them, at the Stations, or on sick calls, or the annual calls, he found it difficult to get behind the bland respect. They wanted all their priests to be people who could be revered. They found it difficult to understand that they were ordinary men with all of the ordinary man's human failings. They found it impossible, it seemed, to separate the man from the office.

It was Donn, with his humanism, that made him see the difference between now and the period that the old parish priest remembered. He talked of the many saints he had seen off on the Mountain. These were the old people whose lives had been hard, who slaved for a small return. Their working lives started at sunrise and ended at sunset. Their fathers before them had been the same. They had worked for landlords who lived on their sweat, but their sons lived on their own sweat. It made a difference to know that you owned the piece of ground you sweated over, but it didn't make it any easier to work the spade and the scythe and the slean. So, the old priest said, these people were given the gift of faith that St Paul had talked about.

Father Murphy wished he had the gift of faith himself, that he needn't be eternally engaging his reason in a question-and-answer session that seemed to go on and on. He knew, but he had to convince his reason that he knew. He supposed it was better to be that way than to be sure in the wrong direction.

So, the old ones got the gift of faith, the priest said, because their lives were so hard, and most of them were putting purgatory over them anyhow slaving in the fields and bogs. But not their children, oh no, they were getting it too soft; so they didn't get the gift and they would have to fight their brains for it, just like the rest of us, and many of them didn't fight too hard. Money was more plentiful. Everybody was eating meat every day instead of twice a year, and they were going to these crazy dances, because there were more and more motor-cars around and they could get lifts. They were even going into the towns to get their hair done, if you please, and the young fellows going to real barbers and paying money, instead of letting their fathers crop their hair with the scissors and the horse-clippers. How could young people like that emigrate and hold on to their faith? They didn't. They threw it away like an old shoe, this treasure that they had inherited, and returned like that Donn fellow up in the Mountain, sneering and corrupting the young ones. Nobody could be corrupted if they didn't want to be, Father Murphy had said. Bull, the old man cried, we are all just dying to be corrupted. Times are changing, Father Murphy said, and we will have to take a new look at ourselves and the young people, find out what they want and how we can help them. Is the Ten Commandments changing, the old man asked? Tell me that. It's not that, but people's approach to them, he said in reply. We will have to see the new way.

I'll tell you a story, the old man said. When I was young my parish priest was a direct-action man. One of the people went a bit off the beam, leaving his family, going into the town getting drunk. Well, my priest went looking for him, and where did he find him but in the bar in a hotel, as drunk as a lord and his children out waiting cold and hungry, and he was so mad with his parishioner that he went up to him and gave him a right cross and laid him out cold. Oh, men, but this was great fuel for the anti-clerical boozers. They brought your man to, and commiserated with him, and said there should be a law against men like that coming into peaceful pubs and knocking out the citizens, but all your man said when he woke up was: who has a better right to bate me than me own parish priest? You see.

I'm not going up to hit Donn, said Father Murphy, laughing, because he'd hit me back and I wouldn't wake up for a week. You see what I mean, the old man said, no respect for the collar, not like the old days. That's the difference. God be with the days you could be batin' the coortin' couples out of the hedges with a blackthorn stick.

It was a matter of education, Father Murphy knew. People were better educated. They were reading newspapers; they were listening to discussions on the radio, they were reading books. The old ways would no longer suffice. Time ago they were more ignorant and more violent and could be cowed into faith through fear of hell and damnation. Their noses were rubbed into hell and death to frighten God into them, as it were, but times had changed. Young people were a bit bewildered, and inclined to indifference. Now you would have to follow the young ones instead of the other way around.

He was slightly upset when he topped the rise and turned down into the valley. He would never get used to the black poles all over the place, almost without design, as if they had been dropped haphazardly from the sky. There was certainly no beauty in them. Before, he would come into the valley, and pause, and admire the peaceful beauty. Now he was too conscious of the poles and the wires and the black gape of the two thatched houses that had their roofs knocked in. The tiled cottages beside them seemed no recompense for the loss. Also he noticed, a narrow ditch had been dug, with earth piled on one side of it, that stretched away up the hills. He shook his head. He stopped the car at the shop, got out and went in.

He was used now to the change in here. It was for the better, perhaps. It was brighter, more cheerful, and all the packaged and gaily-coloured goods on the shelves looked inviting, but where was the smell of cinnamon and cloves and tea and spilt porter? All these smells had been packaged out, he thought, and shops were the poorer for it, and smiled at his own old-fashionedness.

'Is herself in?' he asked Paud, who hooked a thumb at the back.

He went that way, going to the parlour and looking in at the new pub on his right as he passed. Shining shelves and bottles reflected in long mirrors, tall stools. It would have been a place in a town: nearly as asceptic as an operating theatre in a hospital.

He went into the parlour. Here Meela was sitting at the table with Sean McNulty. They were bent over account books.

'God bless the work,' he said.

Meela looked up, smiled and rose to her feet.

'Thank God you called,' she said, 'and got me away from these damned things. I don't understand them at all.'

'Don't believe that, Father,' said Sean.

'It's all the different things,' she said. 'They have my head in a tizz. We are getting things now that I never even knew were invented. Won't you sit down? Will you have tea?'

'No, no thanks,' he said hurriedly. 'I was actually looking for Donn.'

'You'll have to travel to find him,' she said. 'He's up at the Red River. They are finishing off the reservoir up there to-day, I think. They have to get it done before the frost or something.'

'I'll go up and have a look,' he said.

'Will you wait a minute and I'll go with you,' she said. 'I'm sick of these old books, and besides Sean knows more about them now than I ever will.'

'I'll wait,' he said, and she went out.

Sean was uneasy. He moved a pen between his fingers.

'How is everything, Sean?' Father Murphy asked.

'Oh, it's great,' Sean said. 'This job with Donn is a godsend. I like it. Do you know that he has increased the turnover of the business three times in the last six months?'

'I'm not surprised,' said Father Murphy. 'How do you feel yourself – about your own life now, I mean.'

Sean looked at him.

'Maybe a biteen wistful, I think,' he said. 'The lads are all back there now. It's only when you get away from a life like that, that you remember the good parts of it.'

'You wouldn't like to be back there?' the priest asked.

Sean shook his head.

'No,' he said. 'Only if it was for the reason that it is there. I'm happy here. I was afraid I would have to go away. Isn't it a great thing that I didn't have to go away?'

'That's good,' said Father Murphy, 'if it's the way you want it. You don't feel the education you got entitles you to more exacting brainwork than book-keeping for a country shop?'

'Oh, no,' said Sean, 'it's not that way at all. I'm in and out to the town in the car, ordering this and that, new things all the time. Give it ten years and there won't be a thatched cottage in the valley. We are kept going. There's movement. Always Donn is thinking of something new. Did you know there will be two miles of plastic pipe coming down from the reservoir? Isn't it a great thing to think that every house in the place will have running water in a short time?'

'I see you are a disciple,' said Father Murphy, laughing.

Then he felt the delicate touch on his arm, as if he had been stroked with feathers.

'Hello, Father, Father,' said Nan.

'Hello, Nan,' he said, and put his hand on the one that was resting on his arm. 'How are you?'

'I will say a song,' she said.

> I wish I was a grey goose,
> I wish that I could fly,
> Like an arrow to the mountain
> Where the lapwings cry.

'Is that nice?'

'That's very nice,' he said. 'Who taught you that?'

'Mammy,' she said. 'Also *one and one are two*. *Two and two are four*. Is that nice?'

'And who taught you that?' he asked.

'Sean,' she said. She went over to him. He was looking up at her, smiling. She placed her hand as gently on his arm. 'Sean teaches me sums.'

'It's a pleasure, Nan,' he said.

He was looking at her, the priest thought, with the most open affection. It is perhaps a good thing for her to have somebody of her own physical age like that to love her as well as Meela. He thought they made a nice picture, one of innocence. It began to dawn on him how sad it was that a beautiful girl like Nan could never know in her consciousness what it was to be loved by a boy like Sean. He wondered again at the way things were arranged.

'I'm ready now,' said Meela behind him. She was wearing a coat, because it was late October and chilly enough outside.

'All right,' he said and went to her and they walked out through the shop and into the street and into his car. Before they started he looked at her. 'I have never seen you looking so well,' he said. 'Why is the high colour in the cheek and the sparkle in the eye?'

'Haven't you heard?' she asked.

'Heard what?' he asked as he started off.

'That Donn and I are together again,' she said. 'Surely you must have heard – I know what you have for breakfast.'

'What?' he asked.

'Cereal,' she said, 'and a fry on Sundays.'

He laughed. 'Well, even if nobody told me,' he said, 'I would know looking at you. So life is good?'

'Life is good,' she said. 'Life is very, very good.'

'You had a lot of sorrow,' he said, 'it was about time that you got some joy.'

'If you didn't know sorrow,' she said, 'how could you know what joy was? All the bad years are blotted out.'

'And will it last?' he asked.

'Oh, yes,' she said, 'because it was always there; it was just that we were running away from it.'

'He has a powerful personality,' the priest said. 'Has all this opened his eyes, do you think?'

'Opened his eyes to what?' she asked.

'To Who is responsible,' he said.

'Oh, now,' she said, 'you want to give him a lot more time. He likes the story of the farmer's son who is asked who made the world, and said, God made the world but my father said he made a damn' bad job of it because he had a very weedy garden.'

They were passing men now who were filling in the ditch that had been dug for the water-pipe. Cheerful men who leaned on their shovels to wave as they passed by. Meela leaned well out to shout at them: 'God bless the work, Corney. God bless the work, Tim.' She said to the priest: 'Isn't it marvellous the way they are all working together? This never happened before.'

'They didn't have somebody around like Donn before,' he said. 'I know when I go up and talk to him and he will look at me and his eyes will say: This is the sort of thing you should have been doing.'

'Well, should you?' she asked.

'If I had thought of it,' he said. 'But I would never have got the results he did. He bullied the grants and the plans out of people. Made them think he was doing them a favour, saving them money, as he was. How do you distinguish between profane work and spiritual work?'

'Donn says the two go together. He thinks that the body now is more important than the soul later.'

'Do you believe this?'

She laughed at his anxiety. 'Don't worry,' she said.

'The trouble is that there is a lot of the truth in what he says and does,' said the priest. 'He may be right, but somebody has to pay for these things, and I don't mean money.'

They passed two more men and Meela leaned out to shout at them. They waved at her, and lifted their hats to the priest.

'How do you get close to them?' he asked. 'I have been here a while now and I still feel a stranger. All these people are so independent. Like non-conforming conformists. You are the only one I can talk to freely.'

'You know Sarah Magee?' she asked. He thought, and nodded. 'Well, a nephew of hers got married in England and when a neighbour asked her if he had married an Irish girl, she said: "Yerra, he did not, then. He married a girl from Tipperary". You see what you are up against. We will have to leave the car here now and walk.'

He stopped the car and got out, laughing. She had already

started climbing the hill. The weather had been dry and the bog was fairly solid underfoot. All the same he had to watch where he was going. Meela went ahead of him towards the group of men, who had stopped what they were doing to watch their approach. He thought how typical this was of life in the country. No working man would let even a dog pass on the road without stopping to meditate on him.

The place was littered around the reservoir with empty cement bags and pieces of timber. Dino's tractor was there, resting squaways on the hill with its trailer.

They greeted the priest, Dino and the young McNallys and Bartley Folan and Jack Tumelty and Seamus Mooney. 'Hello, Father,' they said.

'You are in time to see the last of it,' said Bartley.

'He timed it well,' said Donn. 'He won't have to take off the coat.'

'Show me,' the priest said.

'Here you are,' said Bartley. They had diverted the river into a new channel. They had sunk the concrete tank, that would hold thousands of gallons, deep into the earth. He had to pull himself up to see the inside of it. It was smoothed with hard plaster. He saw the long grating at the far end to let in the water, and the vent to let the water flow out into the pipes.

'What do you think of that, now?' Bartley asked.

'I couldn't do it better myself,' the priest said, his voice booming in it.

They laughed. The men were lifting the heavy blocks, made in two parts from their forms and were hoisting them on top of the tank.

'Well,' said Donn, 'since the Church is here we better let him run the river in.'

'That would be a blessing,' said Bartley.

'Show me the way,' said the priest.

He followed Donn behind the tank. They had built a concrete run each side of the river. This run was blocked by a heavy wall of cement with a grating in grooves with a handle on it.

'All you do,' said Donn, 'is lift that handle and she is away.'

The priest took hold of the handle, paused a moment.

'May this water bring nothing but good,' he said and lifted and the water rushed into the channel and into the tank. They all turned and looked down, visualizing the water in the pipes, seeking its own level, going to its many branches – and when the women below turned the taps, the water would pour out freely: and the days of the bucket-hauling would be over.

'And all done by people,' said Donn, 'don't forget that,' tapping him on the shoulder.

'And God,' said the priest.

'We did this,' said Donn. 'We did it, and we had fun doing it. And we feel good about it, and we don't want anyone else but ourselves getting credit for it. Eh, Dino?'

'Ourselves and the fish,' said Dino, laughing.

'That's right,' said Donn.

The men were chuckling.

'Mind for God's sake would Mick Dunn hear ye,' said Bartley.

The priest didn't understand.

'Are you coming down, Donn?' Meela asked. 'We'll give you a lift.'

'You'll be able to finish up, Seamus?' Donn asked. 'Anything else you want?'

'No,' said Seamus. 'We are on our way.'

'We'll celebrate tonight,' said Donn. 'I'll see you all in the place after tea. We will have a big celebration. Wives and all. I'll go. I want to be the first to turn on a tap.'

He went down the hill. Meela followed him.

'Well, God bless your work, men,' the priest said.

'Thank you, Father,' they said, waiting for him to go. He felt he ought to say something else, to praise them for their endeavour, their cooperation with one another in a project like this, which was a true charity, but he felt shut out from them; so he just waved his hand at them and walked down the hill.

Donn was sitting in the front seat, turned back talking to Meela. She was laughing. He was smiling and holding her hand. The priest sat in beside Donn.

'Now,' Donn said, 'what do you think of all that, eh?'

'It's excellent,' the priest said. 'The miracle is how you got the money and then got the work out of them.'

'Not me, themselves,' said Donn. 'When they saw what a benefit it would be to them, you couldn't stop them. That's what life is all about, you see. People.'

'Have you paid for the whole thing?' the priest asked.

'We are about £200 short,' said Donn. 'But a few dances and we'll have made all that up.'

'Well,' said the priest, putting his hand in his inside pocket and taking out a bulky envelope, 'here's about £100 towards it.'

'Where did you get that?' Donn asked.

'From various people,' he said. 'Not much of my own. I told them about it. They thought it was a great idea. So that's the result. Since digging ditches is incompatible with the cloth, I wanted to do something and this is the result.'

'I don't want to take it,' said Donn.

'Donn!' said Meela.

'I am people too, after all,' said the priest. 'I am part of the human race. Am I not entitled to help – just because I am a priest?'

Donn thought over this.

'All right,' he said. He took the envelope. The priest started the car.

'You could at least say thanks,' said Meela.

'Why should I?' he asked. 'Everyone gave their work and their endeavour. Why thank one above another?'

'I didn't ask for thanks,' said the priest. 'Don't blame me for that.'

'You know what I mean,' said Donn.

'I know,' the priest said. 'Can I say something else?'

'Try it out,' said Donn.

'Don't put all your money on the people,' said the priest.

'And what is that supposed to mean?' Donn asked.

'No more and no less than the words convey,' said the priest.

'What are you trying to do, spoil everything?' Donn asked.

'Donn, please,' said Meela.

'Why does everything I say grate on you?' the priest asked.

'Why do you say things like that?' Donn asked. 'Don't you know before you say them that they will grate on me?'

'No,' said the priest. 'I'm afraid everything I say grates on you. I'm sorry for that. Also I was told to tell you that the

147

parish priest won't oppose you when you apply for a dance-hall licence in the courts.'

'I should think he wouldn't,' said Donn. 'The police have no objections. The pub and the hall are not connected. There won't be any bad conduct. Why should he oppose it?'

'Maybe he knows more about human nature than you do,' the priest said. 'He has been treating it for a long time.'

'Too long,' said Donn. 'Here we are. Thanks for the ride. You can come up yourself when we have a dance. That should keep the young ones chaste.' He got out of the car. Meela got out and hurried into the shop. He knew she was annoyed with him. He didn't care. He wondered why this young priest could make his hackles rise so easily.

'I intended to come whether you asked me or not,' the priest said.

Donn stood there looking at him. The blue eyes were gazing calmly back at him. If only he would lose his temper, just once, Donn thought. He couldn't think of any reply that wouldn't make the situation worse, so he said nothing more, but went towards the shop, thinking, well the expenses of the celebration can come from the priest's money. That will be something of a jest. That will be putting the priest's money inside the people.

He laughed as he thought of it, going into the shop.

The priest heard the laugh, and was sad.

Interlude

SOME PEOPLE can go away and travel in strange lands and when they come back, and you ask them what they thought about those lands, all they can say is that they were hot or cold or they got the runs in Salerno. The food and the climate and the slow bus journeys are about the limit of what they see and can talk about. They might as well never have left home. All it does for them is to make them glad to return to their own patch.

Man seems to be lost without familiar associations, however poor. What he really misses is the people he knows and can talk to and gossip about. These other poor creatures, talking Italian or French or Spanish or broken English, how could you ever get on a footing with them when you knew nothing about their families and their failings? As for their mountains and their lakes and their blue seas, haven't you them at home?

The point is that the world is filled with the beauty of inanimate things. You can find this wherever you go. It's only the change in the light and hence in the colouring that makes it different to the eye. It's the people you should be watching, Donn knew. Once you broke through the barrier of the language you found the common denominator. They were people. About ninety per cent of them were good honest people earning their bread by the sweat of their brow, finding it hard to make a living, tightening their belts in hard times and living almost profligately when they were in funds. There were shades and gradations in all of them, gloomy or happy, sad or joyful, loving or hating, but mainly interested in themselves. What were monks who shut themselves up in monasteries doing but thinking only of themselves and their own salvation?

If it weren't for the bad ones, life would be boring. You had them to read about and could imagine yourself in their place, stealing or killing or committing adultery with abandon, siring bastards or walking out on their wives. There were notable criminals, notable prostitutes, actresses, entertainers, powerful rich people, politicians. You could live the high life with those in your imagination or commit their sins at second-hand, without suffering the consequences.

Look at a great city with its millions of peoples. Where would the city be without them? Early in the morning, in the tubes, you see them going to work. These will be the overalled people. Later, the better-uniformed ones will be out. You see great powerhouse chimneys pouring out smoke. Take the people out of the powerhouses and from behind the wheels of the transport and out of the offices and what good would the city be? With all its apparent power, it would be a dead thing; and while it appears to be the gigantic master of the pygmy people who scuttle about below its great towers like ants in the shadow of a great rock, it is as dependent on them as a child is dependent on its mother. So they are far more important than the great thing they had built and ran.

This was the secret you have to learn, to realize how important people really were. Tyrants rose and fell because they overlooked this simple equation. The people are the cornerstones of the world, but you have to know them, and since the life span of man is so short, it is easier and quicker to get to know your own people, the people you were born amongst, played with, sang with, laughed with, danced with, loved with, worked with.

Donn looked down from the Mountain on a spring day. He sat on the heather with his gun and his dog and three dead birds and he found the prospect good. The colour of the fields alone was enough to show you how prosperity had grown in the valley. Most of the fields were pushing up the spring grass and it was deeply green, like the colour in the heart of an emerald. That didn't come from nature. It came from artificial manure, from men in the laboratories and in the great factories probing and prying into the secrets of nature; testing the earth to find its faults and to fix them with their concoctions. For wherever in the world a thousand more families decided they would eat meat on two days a week instead of one, it sent a wave of meat-desire over the lands, so that each field would have to feed one more cow, one more sheep, one more pig.

To do this you had to have machinery, and where you introduced machinery you needed less men. But factories had to be built to make the machinery, so the young men could go to the factories to do that. This thought caused Donn to frown. He hated to see any of the young men going. He had done his best to retain them, but there was a point beyond which it was impossible to go.

This didn't seem to be the same valley he had looked at after his return. He had made it look much greener, and in the whole place he could only see four thatched cottages. These were abandoned, all except Bartley Folan's, for he clung to his thatch as he had clung to his still over the years. He would never yield. So people were better off. Looking now he could see five motor-cars outside the tiled cottages. This was good. The young people could get away and come back again. The cottages were neat and clean, each of them with a bathroom and toilet, bottled-gas cookers, new haysheds. Of course the valley didn't look the same, but soon all the people who remembered it as it was would be dead and the new ones would see nothing strange in the changes. They would appear as if they had been from the beginning.

He rose to go down the Mountain.

It was that phrase the priest had hurled at him, how many years ago now, five it must be, the time when they had built the reservoir at the Red River, about don't put all your money on the people. He couldn't understand why this phrase had stuck in his memory, but it had; and he found himself constantly putting up arguments against what he regarded as the cynicism of it. Don't put all your money on the people! He would put every penny he possessed on the people! He knew them now. He was welcome everywhere. He could make them laugh, because he was happy. Happy in his life with Meela, and what he had helped to do for the people, through jibing and butting like a puck goat, and advising and lending and encouraging, and even taking his own coat off and working.

Suddenly, almost from under his feet, two snipe got up and zigzagged away from him, one to the right and one to the left. The dog had missed them, but he didn't. His gun was up and firing, left and then right, and he saw the two birds falling. Reactions still very good for over forty, he thought complacently as he went to collect them. 'You are a dunce,' he said to the dog, who came wagging his tail to him. 'Your scent is no good. You are still inclined to chase after hares. You can't fetch. I don't know why I keep you.' He patted him all the same. He put the birds in the bag and went on down. He suddenly realized that he was hungry. He was looking forward to his meal.

The best investment for any man's money is people, Donn thought. He could have thought more deeply about it. Artificial manure was the work of man, but somebody had to provide the ingredients. Even if they came from the air, the air had to be there in the first place.

And people are queer. Donn should have thought of that too. Their bodies are composed of a lot of chemicals and water, but their minds are their own. They belong to themselves, and each lives secretly in his mind. Man hardly knows his own mind, or where it can take him or where it can lead him.

And there was one person in that valley whose mind was leading him a certain direction.

Many times during the day the eyes of this man followed the form of the girl. He admired her small feet in the summertime, and the shape of her calves, and the suntan on her legs and her arms and her face and the uncovered space above her breasts. He watched the way the sun bleached her hair, and since she was so innocent and didn't know, many times his eyes saw her with her dress raised as she paddled in the lake, so that her shapely thighs were exposed and he could guess greedily at the shape of the rest of her body. Times too in the summer when she went swimming in the pool, he watched her until he came to know every bit of her.

He desired her. This is all right. Most men have a fleeting desire for shapely and pretty women whom they see walking the roads, or at Mass on Sundays, or in a dance-hall, or a coloured picture in a magazine. But they forget quickly.

This one didn't, because the case was odd. This girl was the most beautiful girl he had ever seen anywhere, and her body was as perfect as the body of a woman could be made, but she had the mind of a child. So you see it was a special case. You couldn't go and say to her parents: I am dying with desire for this girl and I want to marry her, if that is the only way to possess her. There could be no answer at all to a request like that.

So there had to be another way, hadn't there? She treated everyone with the distant friendliness which children have. He spoke to her in a joking way, but frowns came on the smooth forehead. She couldn't understand jokes, or pleasantries.

Could she understand anything that happened to her? Do you think? What would her reactions be? She wouldn't know, would she? After all she was practically an idiot? How would she know? It might as well be a little girl that knew from nothing about nothing. Just that something had happened, something unfamiliar. Maybe she would even enjoy it? How did you know? Deeply secret in her must be the longing that would match his own. She had the body and the functions. How did you know that she wouldn't react with pleasure, to something she wouldn't know about or understand, but that she would enjoy without knowing in a way that she was enjoying it? Maybe it would be good for the girl. Maybe it would bring her mind awake, out of the childish bog where it was now. Who could tell? She was like a wild flower, wild, see, that was the word, like a little animal in a way, would you think, who would react like an animal to a normal function of nature? Who could tell about those things? There were girls you could get, careful ones, easy with the virtue, but it wasn't the same at all. They weren't like her. They didn't look like her, and they didn't have this awful daunting childlike innocence, the innocence of the completely unknowing.

One of these days.

His mind fed on her, day and night. He watched her when his work took him to the places where she was. She seemed to him the most desirable person in the whole world. He felt that his life would not be complete until he got to know her, savoured her, and the beauty of it was that it would be all in ignorance. She could never tell. How could she tell about something when she knew so little about anything else?

The more he thought of it, the more feasible it seemed, and his mind was set on how he could go about it.

There must be a way, his mind said, and soon, because I am just plain dying with longing for that girl.

Of course Donn knew nothing about a mind like this in the valley.

Sixteen

FOR A few hours the Mountain was the oddest place on this spring Sunday evening.

There were motor-cars stretching each side of the road for several hundred yards. They had come, their interiors packed with young people, from all over the place.

Nobody had quite believed that this dance-hall venture of Donn's would succeed, but he had sensed the trend and his venture was very successful.

The old men who sat in the pub drinking their pints until closing time, when they would walk home and chat a while outside their houses before going to bed, were still puzzled. The hall was cut off from the shop and the pub. The far end had been added to, and the entrance made there, glass doors, mark you, and a place to hang coats, and flush toilets – one for the MNA and one for the FIR. It wasn't this that really upset the old ones, but the sound of the music that came to their ears through the solid walls. The daftest kind of music ever known to man, all squiggles and ups and downs and blares and bladders. They had peeped at it and watched with awe the gyrations of the young people in the place and had come away shaking their heads.

To most of them dancing was hobnailed boots on a concrete floor, knocking sparks from the cement, jigs and reels, around-the-house-and-mind-the-dresser type of dancing, that stirred your blood and shortened your wind, and separated the fit from the unfit, but this other sort of sleazy stuff, like an eel sliding through grass, left them in a state, feeling old and indignant. It really signalled the end of the old days and the old ways for them. It left them feeling uneasy and unwanted in a quickly-changing world. They never thought they would see the day that these terrible changes would reach their own place. They had heard about them and read about them, but they didn't quite believe them; and here they were now for all to hear and see. It was little of that they recognized, an odd old-time waltz maybe, or *The Walls of Limerick,* or *The Siege of Ennis,* thrown in, they thought, to give the thing a dim look of respectability. And have a look at the fellas up on the stand, and the queer yokes they were playing. You'd think a good melodeon or a fiddle would be good enough for them, but no, guitars and drums and trumpets and loudspeakers and a tall fair young fellow strangling himself with un-understandable words, shaking his body around as if he had St Vitus' dance, and not a note in his head, just screeching like a cock that was going to get its head chopped off.

They didn't mind going into the hall of an evening when Sean McNulty was showing the pictures. That was all right. Two hours of that whiled away an evening, even if you had to shift your backside a lot on the hard wooden folding chairs, or they didn't mind going to it when they were being addressed by a member of one of the Farmers' Clubs or organizations, or a knowing young fellow telling them how to get better grass from their fields, or explaining with repugnant slides what to do in difficult calf deliveries, or how to treat all the repulsive diseases of pigs or cattle or sheep if they couldn't get the vet. All that was good and the hall was of great benefit to them, but they couldn't hold with this dancing, this new unintelligible dancing, mainly because if they criticized it, their children looked at them as if they were speaking heresy and they felt that their world was truly dead and gone and only waiting to be buried.

All Donn saw was a lot of nice young people having a ball. He saw the contrast to his own young days. All the boys and girls were very well-dressed and well-groomed, which was a sign of better times. It was only when you spoke to them and heard their accents that you could distinguish them from the young people at a sophisticated dance in the Town. The noise was great. From his height he could look over heads and he saw Father Murphy up near the bandstand talking to Nan. He made his way up to them, greeting a lot of young people on the way, when they could look up at him from watching their shuffling feet or their clicking fingers.

'Well, Father,' he said, shouting because the blare was right behind him. 'We are glad to see you. Are all the young people behaving themselves?'

155

'They seem to be too busy gyrating to do anything else,' he said. 'Don't you think that all this is far more solemn than it used to be? I mean they are so intent on the dancing itself.'

'It doesn't sound solemn,' said Donn, putting his hand on Nan's shoulder. She looked up and bent her head to rub her cheek against the back of his hand. She enjoyed the dancing. She would look at it for a while and then she would go away. 'So many pretty girls now. Are you sorry you joined the Church when you look at them?'

'No,' said Father Murphy, laughing. 'I have enough to worry about.'

'Will you come in and talk to Meela and have a glass of something or a cup of something?' Donn asked. He was trying hard to be friendly with the priest, mainly because they seemed to knock sparks off one another. The priest hesitated. 'Nobody will lose their virginity while you are having a cup of tea.'

The priest remained unprovoked. 'All right,' he said, and followed Donn towards the end of the room.

They were out in the air and turned towards the house when the noise of the band ended with a triumphant cacophony.

Sean McNulty was dancing with Susan McNally. She had grown into a pretty girl with regular features, but one slightly crooked tooth. She was neatly dressed in a white blouse and a blue skirt. He saw Donn turning and looking back as he went out with the priest. Donn caught his eyes and waved at him, smiling. Sean waved back. He was pleased not to be too near him or Donn would smell the drink off him. He had drunk quite enough.

Susan thought so too. 'Will we go out and get some air?' she asked. 'I'm roasting hot.'

'Yes,' he said, turning to survey the emptied floor. His eyes moved around it at the people gathered at the sides. His eyes rested on Nan. She was looking ahead of her, her hands listless in her lap. He tried to catch her eyes but failed and when Susan came back with her costume coat over her shoulders he walked with her to the door and out into the night. It was good to feel the cold air embrace his warm body. Many other couples had come out too. It was a bright starry night and the moon had topped the hills to the east, three-quarters full. Some couples were just talking, laughing, or smoking. Others of them had walked to the cars and got into them.

'Will we go down to the lake?' Susan asked.

'If that's what you want,' said Sean.

'It isn't what I want,' said Susan. 'I only said. If you don't want to go down to the lake, there's no need to go down.'

'What are you angry about?' he asked.

'You haven't much mind of your own, have you?' she asked.

'What did I do to annoy you?' He was genuinely puzzled.

'Is it because you are working for somebody else and you are waiting orders?' she asked, walking ahead of him. 'Why couldn't you say: "Let's go out"? "Will we walk to the lake?" Why do I have to say things like that?'

'I don't know what you are talking about,' he said.

'Arrah, sometimes you make me sick,' she said, and she walked away faster from him.

He wondered if he would let her go away on her own. He had only taken a few drinks, but they always made his mind slow. He wasn't fitted for drinking, he supposed. He was a one-minded person. He could only puzzle out one thing at a time, give it his whole attention, thinking of two or three things at the same time always distracted him. He liked Susan. She was a very direct honest person. He didn't know if she liked him a lot. He thought she did. He always got on well with her. He hurried his pace and caught up with her. He held her bare arm. The inside of her arm was as soft as the petal of a flower.

'Don't be cross with me,' he said. 'I had a few drinks.'

'You are not a one for them,' she said. 'They make you slow.'

'That's so,' he said, 'and I'm slow enough already.'

'As far as I am concerned you are,' she said.

He thought over this. It was a direct invitation. He didn't like that. It meant he would have to play the next ball. Their feet crunched on the gravel of the makeshift pier. There was a river boat there, turned upside down, ready for the spring painting.

'Will we sit on the boat?' he asked.

'We will not,' she said. 'I'd ruin my skirt.' She turned to face him. She was very close to him. She smelled very nice. He could see the moonlight glinting in her eyes. She put her head on one side. 'Well?' she said.

He put his arms around her. He didn't have far to pull her to feel her body close to him. He kissed her. He realized that this was the first time he had ever kissed a girl. The fact that he was thinking this way was wrong. He should have been lost in the mystery of the first kiss. But he wasn't. He could feel the soft lips, and the tip of his nose was touching the soft cheek.

She pulled back from him.

'It meant nothing to you, did it?' she asked.

'I'm not practised,' he said.

'Do you have to be?' she asked.

'What do you mean now?' he asked.

She turned away from him. 'You don't really care for me, do you, Sean?' she asked.

'I don't know,' he said. 'How am I supposed to know?'

'It would be all over you,' she said. 'You don't really care for me that way at all. I was hoping you would, but you don't, do you?'

'You know the life I led,' he said. 'It didn't train me for this sort of thing, did it?'

'That was a good spell ago now,' she said. 'You are a man. Didn't you know? If you had a feeling for me, you would know, and I would know. You haven't at all, and I'm sorry.'

He walked over and sat despondently on the upturned boat. 'If you say that, then it must be true,' he said.

She stood looking at him. He had filled out in the few years. He was well-built. His deep-set eyes were sad. There always seemed to be a touch of sadness in them. He was fairly handsome. She had liked him from the first time they had met. She had been pleased when she knew he was not going to be a priest but as she saw now there was nothing in him for her. She felt desolate, but then she talked sense to herself. You're not getting me to go into a decline, she told herself, just because this boy I had a fancy for has none at all for me. She wondered why. She was well-built. She could turn heads as she walked the roads. But as far as he was concerned she might as well have been a sack of potatoes. Well, she told herself, the sooner you get over him the better. It will take a certain amount of time, but I will, and since he is not meant for me somebody else is, and after a while I will set out to look for him.

'It's better to know, anyhow, Sean,' she said.

'Is it that easy to know?' he asked.

'You'd know,' she said.

He was silent.

'I'll go back,' she said.

'Let me go with you,' he said.

'What use is it?' she asked. 'Isn't it all over before it began?'

'If you say that,' he said.

'Not if I say it,' she said. 'You know it.'

'All right, I know it,' he said.

She looked at him for a few moments and then she walked slowly back towards the lighted hall. Even down here you could hear the sound of the band.

He watched her walk away. For a moment his heart jumped. Maybe I am doing the wrong thing, he thought, almost in panic. Maybe Susan is the one for me. Where would you get a nicer girl, a girl of good looks and laughter and amazing practicality?

As if in answer to his question he saw the figure of Nan coming down the road. He knew what she would do. She would walk towards the pier and then she would turn left short of it and take the path towards the place where the river came into the lake from the top of the valley. It was a protected spot, a dip near the bank, closed in on two sides by a solid granite rock, moss-covered. There was a cleft as if a giant had cut a quarter out of a granite cake. There was a grassy space where she had stones around in a ring like a fairy circle and in the centre she had a stone seat where she would sit and watch the water where it rippled over stones. Here she would bury dead birds or animals that she found, make small little graves and put flowers on them when they were covered.

She didn't see him. He watched her all the way down, the moon lighting her well, almost making a halo around the whole of her. Soon she had rounded a bend and was out of his sight. She would sit there for nearly an hour on a fine evening.

He couldn't understand her. How could anybody understand her? She must even be a puzzle to her mother. He thought how shocked Susan would be if he suddenly declared: You see I am in love with Nan. It was typical of him, he thought, to be in love with the unattainable. He had been before, and he had been found wanting. He wondered if he had just transferred the love he had had for the one thing he couldn't attain, to another. Was that the kind of fellow he was? Wouldn't her eyes always be blank except when you talked about the most simple things? How could you go to a girl like this and say I love everything about you? If there are miracles in the world, why can't your mind suddenly blossom and understand perfectly what I am saying to you? He could become a poet as he would compare her beauty to the beauty of the natural things around them. He said them often to her in the darkness of the night; silently sometimes when she sat beside him with her hand on his arm. He wanted to touch her, but she had the child's instinctive dislike of being touched, and if he held her hand she would draw it away. If he put his hand on her shoulder, she would bend under it and move away. His reason and intelligence told him that what he wanted was impossible. There was Susan, sane and healthy, and ready to be kissed and fondled, and he had to get caught up with this beautiful child, and feel that his life was tied to her for ever.

'You were watching her,' said the voice of Dino beside him. The boards of the boat creaked as he sat down beside him. Dino was a heavy man now. He had a huge chest, even if his legs were short.

'What are you talking about?' Sean asked. 'Why aren't you back at the hall chucking out?'

Dino chuckled. He was an efficient chucker-out. His ways were short and slightly brutal, but they worked. They had very little trouble in the hall with Dino around.

'They are quiet as sheep tonight,' Dino said. He took a bottle from his pocket. 'Take a slug,' he said, holding it out.

Sean looked at it. He was shaken by Dino's remark. This might dodge the issue. 'Thanks,' he said. He took the bottle, pulled the cork, put the neck to his mouth and slugged. It was like drinking fire. He had swallowed quite a bit of it.

'Ah! Ah! Ah!' he said, bending forward. Dino clapped him on the back, laughing.

'That's Bartley's stuff,' he said, taking the bottle back and drinking himself. He wiped his mouth. 'It's great stuff,' he said. 'It makes giants out of little men.'

'Oh, but it's fiery,' said Sean. 'It's raw stuff.' Its effect on him seemed to be instantaneous.

'I seen you watching Nan,' said Dino.

'What do you mean?' Sean asked.

'Your eyes are never off her,' said Dino. 'I seen that. I do be watching her myself too, you know.'

'You do?' said Sean, amazed, and hurt, like you had one flower in a far field that you thought only you knew about and you could go and look at it privately, secretly.

'Sure I do,' said Dino. 'Have another one.' Sean took it, almost automatically. He drank some, this time more cautiously. 'Who better is there to be looking at?' Dino went on. 'Have you ever seen her equal, have you?'

'She is pretty,' said Sean. 'She is pretty.'

'More than that,' said Dino. 'Man, I do look at her and there isn't a one in the whole province that I'd rather take than her.'

'You, Dino?' said Sean.

'Yeh,' said Dino. 'What a pretty heifer and never to know. I say. You seen those nice legs of her, long and round, man, and upstairs and the nice mouth of her.'

'Stop talking like that,' said Sean, but his voice seemed to be booming in a vault in his head.

'Why?' Dino asked. 'I thought we might help one another. I seen you watching her. Only a while back, and I said to meself: Look, there's Sean and he in the same flux as meself about her, in heat, man.'

'No! No!' said Sean.

'What's the difference?' Dino asked. He was bending close to him saying those things as if he was afraid the stars were listening. 'How can she ever be got? Girls like that don't marry, do they? Listen, you'll go on the rest of your life longing for a one like that, and it'll do you no good and you could go out of your head. Isn't this so?'

'You could go out of your head right enough,' Sean said, almost groaning.

'You see what I mean,' said Dino, 'with two of us on an

evening like this. We go down there and we sort of pet her see. It would work. What would she know about it? Nobody would know, would they, when she wouldn't be able to tell, would they? Are you listening to me, Sean?'

'Are you out of your mind?' Sean asked him, trying vainly to pierce the fog in his brain.

'No, it's a natural, I tell you, with two of us. How the hell are we to go on for ever like this? It can't be done, man. We are men aren't we? Why should they be allowed to get away with it. Nobody would ever know, Sean. On me oath. She's soft in the head isn't she? She wouldn't even know, would she? A few minutes and it's over and nobody the wiser except ourselves; and we don't go out of our minds. You hear? Nobody would ever know.'

Sean had enough strength in his legs to raise himself from the boat and stagger on the pier and try a staggering run back towards the hall, saying 'No! No! No!' flapping his right arm up and down weakly, while Dino looked after him, and raised the bottle to his lips and drank. He grinned after the wavering figure of Sean.

Seventeen

WHEN YOU get a bad cold and you are blowing your nose for some days, you get a sort of lightness in your head. You feel detached from yourself. Voices seem to come to your intelligence from a long way off, as if the people who spoke were at the other end of a valley from you.

Then there are the disturbed dreams that come to you at night, terrifying: but only if they are repeated do they take on the touch of reality, so you find it difficult to separate the dream from the real.

Sean McNulty spent a month like this. He was never quite able to separate the events from his nightmarish dreams of them. During that time he drank a lot with Dino. They would mount the tractor of an evening and set off for the street town.

By the time he got home his mother and father would be in bed. His mother would nag at him for the poverty of his appetite. He would look at himself in the mirror when he was shaving in the morning and scarcely recognize himself. His eyes were bloodshot. He managed to get through his work at Donn's by keeping his head down. He wasn't himself, he was to say over and over again to himself. He didn't know what had got into him.

He wasn't to remember much of this night either. It seemed such a repetition.

They were sitting on the upturned boat at the pier and it was night-time, and there was no moon, but there were a lot of stars. You could see things when your eyes became accustomed to the odd light. Dino passed him the bottle and he drank. They had done that before, he remembered, but there were lights above in the hall and there were many cars and the sound of voices, and laughter and a band playing. Tonight there were no lights and no voices and no laughter and no cars. So he could distinguish one night from the other in that way.

There was a tenseness in the air as if the night was holding its breath. He didn't know why he should remember a thing like that when everything else seemed so unclear, but he did.

It wasn't as if Dino and himself were even talking. There was no sound except the sound of the river behind them where it went into the lake and the gurgle from the bottle as they drank.

Just the sound of Dino's voice coming from a long way, it seemed.

'She's coming out,' Dino said.

It took his mind a long time to understand that.

'Who? Who? Who?' he said, reaching into the recesses of his memory.

'You can just see,' he heard Dino say. 'Coming out from the house. Now she is at the turn off and she is going down there.'

'Who?' he said again.

'Come on,' said Dino.

He remembered that.

'No,' he said.

'She's down on to the path now,' he heard Dino say and then knew that Dino had left him and was gone.

He remembered the effort of getting to his feet and standing there looking after him. He could see him crouched, walking up, and then turning to the right.

He called: 'No, Dino!' but he wasn't sure if he said it or not. He felt sick. He went up the road after Dino, went beyond the pathway, came back again to it, helping his body with his waving arms, and then he turned down the path too.

He didn't remember what he felt. It was like doing something that had been rehearsed. He just wished that he was sober and that his mind was clear. There was something urgent he had to do, or something urgent that he had not to do. Something terrible or to stop something terrible. He remembered feeling that he was too young, too young. Why too young? He didn't know.

His sense of direction was leaving him when he heard the scream. Oh, no, his mind said as he ran towards it. He thought his feet were bringing him there flying, but he was staggering from side to side. Two figures in the starlight. The girl screamed again. He reached them, in a panic. There were to be no screams, that was what he remembered. Don't scream. He put his hand over her mouth. Felt the wet of her lips, felt the teeth biting into the flesh of his first finger. Then she fell, and he was running away. He climbed out of the place and felt the heather and ran towards the line of the hills that he could see feeling his feet going into wet parts, the wetness seeping up his legs, but he just kept running as well as he could, and once when he rubbed his hands together he felt the sticky wetness of blood from his finger and that seemed to make it worse.

Dino was wrong. It wasn't the way Dino had seen it at all. This girl, struggling and screaming. She wasn't supposed to do that.

How can I kill myself? he wondered. What kind of a person am I at all? I ran away. Instead of hitting Dino on the back of the head with a rock. He turned to go back and he didn't know where he was. Somewhere in the middle of a mountain bog.

He fell flat on his face. He stayed there. He could feel the bog soaking into him. He scratched at it with his fingers. He felt the soft brown of it squeezing through his hands.

Then he pulled himself erect.

He peered around him. Below he saw the lights in the houses. He tried to pull himself together. He looked at the lights. He tried to place them in their setting. He thought he recognized his own. He would go home and steal in, and nobody would know he was ever out.

It was all he could think of to do.

He staggered his way across the bog.

He thought he was carrying on a conversation with himself. All he was saying was 'Oh! Oh! Oh!'

Eighteen

DONN WAS tidying up in the bar. He had given Paud an evening off and served there himself. It was a pleasant enough way of passing an evening, pulling pints, filling an occasional half one. It was rarely he was asked for an out-of-the-way drink – brandy, whiskey, and porter, it was usually, with minerals for the young ones who didn't drink anything stronger. The talk was about the price of cattle, the number of bags of manure per acre, some claiming you could put it on too strong and others claiming that you could never put it on strong enough; the death of several sheep and the wounding of lambs by the dogs; the building of the new cottages, and how some of them professed to prefer the old, with all their inconveniences.

It was all pleasant, unsophisticated, down-to-earth, with nobody getting drunk. They saved getting drunk for funerals or weddings or fair days, a few calculated days of the year.

Now they were gone. He cleaned the glasses and washed the stains off the counter with a damp cloth, wondering at himself that he felt quite content with all this. He would finish and he would go into the parlour and he would sit at the other side of the fire from Meela, and they would talk desultorily about things, maybe laugh a little, eat their supper and go to bed. It was as commonplace as it could be, and this was the way he liked it. You shut the doors and you were at home, a good husband sitting in front of the fire, reading a book, writing a few of your impressions about things. No drama in life at all, and the realization that this was the way he preferred it to be. He wondered at the way the fire had gone out of his belly, the discontent, the terrible restlessness. He had had enough of drama, he told himself, enough of trying to analyse why and where. He was heading towards living in a rut, a nice comfortable rut. He had done a lot, instigated a lot of action. He had stirred the place up, and from now on it would keep going with this momentum, with a little prodding here and a little prodding there. He was amused as he thought of this, himself turning into the quiet man. He looked at himself in one of the mirrors with the whiskey manufacturer's name written across it in red, so that you had to look between the lines to see your face. It was a lined face now, creased at the eyes and the forehead, and the broad cheeks bisected by lines that ran from under the cheekbones by the mouth and under the chin. He felt the jowls that were beginning to form under his chin, raised his head, made them disappear. His brown hair, still very thick, was speckled with grey over his ears, but it wasn't all that noticeable. Just a hint of the future, a reminder that the years were passing. He didn't mind now, he wasn't trying to hold them back. Life was good. He was surrounded by love and he had many friends. He was quite willing to pass the rest of his life doing what he was at now. Long life, a quick death, and oblivion.

He heard Meela calling. His hands stiffened on the counter. She was shouting his name. He felt frightened for a moment, the old insecurity flooding back over him for a second. Then he laughed at himself and came out from behind the counter.

She came in the door quickly.

'Donn!' she said. She was breathing hard.

'What is it?' he asked. 'What's wrong?'

'Come quickly,' she said. 'It's Nan. Something has happened to Nan.'

He stared at her. Her face was pale. He suddenly felt cold. In a detached way he thought: I must never again be smug. No man should ever count his blessings if he doesn't want to call down the curses.

'Where is she?' he asked. He didn't ask what was wrong. She turned and walked away quickly and he followed her, through the door and into the corridor. She turned from that into the parlour.

'Nan,' Meela said. 'Nan.' He could hardly see her at first. She was crouched in the corner. He passed Meela and went to her, holding out his hands. She was crouching, her arms crossed over her breasts. Her hair was dishevelled, there were dirt-marks on her face, and a bruise on her right jaw.

'Nan,' he said, 'what happened? Did you fall? Where did

you fall?' Her legs were marked. Her eyes were staring at him. Before he could put a hand on her, she screamed, and she kept screaming.

'Nan!' he said desperately. 'It's me! Your father! Nan!' He had drawn back from her. Now he approached her again and she screamed again. She was looking at him with fear and terror. 'What's wrong with her, Meela? What in the name of God is wrong with her?'

Meela was kneeling beside her, her arms around her. She was saying: 'Nan, it's your daddy! Don't you know your daddy?'

Nan kept staring at him. He went to approach her again and she screamed again. He felt the sweat breaking out all over his body. It was as if she had never seen him before, as if she was afraid he was going to approach her and beat her.

He didn't go near her again.

'What could have happened to her?' he asked.

'I don't know! I don't know!' said Meela, looking at him, waiting for him to solve it. He couldn't. He could only think of one thing. 'I will get out the car and go for the doctor,' he said.

'Hurry!' she said. 'Hurry. Her heart is racing. Nan! Nan! It's all right. Everything is all right now. Do you hear?'

He looked at her again. Her eyes kept staring at him. He went to speak once more, decided against it and ran out of the room. He tried not to think, to put the impression of her out of his mind. She reminded him of a wounded prisoner he had seen when he was a soldier, trapped after a retreat, waiting like an animal to be killed, expecting death and not having anything to defend himself with. But why Nan? And why against him? He loved her. He had won her love. It had taken time. She had obviously fallen. Had she hurt her head? He could see no sign of blood, only bruises, and scratches and marks on her bare legs.

He was so eager to start the car that he stalled it. He sat back and counted four, deliberately, and then got the engine going and drove out of the yard. The headlights cut swathes through the darkness. He drove dangerously, but on this bad winding road he couldn't drive too fast. If he could have made his body an engine he would have done so to get more speed out of the car.

He saw every mile of the road with his mind, where he could go fast, where he would have to slow down before a very bad corner. He was trying to stop himself from panicking, or he would end up dead and be no use to Nan. Nan, maybe it was a brainstorm. Maybe something was happening to the poor retarded mind. Did she have a fall, and was there part of her skull pressing on her brain? Hurry, hurry, hurry, but don't kill yourself. If you kill yourself you will never know and you will have been of no use to her.

Each mile of the road seemed endless to him, seeming to stretch and wind away into infinity. He was hurt. He still heard her scream as he approached her. As if he was the devil. Why? He hadn't done anything to her, just loved her, because she was part of himself, that was all, bemoaning all the wasted years he had been away from her and from Meela. The look of bewilderment in the eyes of Meela. Hurry! And he did, but with caution, one part of his brain rushing, rushing, and the other part slow and cautious and seeing the road ahead and judging each turn and twist of it.

All journeys end, somewhere, some time, and so did his. He stopped outside the doctor's house. He sat in the car for a second, and then he got out and went in the gate and knocked at the door. There was a light in one room on the right. It was a time until his knock was answered. He had to hold himself from knocking, and knocking, and knocking again.

Then the door opened, and the small balding man was there, in his slippers, a book in his hand. He took off his reading-glasses.

He recognized Donn.

'Oh,' he said. 'Something up?'

Donn paused.

'Please come quickly,' he said. 'There is something wrong with my girl. I approach her, she screams. She is bruised. I'm afraid it might have done something to her head. She must have fallen. Will you come now?'

'What do you mean, she screams?' he asked.

'When I go near her,' said Donn. 'I can't understand it. I

love her. She loves me, and when I go near her she screams.'

'Oh,' said the doctor. 'I'll come. You go down the road. Pick up the nurse. Take her with you. I'll go now. I'll be up as soon as you. I can bring the nurse back.'

'Thank you,' Donn said, admiring the man's decisiveness. He left him and went out to the car. He started it and went farther up the road, remembering where the nurse lived, knowing well – because small communities were valuable in this way, that everybody knew where everybody else was and approximately what they would be doing at any certain time.

He knocked here. There was light in the house. Nobody went to bed early, and this was a good thing too. Only some got up early.

She was a small, middle-aged woman.

'Oh,' she said as she peered out at him.

'The doctor said to come with me,' he said. 'There is something wrong with my girl. He wants you.'

She didn't answer him. She left the door open and went away and then she came back with a bag in her hand and a blue coat over her arm. She left down the bag and started to get into the coat. He helped her. 'Thanks,' she said and then went with him to the car. He closed the door on her. He had to drive down quite a way before he could get a place to turn and when he had done so, and got back on the road again he saw the doctor's car ahead of him. He closed up until the red lights were only a few yards ahead of him. His inclination was to pass the doctor's car and race back to Nan, but he didn't. The doctor knew the roads as well as himself, and keeping at a moderate pace he would probably get there more quickly than if they both started a race.

'What's wrong with her?' the nurse asked.

'I don't know,' he said. 'You know Nan.'

'She is a beautiful girl,' she said. 'She has a grand manner. There's nobody that couldn't love her. You think she fell?'

'She is bruised and scratched,' he said. 'I think she must have fallen and hurt her head. I hope she hasn't hurt her brain.'

'Please God she hasn't,' the nurse said. 'I often thought it would be nice to live in the childlike world that Nan lives in, when she doesn't know any different.'

'Something has happened to her,' he said.

'It will be all right,' she said.

That was all the conversation they had. He had to concentrate on his driving, clenching his teeth, because he didn't like the situation he was in, of having to depend on other people. He was used to handling problems himself, thinking over them and deciding what should be done and then forging ahead with them, forcing them to a successful conclusion. This was the way he wanted it to be now, but he saw no way through. He would have to abide by the knowledge of other people.

They stopped the cars outside the house.

He went in the door, straight to the parlour. The doctor followed him, and then the nurse.

Nan and Meela were in exactly the same places. Meela was kneeling, holding the girl in her arms, but her face was not hidden. Nan saw Donn and her eyes widened. He had forgotten. He wanted to go to her and raise her in his arms.

She started to scream, and it intensified as the doctor came to Donn's side and moved towards her. Donn was going to force the issue, but the doctor stopped him.

'No,' he said, holding him back with his free hand. 'You and I will go outside. Nurse, you go over to her, will you? See what happens.'

The nurse walked towards the pair in the corner.

'Hello, Nan,' she said. 'What is troubling you?' Nan kept looking at her, but she didn't scream. She looked at her and then fastened her eyes on the two men behind.

'Sedate her,' the doctor said to the nurse. 'We'll go away. Tell me when she is quiet and I will look at her.'

'All right,' the nurse said, opening her bag.

'Come on,' said the doctor to Donn, pulling at his sleeve. They went out the door again into the night.

'But why? Why?' Donn asked, completely bewildered.

'Smoke a cigarette,' said the doctor. 'Here,' pushing one into his hand, and when he had put it in his mouth lighting it for him.

'I don't understand,' said Donn. 'I can't understand.'

'We'll find out,' the doctor said. 'I can see her when she is quiet.'

'Could it be her mind?' Donn asked.

'It's certainly something in her mind,' said the doctor. 'Can't you try not to think of it for a little while?'

'I could if it was somebody else's child,' said Donn. 'But she's mine.'

'That makes a difference all right,' the doctor said. 'It's marvellous the way ye have changed this village. An old inhabitant would find it hard to recognize it.'

'Yes,' said Donn.

'We'll walk down to the pier and back,' said the doctor. 'Come on. We'll know soon.'

He waited and then started to walk. Donn went reluctantly with him, after listening. There was no sound from the house. The stars were shining, not brilliantly. You would want the cold frosty air to make them gleam.

'What do they say?' the doctor asked. 'It is easy to sleep on another man's wound. Don't be too sad. She looks healthy to me. I think she would look worse if she had hurt her head.'

'What else could it be?' Donn asked.

'We'll know,' the doctor said. 'We'll know soon.'

They stood silent on the pier and smoked. There wasn't even a puff of wind. The cigarette smoke took a long time to disperse. Donn smoked very quickly and then flicked the cigarette at the water. He could hear the hiss as the water quenched it.

The doctor finished his cigarette more slowly and then he threw it away too, listened to the hiss and said: 'Right. We'll go back now.'

They walked back to the house. Now, Donn had a strange reluctance to go back in. He was afraid of what he would hear. His imagination covered a lot of ground, all of it treacherous, all of it sad.

He followed the doctor in. There was nobody in the parlour. They stood there for a few seconds. Then Meela came in the door. She was very pale, Donn saw.

'We got her to bed, Doctor,' she said. 'She is in her room. I'll show you the way.'

'Can I come?' asked Donn.

'No, please,' said the doctor. He took up his bag and followed Meela out.

Donn stood there, feeling helpless. He waited, his mind almost a blank.

Then Meela came back. She walked over to him and put her arm around his waist. He put an arm around her shoulders and the just stood there, without speech. It was good to feel her so close to him.

After a while he said: 'It will be all right. He said it will be all right. He said she would look worse if her head was hurt.'

'Her heart was beating too fast,' said Meela. 'That's all. All the time you were gone. She wouldn't speak. I tried to make her talk, but no matter what I said, she wouldn't speak.'

'She'll be all right,' he said. 'I know that she will be all right.' Only words, because he didn't know. Trying to comfort Meela. Out of ignorance.

He didn't know how long they stood with their arms about one another, until the door opened again and the doctor stood there looking at them. Donn thought that his face was grim. He was a slight man and his face was thin, his light hair was thinning too and he had thin lips.

'Sit down,' he said.

They looked at him.

'Just sit down,' he said. 'Please.'

They went and sat beside each other on the sofa near the window. He thought of Nan lying in what had been Meela's bed, in the feminine room that she had abandoned for him.

'This is not easy,' the doctor said, facing them. 'I don't know how to put it. It's not easy.'

'She is bad?' Donn asked.

'No,' said the doctor, 'not physically. She'll get over it, that end of it, I mean. She is in a state of shock now. You will have to know. She has been raped.'

The word hung on the air, like an ugly lance, poised.

They stared at him.

'I said it brutally,' he said. 'I'm sorry. There is no other way to say it. Her legs and shoulders are badly bruised. But there is no doubt. This is what has happened to her.'

'You must be wrong,' said Meela.

'I wish I was,' he said sadly.

'You are telling me,' said Donn, 'that here in my village in the quiet evening some man has raped my daughter. Are you serious?'

'I'm serious,' he said.

'It's impossible,' said Meela. 'Nobody would do that to Nan.'

'Somebody has,' he said. 'I'm sorry.'

He looked at their faces. How would I feel, he wondered, if it was my daughter? I wouldn't like to believe it either.

'I will leave the nurse for a few days,' he said. 'Will you be able to put her up? The girl will have to be kept quiet, as much as possible. It would be better for the nurse to be here. Is that all right?'

'All right,' said Meela. 'That will be all right.'

'There's nothing much else I can do,' he said. 'The nurse will be able to do anything that is necessary. I will be going now. I'm so sorry. But she'll be all right. The bruises and injuries will go away. Her jaw will be sore for a few days. She will find it hard to eat. She should get soft food.'

'You mean somebody hit her, hit Nan?' Donn asked. He was on his feet. He found it hard to understand what the doctor was saying.

'Yes,' said the doctor. 'That is obvious. She is a strong girl. She must have fought.'

'Oh, my God!' said Meela.

Donn suddenly felt cold.

'I'll be going now,' said the doctor. 'I can't do any more. I'm sorry.'

He walked to the door.

Donn followed him. The doctor stood at the car door.

'Normally I would have to report a thing like this to the police. Is that what you want me to do?'

'They find this fellow,' said Donn, flatly. 'Who is to be a witness? Nan? Can you see Nan being a witness? You would like that, for the sake of justice?'

'I know how impossible it is,' said the doctor. 'But if people knew, a monster like this could be ostracized.'

'You can tell the police or not as you like,' said Donn. 'That's up to you.'

'What are you going to do?' the doctor asked. He was sitting in the car, looking out the window.

'I am going to kill somebody,' said Donn.

The doctor looked at his face, hard to see, just the tight planes and the muscles jutting at the jaws.

He will too, the doctor thought, as he turned the car. He was still there standing outside the door when the doctor passed. He waved his hand but he got no reaction from the figure standing there, with legs braced, looking from his home back at the village, with the lights still in the windows.

He looked at his place and the dark tops of the surrounding hills against the horizon, and he heard the sound of the water, and all he could say through clenched teeth was: 'My own place! My own place! My own place!'

Nineteen

DONN WAS making people uneasy. He knew this. It was what he desired. One by one he visited them in their houses. He brought no joy with him, no laughter. He would sit on a chair near the fire and if they offered him a drink he would take it. Nobody mentioned why he was doing this pilgrimage of visits. He left them in no doubt, just by the way he looked at them.

I knew these people, he thought, but I only thought I knew them. I thought I was safe in the midst of them, that my child would be safe in the midst of them, and yet one of them has done this thing to me. Which one of them? And all the time this phrase of the priest was with him: *Don't put all your money on the people.* He had put all he possessed on them and what had they done to him? They had done this incredible and unspeakable thing to him. Which of them? He was determined to worry it out of them. He would look and stare at them and one of them would give it away. He was confident that they knew. A small tight community like that must know which one of them was capable of such a terrible thing.

The tight jaws and the brooding eyes of him would make anybody uneasy. The free relationship he had worked out with them was vanished. Could it have been Tim Woods, the tall man with the thick spectacles, a slow-moving man? How could it be he? His glasses would have fallen off. Then how about his sons, leaning against the dresser, feet shifting under his probing gaze? They never mentioned Nan. It wasn't a thing they were supposed to know. Nobody was supposed to know about it, yet he knew that everybody did. But because they weren't supposed to know, they couldn't say: Oh, dear man, we are sorry for your trouble and if there is anything we can do, just ask us.

When he left Tim Woods he stood at the door, and then looked back at them, the woman at the fire with the sad look, and the man himself with the light reflecting from his spectacles giving him a totally blank look, the hefty sons with their muscular arms folded, watching him. They had all worked hard, putting in the water, building their new house, helping to build the other new houses. Now they were as cut off from him as if they were all foreigners.

'Give me a name,' he suddenly shouted at them. 'Just give me a name! Tell me that some stranger came over the hills. Just tell me that!'

They could tell him nothing.

'We're sorry, Donn,' Tim said. 'We are truly sorry.'

'I don't want your sorrow,' said Donn. 'Don't give me that. All I want is a name. Put a name on him!'

They couldn't, so he left.

How many visits was that? He didn't know. He was doing two or three a night. During the day he walked, and he would lean on a wall looking at the young men working in the fields, silently scrutinizing them, trying to get a picture in his mind of the one who would be capable of doing such a thing. He wanted to frighten him out of his anonymity.

When he called on the McNultys, Sean was sitting on a chair in the kitchen, looking very pale. He had lost weight in a week, his eyes were deep in his head. He looked sick.

'I thought we were going to lose him,' said Mrs McNulty, fussing around him. 'You could light a pipe off his skin, he was so hot. I had to change the sheets twice a night with all the sweating he did. It was terrible.'

'I'm sorry I couldn't get to work, Donn,' said Sean. 'I sent you a message.'

'That's fine, Sean,' said Donn. 'I got the message. I knew you were sick.' He had inquired about the time. He was sick from that Tuesday. A man with a fever on him of a Tuesday wasn't going around raping girls. He was a bit shocked at himself for even putting Sean in the category. He thought he knew him well. He judged him utterly incapable of a thing like that. So he could relax with the McNultys.

Tom brought him a drink of whiskey.

They watched him in silence as he swirled the whiskey around in his glass, just looking at it. His face was drawn. He could do with a shave. He wasn't wearing a tie. He wasn't the same man at all, Sean saw, his heart sinking. He wanted to confess to what had happened, but he couldn't face it. The consequences following on a confession were too awful to imagine. His mother saw the cold sweat on his forehead and came over to him and rubbed it off with her apron.

'Are you all right, Sean?' she asked. 'Should you go back to bed?'

'I'm all right, Mother,' he said impatiently. 'I'm all right.'

'Do you want to talk about what happened?' Tom McNulty asked.

'Where does talk get us?' Donn asked him, looking up with his eyes bleak. 'All I want to know is, who? Do you know, Tom?'

'I don't,' said Tom. 'Honest to God, Donn, I cannot think of anyone in the place who would be capable of a thing like that. Many of us would be capable of murdering a man, but I cannot think of anyone here who would do ... that. It must be someone from outside.'

'No,' said Donn. 'It was one of you. This was no stranger. This was a person who knew what she did and where she went and where he could get her.'

'Look, Donn,' said Tom. 'Don't you say one of *you*. Don't put us in there with whoever it was. You hear? We are decent people. I don't like to hear things like that said in my house.'

'Find him,' said Donn. 'Just find him, and then there will be only one.'

'Suppose we find him,' said Tom. 'What then? What happens then?'

'You just tell me the name,' said Donn.

'And what happens then?' McNulty asked.

'That's up to me,' said Donn. 'What happens then is entirely up to me.'

'With you feeling like that,' said Tom, 'suppose I knew who he was, do you think I would tell you?'

'Why not?' Donn asked. 'Why wouldn't you tell me?'

'Because I would be afraid of what you would do, and two wrongs don't make a right.'

'Did you say that,' Donn asked, 'when you were out shooting Black and Tans?'

'That was different,' said Tom. 'That was altogether different.'

'It's easy to sleep on another man's wounds, eh?'

'It's not that either,' said Tom. 'Times have changed.'

'How about justice?' Donn asked.

'That is always there,' said McNulty.

'You know in this case there can be none of this so-called justice,' said Donn.

'Well, don't do anything you would be sorry for,' said Tom.

'I couldn't,' said Donn. 'There is nothing I could do in this case that I would ever be sorry for. I cannot think of anything that would make me sorry. My only sorrow is my present ignorance. It's eating me up, like I had worms in my belly.'

He left them.

They looked at the closed door. They were very uneasy.

'God help him,' said Mrs McNulty.

'God help the fellow if he finds him,' said Tom.

'I feel weak, Mother,' said Sean. 'I will go back to bed.'

She fussed about him.

Seamus Mooney and Jill.

They were sorry to see the look of him.

All the children were in bed except for the eldest boy, who was fourteen, who was at the table doing his school exercises, helped by his tongue between his teeth.

So they watched him and talked about trivial things. He was content just to be there. The Mooneys had no young man big enough to do what had been done, and even his now slightly distorted mind could not fit Seamus into the role of rapist.

'If only I could lay my hands on him,' he said, pounding his knee with his fist.

'Joe,' said Jill to the boy. 'Finish up your exercises and go to bed.'

'Arrah,' he said, 'I'm not near finished. Leave me alone.'

To all their surprise Jill went over to him and gave him a box on the head.

'Don't you speak to me like that,' she said. 'Get up. Off with you. Get up early in the morning and do it.'

'Mother!' said the shocked Joe, holding his head.

'Jill!' said Seamus surprised.

'Do what I tell you!' she shouted at her son.

He was so surprised that he gathered himself, folded the copybook and went off to his room.

Jill knew she would be sorry.

'What made you do a thing like that?' Seamus asked.

'If you won't correct your children,' she said, 'somebody will have to do it.'

'That's not the way to do it,' he said.

'Isn't it now? And will you tell me what other way there is of doing it?'

'You know that isn't the way,' he said angrily.

Donn rose and walked to the door.

'I'll go,' he said. 'I'm sorry. I know I am not myself. But I don't want to bring trouble into other people's houses.'

'You don't do that,' said Seamus. 'You are always welcome here.'

'All the same, I will leave you,' said Donn, and did so.

'Now see what you done,' said Seamus to her.

'What have I done now?' she asked.

'Driven the man away,' he said.

'I couldn't be looking at him,' she said. 'He goes through me.'

'Is that any reason to be walloping Joe?' he asked.

'I'd wallop you, if I could,' she said.

'What's got into you, Jill?' he asked.

'That girl and him,' she said. 'Suppose it was our Maeve, what would you do? How would you feel?'

'It's not,' he said, 'so I don't feel anything. All I feel is pity for the poor bastard that did it when Donn lays his hands on him.'

'And what happens to Donn?' she asked. 'If he kills him what is going to happen to him?'

'They'll give him a medal,' he said.

'They'll give him jail,' she said.

'It'll be worth it.' said Seamus. 'If it was me I wouldn't mind being hanged for him.'

'Don't say things like that,' she said. 'Say things and they might come true.'

* * *

In Tumelty's Dino did all the talking.

'Listen, Donn, will I go to town on Thursday and pick up all the stuff? Have you enough on order for a tractor-load?'

'Yes, Dino,' said Donn, 'do that.'

'Do you want the hill field ploughed? It's getting late. I'm going to be very busy. If I don't do it soon for you, it will be too late.'

'Do that, Dino,' he said.

'With Sean sick,' said Dino, 'there is a lot of back orders piled up. If I go and see herself about it will she be able to tell me, do you think?'

'She's the one,' said Donn. 'Go to her.'

'I'll do that,' said Dino. 'They tell me you want more stuff for the shop too. Will somebody make out a list? Will Sean soon be better?'

'I'm sure he will be,' said Donn.

Dino asked all those questions, leaning back in a kitchen chair, his small thick hands shoved into the belt of his trousers. He felt safe, looking at this man. How would he ever know? He would never know. He had panicked for a few days. At a noise in the night he would wake up in fear, thinking it was Donn about to break down the door of the house. He could do it too, he thought. He was a big man, but he was looking shaken. The passing of the days were leaving Dino with a feeling of security. Nobody would ever know. How could they know? How would Donn ever know? There were bruises on his own body, but they were where nobody could ever see them and they were fading away now anyway. Sean would never talk, he knew, because he felt more guilty than Dino. Who would have ever thought that the girl would put up such a fight? As his panic fear left him he began to think with a certain amount of pleasure of what had happened. It hadn't worked out the way he had thought, but it had worked out and maybe the fighting had added zest to it. Just to be careful. Not to let it show in his eyes.

Donn thought of Dino. He looked closely at Dino. Dino had a sensuous mouth, but how could you go by external marks like that? He had seen sensuous mouths on blameless people. And Dino was part of his house by now, with his red tractor parked in the yard. You got used to Dino in the shop, in the yard, even eating his meals in the kitchen.

'I'm getting tired,' he told Bartley Folan. He was drinking Bartley's brew. It tasted like water to him. His mouth and throat were dry. 'I don't sleep much. I get up and walk. I go out into the night and I look at every house in the valley. He is behind one of those sleeping windows, I tell myself. Some one of them. Which one of them?'

'You'll drive yourself to drink,' said Bartley. 'Take it easy.'

'No,' said Donn. 'I must go on. I'll ferret him out.'

'What then?' asked Bartley. 'What then?'

'Ah,' said Donn. 'What then, Bartley? I have seen indecent things done in the world, very obscene things. War does things to human beings. But I have never come against so terrible a thing as this. It is beyond comprehension. It is beyond reason.'

'You are branding the whole people,' said Bartley, 'for a crime done by one of them.'

'It was one of them,' said Donn. 'It was one of them.'

'There are a few hundred people,' said Bartley. 'One of them is only a small per cent. You are branding the whole of them for this one creature. This is not a good thing to do. You will drive them away from you. They don't like to be branded. They are decent people. If they knew who did this they would kick the guts out of him.'

'I will kick the guts out of him,' said Donn. 'Some of them must know. I must keep after them. If I don't, how will I ever find out? I will have to keep after them, accusing them, so that they will be forced to tell me his name.'

'Would you ever try and forget it, Donn?' Bartley asked.

'What a thing,' said Donn. 'Are you my friend?'

'I try to be,' said Bartley.

'With words like that in your mouth?' Donn asked. 'I am dirtied. I feel that they have sent me swimming in a septic tank, a cesspit, and you ask me to forget it. In a night all that this place meant to me, all that I was compelled to do, to make it my place, all this is gone. I could be living in a garden filled with weeds, sleeping in beds of nettles. I made something bloom. I would like to see it rot and die, if this is all that it has meant, that after it all they should do this to me. You tell me to try and forget it!'

'I do, for your own sake,' said Bartley desperately. 'What you will do there will be no going back on. Leave it to a few of us and we'll find out and we'll do things that won't bring more sorrow and passion down on your head. Can't you leave it to us to handle it?'

'No,' said Donn. 'No!'

Meela came in the door.

She stood there in the lamplight. There were dark circles under her eyes.

'I have been searching all over the place for you, Donn,' she said.

'Why? Why?' he asked.

'Just to get you to come home,' she said. 'I want you at home. I am lonely. It is late. Will you come now?'

He thought over it, twisting the glass in his hands.

'I will,' he said. 'I don't want to. She still won't look at me. When I go into the room, she crouches away from me. Why does she think I would hurt her? I want to comfort her. I want to tell her that I'm going to find out who did it to her and I'm going to kill him.'

'That would be a great comfort to her,' she said.

Bartley looked up at the sharpness in her tone.

'You must give her time, Donn,' she said. 'She got a very bad shock.'

'What kind of shock do you think I got?' he asked.

She was going to say something, but she held it back.

'Will you please come home now?' she asked.

'I will,' he said and drank the remainder of the glass. He rose to his feet and walked to the door. He walked straight, but he was drunk. When he got outside and the night air hit him, he staggered. Meela was there and he put an arm around her shoulder. He leaned his weight on her. They walked on the poor road.

'I have to take drink, Meela,' he said. 'I think and I think and I think, and if I don't dull the thinking with drink, I would go out of my mind.'

'Nan won't have a baby,' said Meela. 'She didn't conceive.'

He thought over that. He mulled over it.

'This makes a big difference,' he said sarcastically.

'It makes a big difference to her,' she said.

'She was brutally violated,' he said, 'but that's all right when she didn't conceive.'

'Who are you thinking of?' she asked.

'What do you mean by that?' he asked.

'It was she who suffered this thing, not you,' she said.

'You are peeved,' he said. 'You are talking the way you used to talk when I came back first.'

'I'm sorry,' she said.

'You won't talk me out of it,' he said. 'Bartley won't talk me out of it. All those nice peaceful people won't talk me out of it. I'm eaten up inside, and nothing will free me until I lay my hands on him.'

He freed himself from her and stood looking down the dark valley at the houses below, only visible by the lighted windows.

'Somewhere down there he is, and I am going to pull him out like a rabbit from a short burrow. I am going to expose him. Unless I do I will die.'

'Come home,' she said.

'I have no home,' he said. 'I don't want to go into that place below, because I know Nan is there. It was home, but it was destroyed. Can't you understand this? Everything I found is destroyed. For ever and ever, it seemed, it was going to be, and now all it is is vomit in my mouth.'

'I love you, Donn,' she said.

'Nan loved me too,' he said, 'and now look at her.'

'You should lean on love,' she said, 'not hatred. Do you think I feel indifferent?'

'No,' he said. 'Just Christian. You learned, eh. Offer it up. For what? Until it eats into your guts. I'm not offering anything up. I know what I want, and I'm going to get it, otherwise I can't live. Do you hear, Meela, I can't live. Find him! Just find him!'

'Please come home, Donn,' she said.

Twenty

THE SERGEANT went through the shop into the pub.

He saw Donn sitting there at a round table, the one table in the place. He was filling the chair, his body slightly sprawling. The light from the window was falling on him. He looked a tough customer, his three-day-old beard emphasizing the strong points of his face and jaw.

'Hello,' he said, inside the door, pushing the hat back on his head.

Donn looked at him. He said nothing, so the Sergeant came further in and sat at a high stool by the counter. He rested an elbow on this.

'I came up with the priest,' he said.

'Wherever the corpse is, the eagles gather,' said Donn.

'I'm not much of an eagle,' the Sergeant said. 'Too much fat.' He was wearing a civilian coat and waistcoat, wrinkling itself to contain his big stomach. He wore the blue police pants and heavy, highly-polished black boots. 'Could I get a drink?'

'What kind of a drink?' Donn asked.

'A pint,' said the Sergeant.

'Go behind and get it yourself,' said Donn.

The Sergeant scratched his head, then walked to the end of the counter, went in behind it, looked at the equipment, found a pint glass and put it under the tap of the barrel. He poured himself a pint, taking his time so that he wouldn't make too much froth. He had to concentrate to pour it, but finally got one with a good head. He tasted it.

'That's good,' he said. He stayed behind there. He rested his arms on the counter. 'I get to know everything in the end,' he said.

Donn just looked at him.

'The people up here are ordinary people,' he said. 'Sometimes they get drunk and fight. Sometimes one of them hits another because sheep have trespassed, or cattle, or because a young dog is worrying the lambs. Sometimes they are fined for not having bicycle lights. And of course there is always Bartley making poteen, and he's hard to catch, because it's a hell of a long way to come in the middle of the night, and there's a long and large area to search, so mostly we let him get away with it because he doesn't make too much of it.'

'You should ask me if I'm interested in your recitation,' said Donn.

'Even the little he makes is dangerous,' the Sergeant went on as if he had not spoken. 'I have found that most of the terrible things that happen around here happen when they drink raw alcohol, which is what it is. I am persuaded that what happened to your house happened on that account.'

'You are wrong,' said Donn.

'I might be,' he said. 'I like to think the best of people. I don't like to think there is somebody around who would do a thing like that in cold blood.'

'There is,' said Donn.

'If so,' said the Sergeant, 'it is like somebody giving me a kick in the belly.'

'You have been kicked in the belly,' said Donn.

'I don't suppose you would like to make a complaint and let us find this fellow?' the Sergeant asked.

'There is only one person who could do that,' said Donn, 'and she is not and will never be in a position to make a complaint.'

'That's what makes it so sad,' the Sergeant said. 'I am very sorry. But then there is the law. We must all live by law, however useless it seems at times.'

'Have you children?' Donn asked.

'I have,' he said. 'One married girl and two boys and one girl who would be about the same age as your Nan. Her name is Mary.'

'Suppose a bad thing happened to Mary,' Donn asked. 'Think of this seriously. You find out who did it, what would you do?'

The Sergeant drank more from the pint. He thought it over. 'I will tell you what I would like to do,' he said. 'I would like to castrate him with a rusty knife. That would be only the beginning of what I would like to do. But in the event I would not do anything except let the law take its course. I wouldn't be capable of taking the law into my own hands.'

'And you think everybody should feel like that?' Donn asked.

'It is the only way,' said the Sergeant.

Donn laughed.

The Sergeant didn't like his laugh. He was looking indolent in the chair with his legs spread out, and his white teeth looking all the whiter for the beard, but the Sergeant knew he was a dangerous man, and he could see only one end to this terrible business.

'What would you do,' Donn asked, 'if I found this person and brought him down to you?'

'I would charge him,' said the Sergeant.

'Without witnesses,' said Donn. 'Even if he confessed, how could you charge him? He could tell his tale any way he liked. The girl is over age. She could not tell a coherent tale. You would have to let him go.'

'It looks that way,' said the Sergeant, 'alas.'

'So?' Donn asked.

'Everybody admires you,' said the Sergeant. 'You have been like a dynamo in this place. You got things done. You changed the face of a whole valley. Are you going to wreck all that?'

'The valley was here before the people,' said Donn. 'It will be here after them. All we did was to make it ugly for our own purposes. Now I see it beautiful again, a lonely beautiful valley, without any people at all, the last marks of them covered up by heather and gorse bushes and moss, the hawk resting on ivy-covered walls.'

'Don't do it,' the Sergeant said. 'You have a good life before you. If you do what you have a mind to do, what do you think I will have to do?'

'You will do what you have to do,' said Donn.

'I wish you wouldn't,' said the Sergeant, knowing that it was useless. He drank the rest of his pint. He saw no way out of this one. The Sergeant in his time had smothered many things that were threatening to burst into flame. Looking at Donn, he knew that there was no hope here.

'If you find him and only hurt him a little bit, what harm would that be?' he asked hopefully. 'We could always say that he was run over by a bus and escaped death by the grace of God. He would only be his own witness. That would be fair.'

Donn whammed his fist on the table, making his glass jump. His teeth were clenched.

'I wish you would leave me alone,' he said. 'I don't want help or advice from you.'

The Sergeant was glad to see the priest coming in.

'Hello, Donn,' said Father Murphy.

'You too,' groaned Donn.

'I'll leave ye to talk,' said the Sergeant.

'Pour out a mineral for the priest,' said Donn. 'He is going to have a sore throat.'

The Sergeant grinned, then he took a bottle and opened it and poured the golden contents into a glass.

'Here, Father,' he said, stretching it to him. The priest took it. The Sergeant came out from behind the counter and went towards the shop with his head down. He swung back there.

'We are your friends, Donn,' he said. 'Indeed you have more friends than you think, if you could separate all of us from the guilty one in your mind. If you give us a chance we might do something for you. We may think up ways of finding and punishing this one man, that would in the long run be worse for him than what you have in mind, and less permanent.'

'Goodbye, friend,' said Donn.

The Sergeant looked at the priest, shrugged his shoulders and went out.

The priest toyed with his glass, then he drank a little of the mineral water. He looked up. Donn was gazing at him with a sardonic gleam in his eyes.

'Are you finding it hard to start?' he asked.

'We all like to be liked,' Father Murphy said. 'I cannot tell you how hard it is to talk to somebody you know dislikes you.'

'Does it upset your ego?' Donn asked.

'That's true,' he said. 'I suppose it is a form of pride.'

'How can you talk your way out of this one?' Donn asked. 'After all you probably know who he is.'

'How would I know?' the priest asked, surprised.

'He has probably confessed to you,' said Donn. 'Dear Father, I'm sorry for all my sins. I raped a retarded girl, and I enjoyed it enormously, and I won't do it again until the next time. That's all right son, three Hail Marys and make sure you join the Pioneer Total Abstinence Association.'

He was pleased to see that he had really angered the priest. His knuckles were white where he clenched the glass. Donn saw that he had to make a terrible effort to control himself.

'Isn't there something wrong with your teaching,' he persisted, 'when one of your boys would do a thing like that?'

'Anyone,' the priest said slowly, 'listening to you, would think it was you that was raped and not your daughter Nan.'

'How would you know?' Donn asked. 'How could you even have a conception of how I feel or how Nan feels? You only know the feelings of a father from books. How can you have even a clue of how I feel inside. You have no idea. You cannot even begin to imagine.'

'You treat everything,' said the priest, 'as if it was a visible matter. There are important things beyond even the visible things. Can you see a feeling?'

'Look at me,' said Donn, 'and you will see the result of a feeling. Look at Nan, who is supposed to have no feeling, and you will see the result of feeling.'

'Nan will forget,' said the priest.

'You are a liar,' said Donn. 'Nan will never forget. This thing has changed her body, and her mind. She will never be the same again.'

'She will never be the same, maybe,' said the priest, 'but she will become herself again, and no thanks to you.'

'Expand on that,' said Donn jeeringly.

'It was the fate of many virgins,' said the priest, 'during the early persecutions and indeed afterwards, to be thrown in to die in brothels. Did this make them any the less virgin because they had to die in this unspeakable way? Even in our own day, virgin nuns have been raped and violated because they followed God in their own way and do you think that this has made them any the less unpleasing to God, or any less virgin? There is unseen purity as well as the visible sort. That's what I mean about Nan. She is no less a virgin now than she was before. Her soul is as pure as ever it was. By the mercy of God, she will suffer no permanent results from this outrage. She is not the one I am worried about. It's you that I am afraid for.'

'You are as glib as a medicine man,' said Donn. 'How am I supposed to feel, when my own child shudders away from me when I approach her? She sits in her room all day. I daren't go near her. The way she looks at me, I could die. What do you think I want out of life now, but the man who did this to me?'

'The physical repulsion she feels will pass,' said the priest.

'No,' said Donn, 'I have seen her. I have seen the look in her eyes. This is what it has done to her, and it will never go away.'

'I will bring her in here to you,' said the priest.

'You couldn't,' said Donn. 'She hasn't left her room. Have you seen her?'

'No,' said the priest. 'I only talked to Meela.'

'Well, just go now and talk to her and bring her here to me,' said Donn, looking at him balefully. 'Just go and let us see you do it.'

What have I let myself in for? the priest wondered.

'Well, go,' said Donn. 'Go! Let us see your magic.'

The priest had no option. He put down the glass, and went out the door into the kitchen. Meela was there helping Bridgie. She was chopping carrots. She looked up.

'Well?' she asked. She saw he was disturbed.

'I will have to see Nan,' he said.

'I told you what will happen,' she said.

'I will have to chance it,' he said. 'Will you come with me? Stand behind me. See what happens.'

She thought over it.

'All right,' she said. She wiped her hands on her apron and led him into the corridor. 'What do you think of Donn?'

'I never know what to think of Donn,' he said. 'If this works it might be something. You know what's going to happen if he finds out?'

'No,' she said, 'but I'm afraid.'

They came to the room door. It was closed. He put his hand on the knob. He took a deep breath, closed his eyes for a moment, and then opened the door and went in. Nan was sitting on a rug at the foot of the bed. There was a low table near her. On this was a copybook and she was scribbling listlessly in the pages. She looked peaked. She had lost weight. Her eyes seemed to be deeper in her head than he remembered and when she turned to look he saw the panic that flared in them. She crouched, her hands on her knees.

Now, he thought.

'Hello, Nan,' he said softly. Outside the door Meela put her hands over her ears and turned away. 'I came to see you,' he went on, gently, without moving, just the things you do in order to get a wild pony to come near enough to you. 'I haven't seen you for a long time.'

Her mouth opened. He was waiting for some sound of terror to come from her. He could see the pulse in her neck beating madly. He was holding his breath. Then slowly the panic went out of her eyes, her lips closed on her teeth, her body seemed to relax, and a look of recognition came into her eyes. He ventured to move a step towards her. For a second she seemed to tighten up again. He waited until that passed and ventured a further step. Her reaction was less pronounced. One more step and she had accepted his appearance, but he didn't move any closer to her.

'The sun is shining,' he said. 'All the birds are singing. It will soon be summer.'

This got to her. She turned her head on one side, listening. The birds were singing. She looked back at him and she smiled. She actually smiled.

He held out his hand.

'Will you come and see the sun shining?' he asked.

She considered this. She looked at the copybook with the scribbling on it. She picked it up. She held it out to him. He took it in his hands and looked at it. The scribblings were very vague, but they were definite.

'That's nice,' he said. 'I don't know what it is, but it is nice.'

He smiled at her. He handed back the copy. 'Now would you like to come out and look at the sun?'

She put her head down. He noticed that her hair seemed to

be lustreless. He wanted to put his hand on her hair and stroke it back to life – if such was possible.

She looked up at him. Slowly she got to her feet. He still had his hand held out to her. She looked at it, and then slowly she put forward her own hand and rested it in his, waiting. He gently closed his bigger hand on hers and moved to the doorway. Meela was gone. He thought she might be. Meela was very intelligent. Nan walked with him into the corridor, into the kitchen. Meela had her back turned to them. Bridgie had a meat-knife in her hand and her mouth opened as they came in the doorway.

'Nan and I are going to look at the sun,' he said.

They walked from the kitchen to the door into the pub. He paused here. Now what in the name of God is going to happen? he wondered. He opened the door. He went in. She came after him, still holding his hand. For a moment his body hid her from Donn, who was still in the same place.

'There's your daddy,' he said softly. 'Won't you say hello to your daddy?'

She saw Donn. He thought the priest had come back on his own. Now he saw her. She was looking at him. He straightened slowly in the chair, bringing his body upright just as if he was coming out of a trench to view an alien landscape. His heart turned over as he saw how pallid she was, and how big her eyes seemed. He couldn't move. He just gripped the edge of the table with his big hand, as if he would like to powder the timber. He watched her. She looked at him, and then freeing her hands from the priest's she came towards him. There was no fear in her eyes, he saw with wonder.

She didn't talk, this was what registered with him. She came towards him and stood in front of him. She was above the level of his eyes.

'Hello, Nan,' he said.

He put his hands very gently on her shoulders. She smiled at him. But she didn't say hello. She wasn't speaking.

The priest came close to them.

'Your daddy will show you the sun shining,' the priest said. 'Wouldn't you like that?'

She thought over it, smiled and nodded her head. Donn's

teeth were clenched hard, bulging the muscles of his jaws.

'I'll be going now,' the priest said. 'The Sergeant is waiting for me.'

He turned to leave.

He was at the door when Donn said: 'But she doesn't speak.'

The priest looked back at him. He was like a lion with his mane of tousled hair and bearded face, his fierce eyes. The priest sighed. You might as well try and stop a lion, he thought, with silken threads.

'She will,' he said. 'She will.'

Then he left them.

'We will go into the sunshine?' Donn asked. She nodded. He rose carefully to his feet and walked towards the door. He put out his hand, expecting her to reject it. She didn't. She put her hand confidently into his. Somehow this made him feel worse.

He should have been overjoyed.

They walked through the shop into the street. The sun was shining blindingly. It was glittering off the lake, sparkling off the tumbling river. Behind him he could hear the priest's car starting up and going away. He looked at the pale face of his daughter. She was looking around her as if she was seeing all the beauty and peace for the first time.

Beauty and peace, Donn thought savagely, beauty and peace. The look of her only made him feel worse.

I'll kill him! I'll kill him! I'll kill him! he thought.

Twenty-one

HE FOUND out on an evening in early June.

For the few months until then he was going around in a sort of dream, induced by drink and brooding. He had no interest in the business or what was happening to it. Sean was back at work, still looking pale and thin and avoiding Donn's eyes. That was no wonder because everyone else in the place was doing the same thing. Sometimes he would come to him, seek him out wherever he was, and he would say: 'We are short of such a thing, and such a thing, will I order it?' Donn would say: 'Yes. Do whatever you like.' In other words he was not much of a help. Many of the men stopped going in for a drink of an evening. Instead they would crowd into a motor-car belonging to one of them, or sit on the trailer of Dino's tractor and go into the street town. They didn't like to be in there having a peaceful drink with his eyes boring into their backs.

He didn't know this. He didn't care.

This evening he got out the car and set off for the big town. He did this now and again, just to get away from the valley and the people, all the people, including his own. He would spend some hours in there, sometimes talking in one of the plush lounge bars, where the conversation seemed so unreal and so inapplicable to his own mind and way of life. It could have been another world.

It was a beautiful evening. Not that he noticed it much. The sky was clear and for a few moments it reminded him of Italy with the sort of umber colour all around the horizon and that blended into an Italian sky-blue, which tapered off into the black-blue of the night sky above it. It promised another beautiful day tomorrow. He was thinking, something will have to happen. I don't think I can stand this strain much longer. The easy relationship with Meela was dead. He knew it was his fault. They couldn't get back on the plane they had reached, the comfortable companionship. That was broken. He knew who was responsible for it. He kept away from Nan. The sight of her only stirred the fires of bitterness and helplessness that it burned in him.

The car gave a few coughs and stopped. He sat a few seconds wondering about it, and why it should have stopped. He fiddled with the knobs. He pressed the starter. The starter worked, but it got no results. Then he looked at the petrol register and it was set at empty. He sat back and reviewed the situation. He was about a mile and a half from the house. He could go back and get a tin of petrol from the pump and walk back with it again, then continue his journey and get his tank filled in the town. Was it worth it? He decided it was. He got out of the car, holding the wheel, pushed it to the side of the road where it would not be an obstacle, banged the door shut and set off back the road walking into the multi-coloured evening. It was quite bright. It was nearing the longest day in the year and the sky would never get quite dark. The moon was due in an hour.

He filled his lungs with air. He could smell the bog and the maturing meadows, ripening for cutting, and reeds and rushes and the faint smell of wild mint and thyme. If it was left alone, he thought, and never touched by man, you could come into it and smell it, or look at it like you would go into a museum and see the treasures of the past. But man was here and man had left his mark on it, soiled it with his seed.

It was a very still night. His footsteps sounded loud and sharp on the road.

Sean was sweeping out the hall. There had been a meeting there last night. He hadn't been able to get around to it during the day. Now he had all the chairs folded and put away up near the bandstand. With a soft brush he was sweeping up the debris, working from the sides towards the centre where he had a shovel and a big cardboard container. There was dust from shoes, mixed with bits of dried dung with the shape of the shoe heel embedded in them. Cigarette cartons and red empty matchboxes. Sweet papers, a woollen glove with a hole in the first finger. He wondered who would be wearing gloves on a night like last night which had been fine and clear. Clips from a girl's hair, a blue ribbon, still tied in a knot, that had fallen from a young girl's ringlets; two pennies and a threepenny bit.

He was bending to pick up those when he heard the door into the hall opening. He had got out of the habit of looking when he heard doors opening. He didn't want to look into Nan's eyes, or Donn's or Meela's eyes for that matter, so he had mastered the habit of thinking before looking. Now he always thought first. He had a feeling that if anyone of them looked into his eyes they would see the whole story written there. He didn't want that. It was a terrible thing to be burdened with a guilty secret, one impossible to divulge. At times he thought it would be a great release if it was known and let the consequences occur. Maybe one could begin to live again.

'Hello, Sean,' said the voice of Dino.

Sean was shocked. His hand picking up the pennies tightened. He thought his stomach was turning to water. He felt slightly sick. He hadn't seen Dino since, just a figure in the distance, mounted on the seat of a tractor, a distant silhouette on the horizon.

He looked up. Dino was leaning against the door, his hands in his pockets, a grin on his face. He was in his shirtsleeves and his arms were very brown, like his face.

Sean couldn't say anything.

'I haven't seen you for a long time, Sean,' Dino said.

'No,' said Sean, 'no.'

'Is it keeping away from me you are?' Dino asked.

'I don't know,' said Sean. 'You just weren't near.'

'I'm near enough always,' said Dino. 'I'm afraid of you.'

'Why are you afraid of me?' he asked, in wonder.

'I'm afraid you are a weak fellow,' said Dino. 'I'm afraid you might get religion and say out something that wouldn't be good for you.'

'Why would I say out something that is unspeakable?' Sean asked.

'What does that big word mean?' Dino said.

'It means just that,' said Sean. 'It means unspeakable, unspeakable, unspeakable.'

'You won't forget you were there, will you, Sean?' Dino asked, coming closer to him and squatting down. 'You were, you know.'

Their eyes were on a level.

'No, Dino,' he said. 'I won't forget that. I won't ever forget that.'

'Even if you did nothing but put your hand over her mouth and then run away, you were there. Don't forget that. Even if you ran away like a rabbit and left me there on me own with her, you were there, don't forget that.'

'I won't ever forget it, Dino,' said Sean.

'I just want to keep reminding you,' said Dino, 'just in case you would forget.'

He saw the hatred in Sean's eyes, a blaze of violence, that came and went away again.

'You couldn't do anything,' he said. 'I could pound you. I could hurt you, and I would too. You cannot get away from it, you were there and if you didn't get what I got, you had the good intention Sean, don't forget that.'

They were both squatting, like men playing cards on a floor.

'You have to keep your mouth shut,' Dino went on. 'I don't know how you talk to your conscience. You were drunk, eh? You weren't used to drink. Dino gave you a drink from a Bartley bottle. Is that it? So you weren't really responsible. This is the way you might think. Well, I'm telling you not to think. There is no escape for you that way. You were there, because you wanted to be there, and if you were a chicken in the end it doesn't matter. See that, Sean. I'm telling you that so you keep your mouth shut. There's you and me. We were both there, and if there is a whisper about me, I'll know where it came from and I'll look after you. I swear my solemn oath I will.'

He wasn't talking loudly. He was talking in what he thought was a low tone, but it was sibilant and enlarged by the acoustics of the hall, and every word of it was clear to Donn, who stood in the doorway that led from the kitchen: and Dino looked up and saw him.

The petrol pump had been locked, so he went into the kitchen to look for the key which was on a rack near the fire.

Meela was there. She was tidying. Meela was always tidying or brushing or scrubbing. She could never stay still except when she wanted to. She saw dirt and disorder where nobody else ever saw it. She would point it out to you as she cleared it away.

'Where is the key to the petrol?' he asked.

'It's not there,' she said. 'Sean must have it.'

'I ran out of petrol down the road,' he said, thinking they could be two strangers and bemoaning it without being able to do anything about it. 'Where's Sean?'

'He went to sweep up the hall,' she said, wondering at how he had changed, if this could be the Donn she had discovered, such a short time ago, it seemed. Come and go. Was there any solution at all for him?

'Meela,' he said.

'Yes?' she asked.

What did he want to say? I am not myself. I don't understand. I cannot forget. I cannot let this thing go. There must be somebody who will punish evil. There doesn't seem to be and so I will have to do it myself, and I can't rest or eat or sleep until it is done. A bad apple in a barrel of apples, a bad potato in a pit, a wet spot in a cock of hay, all these lead to the ruin of the whole, and if this evil person is not punished what will happen to the rest of us? She would then say, a bad potato or good leaven, which is the more potent?

'Nothing,' he said, 'nothing.'

He went to the door into the hall. He heard voices when his hand was on the knob. He heard the voice of Sean saying '. . . unspeakable, unspeakable, unspeakable.'

He wondered what could be unspeakable, and then he heard Dino's voice and, very slowly and almost uncomprehendingly, the sense of what Dino was saying sifted into his understanding. He opened the door a little and the sibilant words came through to him. He didn't know that they were coming through to Meela too, who stood behind him, listening to the voices, scarcely able to believe what she was hearing.

Dino!

The squat powerful young man. Virile, lightly educated. A young man with a one-track mind. He thought of him as he listened. He didn't want to believe him. He had helped Dino. Dino was nearly part of the home they had built. It couldn't be Dino. And yet there the words were. And Sean. He had to shake his head. Sean was there. Think of the pale boy in the kitchen with a fever on him, the eyes avoiding his own. Dino, yes, he thought savagely. Dino's dialogue was limited, but spattered with sex symbols. If he queried Donn about his travels, it would be about girls. One question, he remembered, 'was it true that the girls in Italy during the war would give it for a bar of chocolate?'

He felt the cold rising from his feet and going up through his body into his head. He tried to get a picture of Dino in his mind, his appearance, his face, how he looked, how he walked.

He couldn't do it. He could conjure up no picture of him, so he opened the door to get a look at him.

He stood there and Dino looked up and saw him.

Donn didn't need the look of dismay in his face, he had heard his words. He just wanted to look at him.

And he looked at him.

And Sean saw Dino's looking and rising to his feet, staring at the door into the kitchen, and he looked up himself and slowly got to his feet, and his whole being was full of terror as he saw the look on Donn's face.

He shouldn't be here, Dino was thinking, he shouldn't be here at all. Didn't I see him going off in the car? I wouldn't have come near Sean if I hadn't seen him going off in the car!

They held this position for what seemed a long time. Dino knew that Donn had heard enough. There was no talking his way out of this. He thought frantically of what he would do, and only one answer came to him: Get out of here as fast as you can because your life depends on it.

He turned and ran to the door of the hall and out into the night.

And because Sean could think of nothing else that he could do, and because he was genuinely frightened by the look on Donn's face, he threw down the brush, and with his hands held out in front of him as if he was pushing away a fog, he ran after Dino.

Donn coldly evaluated what they would do. If he was in a similar situation he would take to the hills. He knew how fast they could go, and how long it would take him to cut them off and pursue them. He had time.

He turned back into the kitchen, and going to the fireplace he reached for his shotgun. He took it down, and went to the cupboard beside it. He reached his hand into the yellow-and-red cardboard box and he took out two cartridges. Opening the gun, he pressed them into the breach, clicked the gun shut and then turned back to the door.

The door was closed and Meela stood in front of it.

'Don't, Donn,' she said.

'Get out of the way, Meela,' he said, quite calmly.

'Don't do it, Donn,' she said. 'Now we know, everyone will know, and they will have to go away. The people's knowledge will shame them. That will follow them all their lives. Leave it like that. Nan is getting back to herself.'

'Get out of the way, Meela,' he said.

'Donn, if you love me,' she said, 'let them get away. You went away on me before although you told me you loved me. Prove it, please Donn, prove it now, because if you go away it will be another long separation and I can't stand it any more. I have had enough all my life, Donn, please. Stay with me now. If I am more important than vengeance, stay with me. If I am more important to you than Nan, stay with me.'

'Meela, if you don't get out of the way soon, I will force you,' he said.

'What are you doing?' she asked. 'What good will this do to Nan? All it will do is take you away from us again. Who will you be hurting? You won't be hurting them. You will be hurting us. What kind of reward is that?'

'I have to do what I have to do,' he said, shouting now. 'There is no other way except my own death. I can't bear with this. Now I know, I will purge it out of me.'

'Yourself is all you think of,' she said. 'You are hurt, so you must do something about it. Don't go out thinking you are doing anything for Nan. You are not. You are not doing anything for me. You are doing it for yourself, just for yourself, nobody else, nobody else.'

He reached for her with his free hand and pulled at her shoulder. She clutched the sides of the door with her hands. He would have to exert pressure to pull her away, he saw. He rested the gun by the side of the door and used his two hands on her.

She was very close to him. He could feel her body straining against him. I love her, he thought, but in an abstract wondering way. He had to lift her off her feet to make her release her grip. He put her on her feet again.

'Donn! Donn! Donn! Please!' she said.

He left her and took up the gun and walked into the hall, towards the doorway that was still swinging a little after Dino's and Sean's violent exit.

She followed him.

'I can't take any more, Donn,' she said. 'I won't stay to face this. I have had to stay to face too much already. I won't do it. Come back, Donn, or I won't be here afterwards. Do you hear me?'

He went through the doorway and she followed him.

'Donn! Donn!' she called, pleadingly. 'Please come back to me now, Donn. Donn!'

She followed him into the night.

She looked.

He was striding away towards the hill. The moon had come up on the eastern side and was floodlighting the valley. Free of the houses, she could see the figures fleeing into the bog plain. They were separated about thirty yards. She could distinguish the long lean figure of Sean and the squat bounding figure of Dino. The bog was slowing them, but they were leaping from tuft to tuft. She saw Sean staggering and almost falling and recovering himself again. Dino was well ahead of him now. He would always be ahead of someone like Sean. He was bounding on his short legs.

Then she saw Donn as he came into the plain. He was not hurrying and this made it worse. He was striding, slowly and determinedly as he did when he was out hunting wild birds.

She could see the silhouette of the gun in his hands.

'Donn! Donn!' she called plaintively, like the cry of the curlew on a frosty night.

It had no more effect than the sounds of her other calls. It didn't stop him. He kept up his even stride.

With despair in her she turned and went back into the hall.

Twenty-two

YOU CAN hate in cold blood or you can hate in hot blood. You can hate for no reason at all. You can kill when you are afraid for your own life, as in war, but Donn thought no man had more reason for killing than he had as he tracked the two of them towards the tall hills. The sight of the innocent girl was in front of him, shocked, scraped, bruised, and making incomprehensible sounds through her hurt lips. There was no punishment in store for them except from himself. He wanted to get close to them first, to be able to see their eyes before he executed them.

The ground was rising and they were slowing down, particularly Sean, who wasn't used to running on soft ground. He was staggering now and again, helping himself with his hands, but each time he stumbled he lost precious seconds of running time. Donn knew the ground very well. He had shot over every inch of it. A glance showed him where he could put a foot without sinking. The dark green or light green of the moss covering the soft spots told him if it would bear his weight; the tufts of sedge and heather were another indication of ground that would take his weight, so that despite their best running he was closing up on them. He knew exactly the spread of shot from a cartridge. He had experimented many times. He had killed a lot of birds to prove his knowledge.

They should have run to their houses and barred the doors, he thought. This way he would not have been able to get at them. They could then have screamed for the law to protect them. But to do this they would have to confess the reason for their seeking shelter – and even for a beast like Dino this would have been too much.

The ground rose higher and higher. In twenty minutes they would be silhouettes on top of the surrounding hills. He couldn't let them get that far. Even though it was easy to see in the glaring moonlight, there were many hiding places and hollows on the other side where they could go to ground, and he would want a dog to nose them out: and he hadn't a dog.

For the first time since he came out, he suddenly ran. They seemed to sense this, and with a terrified look over their shoulders they tried to increase their speed, but their running was panicked now, and only made them stumble. He was the right distance from them. He paused and raised the gun to his shoulder.

He fired at Sean, and saw him drop. He ran again, in a straight line, after Dino. When he got close enough he stopped again and raised the gun. Dino looked over his shoulder and as he pressed the trigger, Dino dropped and when the sound of the shot echoed in the bleak land, he rose to his feet and ran again. And Donn hadn't another cartridge. He stood and thought of this, and then thought: It is just as well. Now I will catch him and kill him with my bare hands. There would be much more satisfaction in that.

So he ran.

And Dino ran, knowing that his life depended on it. He knew that Donn was only about thirty yards behind him. He was young and he was fit. It never entered his head to stop and fight. Each moment he was expecting the sound of a shot. He didn't dare to stop again and look over his shoulder. He had to get to the top of the hill and over. When the shot didn't come, he thought jubilantly, he has no more cartridges. So he paused and stood and turned to look. Donn just came running, so Dino knew he had no cartridges, and that he had a chance, so he increased his pace as much as he could. If I get to the top of the hill I am safe, he thought. Down there in the middle of the bog plain littered with lakes and crevices near them, it would take an army to find me if I can get to ground.

Donn ran hard. He was encumbered by the gun, so he threw it away from him. Without that extra weight he knew he could travel more quickly. He kept his eyes on Dino, and willed himself to draw closer and closer to him.

After five minutes he knew that he wasn't drawing closer to him and this dismayed him. He found that the calf of his left leg was aching, and that his lungs seemed to be on the point of bursting. How could this be? He couldn't imagine this ever happening to him, that a fellow like Dino could outrun him on the hill.

He gritted his teeth and increased his pace. But the muscle in his calf seemed to be tightening. Then it was agonizing. He had to stop and rub it with both hands. It seemed to have shifted out of place. He rubbed it desperately, rested panting for a few seconds and then had to limp his way to the top of the hill. It was a broad flat top that stretched away for a few hundred yards before it started to drop on the other side. He had to limp his way across this and when he got to the place where it fell away he stopped, because the whole plain below was covered with a June mist, about man high, that had risen from the ground and covered many acres of the place below; and Dino had run into the mist.

He stopped and listened.

He could hear nothing. The ground was so soft it would muffle the sound of running feet.

I'm twice his age, he thought then, that is what's wrong. I keep thinking of myself as a twenty-year-old physically. It's not true. I am near middle age. He saw a rock and he went to it and he sat on it, drawing deep breaths, trying to quell the racing of his heart and the bursting of his lungs and the pain in his leg. It was the first time he had thought of his age. He thought of it now. He pounded his leg with his fist as he thought of it. He knew he was helpless; that he would have to let Dino go. But now that he knew, there would be another day.

He stood and shouted that into the mist.

'Dino!' he called. 'There is no escape. I will find you. Wherever you are or wherever you go I will find you. I will find you! I will find you!'

He heard his own voice come echoing back to him. He didn't expect Dino to answer him. He would be clever enough to know that he might betray his hiding-place. He didn't have to find him, he suddenly thought then. When he had been in the yard he had seen Dino's red tractor drawn up there. Dino loved his tractor. It was all his. It was more precious to him than anything on earth. All he had to do was to leave the tractor in the yard and wait for Dino to come back for it. Dino would come back. He could cross the plain below now. Five miles of it and he would come to a dirt road that wound through it. On that road he could go east or west, and from there wherever he liked, but Donn knew that one day he would come back for the tractor, and however long it took, he would be waiting for him.

He stood there for a few more seconds and then he turned and started to walk down the hill.

The pain in his lungs had eased, but the muscle of his leg was still aching. The coldness had left his mind. He felt confused. He wished he had a drink of whiskey. He thought of the raw taste of it in his throat. His mouth was dry. He wondered who he was. He had been all his life asking who he was, what part of him was real, and what part of him was imagined.

He thought of Sean. He tried to recall the conversation he had overheard. It had absolved Sean of guilt, but not of all guilt. He had an affection for him. Even now he found it hard to believe he was involved in it, or why he had been caught up with it. It was so contrary to his educated gentleness. Why hadn't he fought for Nan? He was there. He should have died before he had let such a thing happen to her.

He hoped he hadn't killed him. He thought he hadn't. He thought he knew where he had put the shot, but suppose he had been wrong?

He veered his footsteps to the right, so that he could come on him where he had seen him fall. It wasn't a fit of softness, he told himself, it was just that he wanted an answer. He had a good eye for ground. He had got used to it, by marking the fall of a shot bird. It had been a new experience to drop a man instead of a bird. Not quite, because he had seen them fall before, but that was a war. This was a war too, if you thought of it. Such incomprehensible evil. He would get it out of him. Clutch his hair in his fist and drag back his head until his neck would nearly break, and say 'Tell me!'

He saw the mound he made, just a little different from the other mounds. He went towards it. The mound was motionless, he thought, but he didn't lose a heartbeat. If that is the way it has to be, then that's the way. He thought of Sean's father and mother. He bent over him and he saw his open eyes in the moonlight.

'Are you going to kill me now?' Sean asked.

'Why did you run?' he asked.

'I was afraid,' he said.

'Where did I get you?' he asked.

'My leg,' said Sean.

It was stretched out. Donn looked at it. You could see the blood glistening dully in the moonlight. Suddenly Donn felt a wave of pity. He wondered why he felt this. Then he saw that Sean was clutching the shotgun.

'Where did you get that?' he asked.

'I crawled over for it,' he said.

'Why?' Donn asked.

'If you didn't kill me,' he said, 'I would say that I had the gun and had an accident with it. I would say that I shot Dino and that I wounded myself.'

'Why?'

'Because the guilt that I feel should be paid for,' he said. 'Why should you be blamed again, I thought? You have suffered enough for all this. Where is Dino?'

'He got away,' said Donn. 'Was he the one?'

'I was as bad,' said Sean. 'I should have stopped him. I just ran away.'

'Why?'

'I cannot tell you. I am weak. I have always been weak, and afraid of nearly everything.'

'How could you? You had an affection for Nan. Tell me how?'

'I don't know. There is nothing in life I love more than her. But no hope. Can you understand this maybe? I know you can't. It was all mixed up. I cannot explain. Something out of reach. Always I have been trying to get something out of reach. I wish you had killed me.'

'But you were there, with Dino. What did you do?'

' "Don't scream! Don't scream," I said. "Please!" I had my hand on her mouth. Her teeth bit into my hand. I have a scar. Now I rub it and it aches, all this time and I wishing I was dead, and not dead because I want to atone for it all, some way, somehow.'

'You could have stopped him?'

'Yes. There were stones. I could have hit him with a stone. But I ran away, ran away.'

Suddenly Donn caught the front of his coat in his two hands, pulled his face close to his own and shook him.

'Why? Why? Why?' he shouted.

'I love her,' said Sean.

'Love!' Donn shouted. He raised his hand to hit him, and then stopped when he saw that Sean wasn't even flinching from the blow. He let him fall back. Now he found that his limbs were trembling. He got to his feet and walked away from him. He wondered if he would walk away and leave him. He thought of this. Then he knew that he couldn't. So he turned and went back to him.

'Get up on your feet,' he said.

He stood back from him and watched him. Sean helped himself upright with the aid of the gun. When he was standing he tried to rest his body on his right leg. He fell, muffling a cry of pain. Donn watched him as he tried again. This time he got to his feet but he didn't rest his wounded leg on the ground. He was using the gun as a crutch.

'I will be all right,' he said. 'I will be able to get down.'

Donn knew that he wouldn't, unless he crawled. He was in a dilemma. He didn't want to touch him. He felt a terrible repulsion for him, but he made up his mind. He went close to him, caught his free hand, and hefted him on to his shoulder. He shifted him to a comfortable position and then set off down the mountain.

'I am not doing this for love of you,' he said. 'I want Dino. What reason are you going to give for being on the mountain with a gun at this hour? What were you shooting?'

'Grey crows, anything,' he said.

'You can tell your tale,' said Donn, 'because I can't think of a better one. It will keep things quiet. They will settle down. And when they settle down, Dino will get his courage up and he will come back. There is a reason he will come back, and when he does I will be waiting for him. I will leave you at your door.'

'Thank you,' said Sean. 'I was thinking how the world is going around. Terrible things happen. Men turn into animals, like myself and Dino, and people don't know. They just go on doing what they are doing and they don't know. And the stars and the sky and the moon are the same over everybody.'

'Don't speak to me,' said Donn. 'I don't want to hear you speaking to me.'

When he got home the lights were on and the doors were open. He had forgotten a lot of things. He went into the shop. Paud was not there. It was his night off. Sean had been looking after the shop that night. He went into the kitchen. There was nobody there.

He saw Meela's coloured apron on the back of a chair. He went to it and took it up and fingered it. Bridgie was gone home.

He went into the corridor and he called softly: 'Meela! Meela!' There was no answer.

He went to Nan's door and opened it. It was lighted only by moonlight. He went in and saw that she was in bed and sleeping. One of her arms was outside the bedclothes. She was sleeping on her back. He gently put her hand back under the clothes. He looked at her helplessness and a flood of rage came over him again so that he began to tremble.

'You will never know, and never care,' he said, 'but I got one of them, and soon I will get the other one and all this evil will be blotted out of your mind and my mind. You'll see.'

He left her then and went to his own room.

It was untidy.

This was unusual.

He started to search it and found that all her things were gone, all the personal things belonging to her, clothes, books, perfumes, all the little knicknacks were gone from the dressing table, her books from beside the bed.

Only slowly did it begin to dawn on him. He heard her voice as she tried to stop him going out of the door. She had meant it, he thought. It hadn't entered his head that she had meant it. He went out into the other rooms, to the closet where she had kept her heavy clothes. It was empty. He went into the living room. That too was bereft of her things.

How had she gone? She knew about the car. He supposed that she had gone with the petrol and got the car and come back again and loaded her things. She could drive. She had gone away. She would send the car back to him.

He went into the empty pub and he got a bottle and poured himself a drink. Let her go. She didn't understand. But he felt bleak. This was the way it would have to be if men had missions. They couldn't expect other people to understand. Let her go. If she wanted to come back, she could come back, but she would never find him beseeching her.

There was only one thing that mattered. He went to the back and looked out into the yard. The tractor was resting there in the moonlight waiting to drive out the gate of the yard. He thought of this. He went out of the pub and into the yard, and into the shed where they kept those things, and he got a padlock and he went to the yard gate and put it on to the small hole and clicked it shut. Now. Dino would have to come for his tractor, but he couldn't fly it over the gate. Some night he would come back and try: and Donn would be waiting for him.

He went back again into the pub, and poured himself another drink and he sat there at the table where he could see the yard and the tractor.

Leaving her child, he thought. There is a heartless mother. But I'll look after Nan. She is safe with me. And I'll look after Dino. Let her go away. Maybe light will dawn on her and she will see how foolish is her action.

He had been without her for a long time before and he had got on. All feelings of sentiment could be quelled. She didn't allow him to explain. If she loved him enough she would stick with him no matter what happened. Why couldn't she have seen the vital necessity for all this?

He drank and looked at the moonlight on the red tractor.

Twenty-three

IN LARGE communities it is called rumour, but in small communities it is knowing. You cannot hide real events and call them by another name, because men are not fools and if you give them the evidence of their own ears and eyes, and even with a minimum of intelligence they can piece together all the facts.

So the people sympathized with Tom McNulty because his son had been foolish enough to go shooting something in the middle of the night on the side of the hill, and his gun, which he had borrowed from Donn, had gone off when he was pulling it through a furze bush and had wounded him in the leg, but thank God he wasn't that badly hurt, and he could be dead. People had heard two shots that night, but that was Sean blasting at the grey crows. They nodded sympathetically at this, even if it was the first time in their lives they had ever heard of anybody shooting grey crows in the night-time.

They also knew that Dino Tumelty the same night had decided to go off to England, his father said, and he was getting great money over there doing something, driving a bulldozer, they believed, and he wrote to them every week, even if the postman didn't deliver the letters, but then maybe it was the grey crows that brought them.

Also whatever had happened that night, it was a strange thing that Meela had gone away, down to her dead father's cottage near the street town. This cottage had been occupied for some time by a schoolteacher and his missus who had recently retired. She had taken up her abode there, nobody knew why, and she hadn't been seen in the village since.

You can do nothing in small places without being seen, and if Bartley told the tale of seeing three men, two pursued and one pursuer, on the hill that evening, you could always put it down to the fact that he was drinking too much of his own brew, and besides he didn't press the story, just offered it as a sort of fairy tale. So if in the privacy of their homes men knew that Dino was the one, and they couldn't fit Sean into it at all, abroad they accepted the account of what was supposed to have happened with bland belief.

It was difficult to explain away the behaviour of Donn and his curious apathy. They all knew he was a man of action. He was odd, of course. He had always been odd and unpredictable. Who wasn't odd if it went to that? – and you had to respect people's oddities. They had thought they had a new man on their hands for the past few years. He was like a human eruption, the way he moved and the things he did and the things he had got done. Admittedly if your daughter is brutally raped you cannot feel the same man again, but it can be carried to excess. Most men would have gone after Dino – that was understandable – and beaten the fair hell out of him, and people would have helped in this if necessary, because nobody could hold with what he had done, but what was the sense in wrecking your own life and other people's lives on account of it? That was carrying the thing too far to be wholesome.

It was a sad thing to go into the place now and behold him and the state he was in. He was as unapproachable as a lion in a cage you would see in the zoo. There wasn't a soul in the place that didn't want to stretch out a hand to help him, if he wasn't afraid it would be bitten off at the wrist, so they had to end up avoiding him, and sending the children to the shop for whatever few things they wanted. They knew about the tractor in the yard and the padlock on the gate and about Donn in the pub sitting at the table looking out of the window. It was the end of June. The fine weather had gone and there was a lowering sky, with the grey clouds resting on the top of the hills. This cloud cover never seemed to lift. For several weeks they hadn't seen the sun, and this is depressing on the spirit. It seemed that the whole village was under a pall, waiting. Waiting for what? They didn't know, but it wasn't good whatever it was. It was a gloomy month and men yearned for the sight of the sun that seemed as if it would never appear to them again.

Donn knew he was foolish. No man will deliberately debase himself, and that was what he seemed to be doing. He knew that what he should do was to destroy the red tractor, set fire to it and in that way mete out punishment that would wound Dino to the quick. He should go and ask Meela to come back. Then he would set about putting the place in order again. He knew it was falling into decay – so quickly built, so quickly dying. He knew all this, and he would say: maybe I will do it tomorrow; knowing that he wouldn't, that he would just sit and watch and wait for Dino. He felt that unless he pounded him he would never be the same again, that unless he beat him to pulp he could never call himself a man again, and he went over what he would do to him in his mind, until the blood pounded in his veins and he would hurt his hand hitting the table.

He was sustained in this resolve by drink. He knew he was drinking too much, but he had to have it. It dulled the suffering edge of his mind, and kept the pictures there slightly blurred, so that they did not become entirely unbearable. Sometimes he saw himself in a mirror as he passed from the pub to the kitchen to eat indifferently the food that Bridgie prepared for him. Red-rimmed eyes and an unshaven face that was becoming a little gaunt, with deepening hollows under his cheekbones. All in a few weeks. Who is winning, he would ask himself, Dino or myself? It doesn't matter now, he thought, because I will win in the end. At times he even forgot what it was all about, and why he was sitting at a table looking out of a window at a tractor. He would be bemused, and he would have to think back to the reasons for this extraordinary behaviour. It wasn't like him to be in the one place for so long. He was too energetic and too virile, but he still felt the energy and virility in his body and he was saving it for the outburst that would have to come, so he told himself that although he appeared inactive he was really throbbing with activity.

Nan was the one who caused him doubt.

He watched her now coming in to him. It was a dull afternoon. The pub was in shadows. There was no light on. He hadn't taken too much drink. She came in from the hall outside, where she would often play. She rarely went outside at all now. He remembered the day the priest had coaxed her and coaxed him to take her into the sunshine. There was nobody to coax her now. Her mother should have been here to do this and to look after her. He saw Nan and he wanted to get away from her. He couldn't comfort her until this thing had been resolved, purged from him.

She walked slowly from the door of the hall. She had her hands in front of her, clasping them, looking down at them. Her head was bent. She came over towards him and sat on a chair and suddenly looked at him. She had her head on one side, as if she was saying: what's wrong?

'There's nothing wrong,' he said now. 'You understand that? Everything will be all right.'

It didn't satisfy her, he saw. There was a puzzled look in her face. How could he explain it to her? Her mother had failed her.

'Soon, soon,' he said, 'the sun will shine again.'

She was looking at the glass in his hand. She would look from the glass to his face and back again to the glass, and when she looked up finally, he was suddenly stabbed with a feeling of pity and frustration.

'Go and play, Nan,' he said. 'Please go and play!'

She hung her head and rose up and walked away from him out towards the hall. Now she had her hands behind her back and she was kicking with one foot at the floor as she walked. I'm not failing you, he shouted after her silently. Just wait until all this is over. I can't play with you now, but I will. I will give you all my days, you'll see. His reason was asking him who he was trying to convince, her or himself. He knew the answer, but it was no help. He was tied by his own determination.

Nan went into the hall. She felt sad. She went over to the old piano near the bandstand. The lid was open. There was dust on the yellowed ivory keys. She plonked her finger on a note. It rang out of key. She looked at the dust on her finger and then wiped it on her dress, then she leaned against the wall beside the piano and let her body slide down until she was sitting on the floor of the bandstand, beside the piano, so that when Sean came to the front door of the hall and looked in, he did not see her through the glass.

He was surprised to find that the door was open, and when

he came to the doors of the porch inside he saw that several panes of glass were broken and littered the floor. He came in and looked at the hall. He shook his head. The litter he had swept up on that night was still gathered in the centre of the floor. There was a lot of dust and debris that had been blown into the hall. The glass of the doors had been broken because the doors had been left open to the swinging wind. He looked at the windows. They were dirty, and already the spiders had begun to weave their cobwebs of neglect.

He knew where he would find Donn. He only paused a few seconds before he set off across the floor to the door that led into the pub. He was quite calm.

He didn't know that Nan was watching him, hidden from him at the side of the piano. As he walked now he had to drag his right leg slightly on the floor. It was stiff. It would always be stiff, they told him – torn cartilages, and a busted kneecap. It would never be able to bend again, not much. Maybe over the years he would be able to get a bend in it, but it would take time, and in the meantime he had to drag it a bit since he hadn't got the knack of lifting it and throwing it out to bring it in front of his stride.

It was this wounded walk that Nan watched closely. She looked from his leg to his determined face and as he got to the door she rose to her feet and looked after him. Wounded walk, wounded bird, wounded rabbit, wounded cat, something that had been injured. His name came into her mind, Sean, Sean, and two and two are four, two and two are four. She saw him opening the door, pausing and then going in, and she walked softly after him. The door didn't close fully behind him so she stood there and she could look in. At first his back blocked her view, but as he hobbled his way across the floor, she could see him better, and see her father, and she saw the look of surprise on his face, and then she saw his face getting a hard look, and her heart beat faster.

'What do you want?' Donn asked him.

Sean stopped where he was.

'I want to talk to you,' he said.

'Are you dragging your leg to impress me?' he asked.

Sean considered this.

'No,' he said. 'I am dragging it because I have to. Later on it won't be as bad as it is now. I don't want to impress you.'

'And what do you want?'

Sean came closer to the table.

'Can I sit down?' he asked. 'It's painful when I am standing too long.'

Donn examined his face. It was thin and pale, and there was a lock of hair falling over his forehead. But his eyes were calm and looked straight into his own without flinching.

'As you wish,' he said, and Sean pulled out a chair and sat into it with a faint sigh. It had been quite an effort to walk from his house over here. Nearly every step had been painful, and at times he didn't think he would be able to go all the way, but he had persisted.

'In the hospital,' he said, 'I had a long time to think. It's a good place for that, also it shows you that no matter how badly hurt you are there are hundreds worse off.'

'If you are going to give me lectures in philosophy,' said Donn, 'don't.'

Sean smiled.

'How would a one like me know anything about philosophy?' he asked. 'I just wanted to tell you this, about the thinking I did. In the old, old days, if a man injured another man he was forced to make personal reparation. Is this true?'

'I'll grant you that,' said Donn.

'I want to make reparation to you,' said Sean.

Donn laughed.

'You don't think a crocked leg is reparation enough?' he asked.

'No,' said Sean.

'Well, I think it is,' said Donn. 'You did what you did and I did what I did, and we will cry quits, so you can unload me from your conscience and get on with your life. Just go away somewhere and start working and forget, that's all you have to do.'

'Apart from anything else,' said Sean, 'I would find it hard to get work with a bad leg. Few employers want to see things like this under their eyes.'

'What are you trying to say?' Donn asked. 'Are you twisting

the book and telling me that I owe you something?'

'Since you put it like that,' said Sean, 'I say you do, but I didn't mean it to be like that.'

'How much do you want?' Donn asked. 'Will we agree on a price or will you take it into court and decide? Is that what you are after?'

'No,' said Sean. 'This is just something between you and me. I just want to come and continue working for you as if nothing had happened.'

Donn laughed. It was not pleasant laughter.

'You think just because you say nothing has happened, that nothing really did happen. Do you think that deeds can be wiped out by words?'

'No,' said Sean, 'but I think that deeds can be wiped out by deeds. I don't know how much I owe you for what I did to you. How can a thing like that be measured by price or by penalty? All I know is that I want to come and work for you, in the hope that some day, I don't know how far off, you will say: All right, you have wiped out the debt that you owe me. This is all I want to do.'

'This is the result of your few years in a seminary,' said Donn. 'It smacks of the Bible. What do you want to be, a bondman or a flail? What do you expect? Every time I look at you I will remember. Is this what you want?'

'No,' said Sean. 'I want you to get to look at me and to get over me and eventually forget that I did you an injury. I am trying to repay you. I have thought over it and this is the only way I know how. You must have some mercy in you. You must know enough about me to understand how much I hate myself for what happened. If necessary I am asking you to have pity on me, because I thought and I thought, and this is the only way I will find a little peace, so I ask you as well as I am able, and indeed, I will beg of you, if that is what you want, to give me this chance. It is the only way I will find a bit of peace, and I ask you to help me find it.'

He had rested his elbow on the table and his forehead was resting in his hand. Donn regarded him.

'Look at me,' he commanded. Sean did so. Donn saw that there were beads of sweat under his eyes, and down the side of his jaws. 'Are you really sincere in this?' he asked. He couldn't believe it. It seemed most illogical to him. Sean should hate him. Even weak men should hate the people who injured them. His weeks in hospital should have brought him to an awareness of this. Every ache and pain should have hardened him in his resolve.

'I think I am sincere,' Sean said. 'I am impelled to it.'

'You aren't nurturing feelings of hatred and revenge by any chance? You are not trying to get back into my house so that you will pay me back for the things I did to you? Is your mind that complicated, like the minds of most men? How can I believe you?'

'I don't know,' said Sean. 'The only person I feel hatred for is myself. If you will let me do this, in time I may not hate myself so much, but this is the only way I see to find out. As far as I know, I am sincere, and I have no other motive except what I have told you.'

Donn kept looking at him.

'And Nan,' he said softly, menacingly.

Sean didn't avoid his eyes.

'I owe her even more than I owe to you,' he said. 'I don't know how to repay it to her, but in time maybe I will even discover how to do that.'

'You puzzle me,' said Donn. 'You are not the same person as you were before.'

'I am,' said Sean, 'but all that has happened has made me see life a bit more clearly. Maybe I even see some sense in it, something to aim at. I don't know. Just help me with this, and I can promise you with my life that you will never regret it.'

'Why should I trust you?' Donn asked. 'I have given up trusting anybody. Who is there that can be trusted?'

'Few people on earth,' said Sean.

'Don't go metaphysical,' said Donn.

Sean stayed silent.

'All right,' said Donn. 'I don't trust you, but you can do this thing if you want to. I wouldn't do it if I were you, but I'm not. I tell you that turning the other cheek never got man anywhere but into more trouble. I have something to do, and I will do it. I don't know how long it will take. I haven't time for other things. Maybe they are gone to pot. Go and see Paud. Do what you think is necessary. All I ask is that you keep away from me as much as you can. Don't let me see too much of you.'

He filled a glass. Sean was slightly shocked to see that his hand was not clean and that there was dirt under his long fingernails. The thing you always noticed about Donn before was his immaculate cleanliness. Donn noticed his look.

'Go away!' he said.

Sean rose to his feet.

'Thank you,' he said and walked towards the door that led into the kitchen. Donn took one look at his dragging leg and then turned his back on him to gaze into the yard.

Nan hadn't understood all that was said. It puzzled her. She was vaguely upset by the absence of her mother. There had been nobody to stay with. Bridgie was too busy in the kitchen. She was uneasy in the presence of her father. Sometimes she heard him talking to himself and this upset her. Sean seemed somebody familiar. She remembered him teaching her sums, getting a packet of sweets and emptying them on the table and making her count them.

Her father wasn't looking, so she opened the door softly and walked through the door into the kitchen. She heard the voice of Sean, talking to Bridgie. She heard Bridgie say: 'In the shop,' and then she opened the door and Sean was walking out of the door into the shop. Bridgie didn't see her. She was bent over a pot on the floor doing something, so Nan went towards the shop door and opened it.

'Hah?' Paud was saying.

'What do you want?' Sean was saying. 'What is in short supply?'

'That,' said Paud. 'Every feckin' thing. I say to him: We want this and we want that, and he says all right, but what do I do? When she was here, she would write it all down in a little book. But she's not here, only him – and all he does is watch out the window like an old granny.'

Sean was looking at the shelves. The goods on them were scant.

'We'll soon fix that,' he said.

'Are you coming back then?' Paud asked.

'Yes,' said Sean. 'Not today. Tomorrow. I'm tired. I want to go home. Early in the morning I'll be back and we'll make out a list of everything you want.'

'Man, that's great,' said Paud. 'What's the use of having nothing? You can't sell nothing. Coley Collery is back with the travelling shop again. Did you know that? He has a new van. People are buying from him. They have to.'

'All right,' said Sean. 'I will be here in the morning. I can take the car and go and collect a lot of things myself.'

'Ah, that's the stuff,' said Paud. 'I do get sick of saying to people: "No we haven't that. It's ordered," when it isn't ordered. Even if telling lies was any good, but it isn't. You're sure you'll be here in the morning?'

'I'll be here,' said Sean. 'I promise.'

'Man, that's great, now we can get going,' said Paud. 'I don't know what happened. Time here it was like we couldn't keep up with everything, now we haven't time to keep up with nothing.'

'Things will get a little better now,' said Sean. 'I promise you.'

'Good,' said Paud. 'I was thinking of going myself. I don't like to be this way, on me oath. Now it will be all right. Did I tell you Bridgie is going to have a baby?'

'No!' said Sean.

'It's true,' said Paud. 'Great day for the McNallys. I bet he'll be a whopper. Bridgie will have to leave here soon. What can she do? She can't be working with that on top of her.'

'Not yet,' said Sean. 'She doesn't have to go yet.'

'She'll have to go soon,' said Paud, his jaw tightening.

Sean saw the signs. When people like Paud tightened their jaws there was no argument you could oppose to them.

'Give us a bit of time,' said Sean, 'just a bit of time and we will have everything going smoothly again. I'll be back in the morning.'

He walked to the door of the shop and went out. He was thinking of the things that would have to be ordered, an awful lot of them. He was thinking if Bridgie left could they get somebody to take her place, and he had an uneasy feeling that they could not. Who would want to come and work for Donn in the present circumstances?

Nan watched him go out of the shop, and then she walked across the shop to the window. It was built halfway up to display goods, but she could peer over the top by standing on her toes. Paud looked at her without wonder. He was used to her in the house, wandering from place to place.

She could see Sean making his way painfully along the road, pausing at frequent intervals to rest his leg, and breathing deeply before starting off again. Each step he made required a great effort on his part. He didn't use a stick, as he felt it might draw attention to his plight.

So Nan looked at him and felt sad for him but she was aware of the knowledge that he was coming back in the morning. That was nice. She was sad for him, but he would be there and maybe he would play sums with her. She kept watching him until he was out of sight.

Twenty-four

THIS AFTERNOON in early July Sean became restless and uneasy and decided to go out. The persistent cloud cover over the valley had lasted almost a month. Sometimes it drizzled, a persistent soft drizzle that would wet you just as effectively as a heavy shower if you remained out long enough in it. It wasn't raining now but the clouds were depressing and the air was close. He shut the books with a bang. It was easy to keep them. He marvelled at how quickly a prosperous business could go down if it was neglected. In a way it was like a garden running to weeds and everyone knew how fast that could happen if it wasn't kept hoed. If Donn only knew. He needed Sean. He couldn't go too fast. The business was already in debt and he had had to do his ordering within the scope of credit they would be allowed and the sales they could make.

He sighed and put his chin in his hand and, looking out of the window, stiffened as he saw Nan looking at him. She was making him uneasy. He would see her in a door looking in at him, or at the window as now. It seemed that her eyes were always on him. He didn't know why. He was afraid that she remembered something about that night and that he was there and she was watching him in order to be sure that she would smell him or something, recognize something about him that was terrifyingly familiar. It left him feeling bleak.

How could he know that she wanted to speak to him; that she wanted him to say: Come here, Nan, and I will show you how to play sums, because that was what she associated him with. He rarely met her eyes. He found it hard to do so. The thought of going near her and touching her hand, say, made him shrink.

He rose to his feet and went out of the room. He went into the pub and looked around him, as soon as he left the room, Nan left the window for the door and opened it and came in. She paused there and then followed him softly through the door. He had left the pub door open after him, so she stood there and looked in.

Sean went behind the counter. Donn was beginning to look like a carved figure sitting at that cursed table. He was wearing a shirt that could do with washing and Sean could only see the back of his head. His hair was too long and tousled. He wanted to say to him: This is no good. This is the height of futility.

He didn't of course.

He went behind the counter, saw that all the glasses were clean, turned the tap tighter to stop the water dripping in the steel sink. He got a cloth and rubbed the counter top, wondering where all the dust came from. He tidied a few bottles on the shelves and came out on the floor again. He looked at the place critically. It didn't look too bad. All it lacked was customers, and how the hell would the customers come with that brooding figure looking out the window?

Donn saw him in the glass of the window, reflected there. He saw him come in and go behind the counter and start fussing. He noticed that his leg movement was easier than it had been. He saw him come out and walk the floor, look at him and then walk slowly out the door into the kitchen.

Nan saw him coming and pulled back so that when he opened the door she was standing behind him. He closed the door, not looking, and so he didn't see her. She watched him and then she came into the pub. She saw her father. She went towards him, paused and then decided not to go near him. He noticed this. He watched her in the window. She did what Sean had done. She went in behind the counter and she came out again and then she stood in the centre of the floor, thought, and went into the kitchen.

He wondered about her. He had noticed the way she followed Sean. He wondered why. When she left the place, he rose to his feet. He rubbed his hands on his face and his forehead, tried to soften his dried mouth with saliva and then walked after Nan.

Sean had gone through the kitchen into the parlour again. He took the books and put them over on the table near the window. He looked out. He could see the clouds low on the hills. The water of the lake looked grey and the river winding out of it was the same grey colour. All the colours of the fields seemed to be drab. They wanted the kiss of the sun to make them blaze and brighten. He wished the sun would come out. Maybe all the old sores would be healed.

He went to the door and stood outside looking. He breathed the air. It was not refreshing. All the same, he thought, I will walk for an hour or two. I will walk by the river and the climb up there will strengthen my leg. He set off, down towards the lake and the river. It was easier to walk now, he noticed. He was acquiring the knack after many days of pain and cold sweat. He just had to treat it a little delicately, and not put too much strain on it, and he could get along fairly well.

Nan came in and looked out of the window. She saw him heading down to the lake, so after thinking a little she too went out the door and stood there until he reached the lake and turned right to walk by the river. Then she set off and followed him.

Donn was at the window and saw this. He saw Sean turning up by the river and the girl setting off to follow him. What's this, he wondered? He opened the door himself then and stood in the grey light. Even its dimness hurt his eyes, so that he had to rub them with his fingers. He thought: Dino will hardly come in the broad daylight. For he had come one night. Only Donn knew this. He had stiffened when he heard the sounds at the gate. He knew that Dino had come and that Dino had shaken it angrily when he found that it was padlocked. He had gone away then, Donn knew, tensely waiting there in the darkness, that he would come back – but not in daylight. A rat like Dino would have to have the cover of night.

Sean was out of his sight, Nan nearly so, when he decided to set off and follow them.

All of Sean's thoughts as he followed the river were devoted to walking the rough ground with his bad leg. Parts of the ground were uneven, parts were rough and boulder-strewn. Sometimes the bank of the river rose and there was no way to pass, so he had to climb the bank and walk on the rough ground there until he could get back again to the river. This posed many problems of movement, because any time he had to rest his weight on his bad leg it hurt him badly enough to make him suck in his breath, pause until the spasm of pain passed, and then, wiping the sweat from his forehead, move on again. But, like everything else, he gradually became accustomed to it, and found ways to avoid the pain.

He was so intent on this that he never once looked behind him or he would have seen Nan following him. She paused when he paused, stopped when he stopped, and went on when he went on. She knew what was happening to him. She was used to watching, and feeling sad for, wounded birds and animals. She didn't know how Sean had come to be wounded. She didn't wonder about it. She just saw that he was. She couldn't remember that one time his leg was as good as her own. She felt a pity for him.

Donn stopped once and went to the river and, bending down, took up water and scooped it in his hands and rubbed it on his face and neck. The coolness of it was shocking but he wanted to be able to see what was happening ahead of him. He was puzzled at the behaviour of Nan. She didn't look back either. She just kept her eyes glued on the figure of Sean. He saw her pausing and stopping and going on, but never once looking back – although he took care that if she did look back she wouldn't see him. The fresh air felt strange to him. He noticed with some wonder that his legs were beginning to ache from disuse. He held out his right hand and there was a slight shake in it. This disgusted him.

When Sean came to forget his leg, he started thinking. He thought of his father and mother and their silent puzzlement. He had not actually told lies. He had said he had an accident with Donn's gun. This was true. He evaded the question of why he had the gun out at night. Just that he had it. If he had told them the truth, two or three things would happen. His father had a temper and determination. He would probably have attacked Donn. He was a fearless man when he felt he was in the right. Sean didn't like to think what the result of that conflict would be. If he told them about his part in the cause of it all, he would have filled his father with such disgust, that he would have had to leave home. He didn't want to do that.

So it was a case of least said, soonest mended, as far as his parents were concerned.

Finally he had reached as far as he could go by the river. It was a sandy place with the bank rising high behind him. He sat here with his leg stretched out comfortably, and he looked at the river rushing over the stones. He took up a small pebble and threw it at the water. It barely disturbed it. The moving water absorbed the mark the pebble made in a few seconds and then there was no sign of it.

That's man passing through life, he thought. Short, and all the marks of him wiped out almost as soon as he has made them. He wondered at his own calm. He knew what he had in mind to do, and he was going to go ahead and do it. There was no more will I, won't I. He knew what he would try to do and if he was blocked in one way, he would set about trying to do what he thought was right in another way. He couldn't see how at the moment. If you could believe that all things were ordained, and that men thwarted a universal plan when they distorted it with what was called sin but was more than that, then you could see a reason for everything, even in what he had done, and what had happened to him for the doing of it.

Nan lay full-length on a high bank away from him and watched him. She saw him throwing the pebble into the water. She pulled a blade of sedge and chewed it and liked the tang from it.

It is unlike Nan, Donn thought, as further back he watched her. Why does he seem to fascinate her?

On the still air of the evening Sean heard the bleating of a lamb. It wasn't a new-born lamb; the sound of the bleating, although far away, was too strong, although a newly-born lamb has a good loud bleat. This call was mature but not fully mature. He listened closely. It came from behind him and off to the right. He waited for it to stop but it didn't stop. He tried to think of the reasons that the lamb might be continuing to bleat. Not for its mother; it would be too old. Not because it was being harassed by a dog, because there would be less bleating and the sound would not be coming from the same place.

It kept up, so finally he rose to his feet and climbed the bank and looked around him. About five hundred yards away across the side of the hill he saw one or two sagging posts. Oh, no, he thought, I hope to God he is not down there. He started to walk across the heather and the rough ground in the direction of the posts. The posts were surrounding what was called the Pookey's Hole, a cleft in the earth for which men could not account, a fairly narrow slit like a gaping wound, that had been made before the memory of man, when something below had shifted, and the earth had opened. It was fenced off, to save animals falling into it, but since it was a commonage, and many people were involved, everyone left it to everyone else and so, he saw as he came close to it, several of the willow posts were rotted, access easy, and so when he walked to the edge and looked down he was not surprised to see the lamb jammed between two sides of the cleft where it narrowed. The lamb was struggling, kicking the air with its legs.

'You silly creature!' Sean shouted down at it, and then without giving much thought to it he started to let himself down into the hole. It was fairly steep, but easy enough. At the top there was the bog-earth topped by thick heather, and then there was jagged granite rock, and clefts where thums of heather grew, with coarse grass and wild orchids. It was about twenty feet to the floor of the cleft, which was inches deep in water and mud, and when he stood there he was almost on a level with the face of the lamb – which was not so terrified of his ridiculous situation as of the sight of the man so close to him.

'Now,' said Sean, surveying him, 'you're an eejit, and I'm a worse one. I shouldn't have come down. I should have gone back first and got a rope and then come back with help.'

There was no use freeing the lamb. As far as he could see he wasn't hurt. His short thick wool had protected him from harm, he was just hung up. If he freed him he would be running around like a hare. There was nothing he could do but get up to the top again.

He tried to do this, and found that it was virtually impossible. Coming down he could let his bad leg hang, and not use it much. Going up, he would need it. He tried and found that he could not get up without it. He got up a few yards, pulling himself with his hands, but the effort was too great, so he had to let himself down again and lean against the other side of the cleft, practically breathless.

He was looking up when he saw the face of Nan, peering down at him. She solemnly looked at him and then looked at the lamb. Sean was never more glad to see anyone. In another few minutes his thoughts might have become very gloomy.

'Sean!' she said down to him. 'Is the lamb hurt, Sean?'

'No,' he said. 'He is not hurt.'

'You will bring him out,' she said confidently.

'I can't,' said Sean. 'I can't climb with my leg.'

He saw her trying to think her way through this. She was lying with her head over the cleft, the hair falling around her face. He saw the frown gathering between her eyes.

'You must get out the poor lamb,' she said.

'You will have to do it,' he said.

She didn't answer him. She waited for him to go on.

'Go back to the shop,' he said. 'Get rope from Paud. Cart-rope. Do you understand. Bring back cart-rope.'

She thought. Then she smiled. 'Oh,' she said. 'Cart-rope.' She rose to her feet. He thought she was gone. Then he saw her leaning over the cleft again. 'You will be lonely,' she said sadly.

'No,' he said, shaking his head. 'I will be waiting for you.'

She smiled at him, and then she was gone, and he had a vision of her racing down the hill as she had done many times before. It was only then that he thought of it: Nan was talking.

Donn, up above, was startled too. He was back from the Hole behind a clump of rocks. He had overheard the conversation. He knew what had happened. He had been shocked to hear Nan talking. Nobody had heard a word out of her since that night. Now she had talked to Sean. He had heard her. I tried to get her to talk, he thought bitterly, and she wouldn't open her mouth to me. He wondered what he should do. He could easily now go down the Pookey's Hole and get Sean and the lamb out of there. But he didn't. He watched the figure of his daughter racing down the hill, her arms outstretched, balancing her body. He noticed that her limbs were white. He remembered another time on this hill, a good time, when she ran away – was it with Sean – and all her limbs were burned brown by the sun.

He was tempted to get Sean out of the Hole. Then she would come back and he would say: Look, I, your father, got Sean and the lamb out of the Hole. Would this be good? Would it be the right thing to do? Why did he want to do it? Was it because he felt jealous of this movement of hers towards the young man who had injured her? I will have to stop all this drinking, he thought then, it is putting curtains over my thoughts. Not now, but soon, soon.

He stayed where he was. Had he been wrong to let Sean come back? The sight of his dragging leg had a lot to do with it, also that he had shown courage in coming back. You had to admire people with courage – even if he had shown very little of it before when it was really needed.

Sean thought: she doesn't know, otherwise she would not be looking at me like that. Could children forget? He thought not. He could think back now to when he was a child and the things that had frightened him were as clear as the day they had happened and also the people who had caused him to be frightened. Was it a boon that she couldn't remember, or was it wrong? One day would it suddenly dawn on her and cause her to scream and draw away from him as she suddenly associated him with her fear and shock? He found himself sweating. He went over to the lamb and rubbed his head to try to comfort him. The lamb resisted at first, but slowly calmed under the scratching fingers. He bleated a little, not as loudly as before.

Donn saw most of Nan's progress. At times she was lost in the folds of the ground below, since distance made her so small, but as she came nearer, he saw that she had a big coil of rope over one shoulder. It was uncomfortable, and she shifted it from shoulder to shoulder, but all the time she kept up a good pace. She didn't see him, but as she came close to the Hole he saw that her eyes were shining. At times she would laugh, shifting the heavy rope. He saw that it had left red marks on her bare arms, and dirtied her dress.

'Sean! Sean!' she said, bending over the Hole. 'Here I am.'
Sean said nothing, looking up at her excited face.

'Isn't Nan good?' she asked.

'Nan is perfect,' said Sean.

'But good?' she asked.

'Very good, very good,' he said. 'You hold one end of the rope and throw the rest down.'

She had to think this out. She pulled away fumbling at the coils of the rope. 'Now,' she said, and threw it down to him, holding the other end. She kept looking over. Sean went to the lamb, got under where he was wedged, lifted him free by his shoulders, and grabbed him as he tried to jump away. He got him away from the narrow part, turned him on his back, and tied the rope around him so that it made a cradle under his belly. This wasn't an easy job. He heard Nan laughing and looked up. She was laughing heartily.

Donn heard her laughing too, and came out of his hiding to look at her.

'Sean and the lamb are funny,' she said, putting her hand over her mouth. He smiled up at her.

'Will you be able to pull up the lamb?' he asked.

'Oh, yes, yes,' she said.

'Put the rope around you a few times,' he said, 'and then walk back.'

She had to think this out too, but she did it, Donn saw. She put the end of the rope around her waist, like a belt, and knotted it and said: 'I will walk back now, Sean.' She walked back. He held the lamb in his arms and raised him as high as he could, and then he saw her pulling, taking the strain, and the lamb, bleating now indignantly, started rising to the top.

Donn wondered if he should go and help her. She slid once, and fell and then rose again, laughing. She was having a great time raising the lamb, so he stayed where he was. Finally she fell on her back and the lamb appeared out of the Hole and started to run around jumping and bleating, trying to free himself. Nan was laughing. She took the strain on the rope, and gathering it in hand over hand, instinctively, she walked towards him. He ran around her. He could have wound the rope around her body, but she turned with him. 'Don't, don't, don't, lamb,' she would call, and then laugh again. Finally she got within reach of him. He struggled against her, but she managed to loosen the loop that held him and, freed, he ran away, calling and calling, and jumping until he was out of their sight.

Donn grinned. Nan was sitting on the ground, her legs spread, her hands behind supporting her, trying to get her wind. Then she got up hastily, sobered, and went over to the Hole.

'The lamb was funny,' she called down. 'You should have seen the lamb.'

'You are a great girl, Nan,' Sean said. 'Now put down the end of the rope to me and do the same as you did for the lamb. It won't be as hard. I just want you for a spare leg.'

'Spare leg? Spare leg?' she asked. 'Oh, I will pull Sean like the lamb.'

'That's it,' said Sean. She got the rope and she threw it down to him. He tied it around his waist. 'Now, Nan,' he called, and when he felt the strain, he started climbing. With the support of the rope it was easy going, and he soon clambered out of the Hole.

She was standing several yards away from him, the rope wrapped around her waist. He looked at her. He didn't want to say: Do you know you have broken your silence.

'Thanks, Nan,' he said. 'If it wasn't for you I might have been down there for a month.' He started to coil the rope around his elbow. As he wound it she came with it. He didn't want her to get too close to him. Her nearness made him feel ashamed.

'Give me the rest of the rope now,' he said.

She unwound it from her waist and handed it to him.

'Sean was good,' she said, 'to get the lamb.'

'It wasn't Sean,' he said. 'Sean made a bloody mess of it. It was Nan that got the lamb, and Sean as well, out of the Hole.'

She stifled laughter by putting her two hands over her mouth.

'The lamb was funny,' she said. 'Sean was funny.'

'And Nan was funny,' said Sean.

'Oh, yes,' she said. 'Oh, yes.'

He had the rope coiled now. He put it on his shoulder.

'Will we go home and tell Daddy about the lamb?' she asked. She noticed that he wasn't looking at her, so she came forward and bent to look up into his face. As he saw the innocent eyes, looking into his own, he found that he was without words.

'Will we? Will we?' she asked.

'Yes, Nan, yes,' he said.

She took his right hand into hers, confidently. He looked down at it. One of her fingers was pressing on the scar on his finger. It was hurting.

'Come on,' she said, 'come on!' pulling at him, so he gave way to her, and thinking many things he set off with her down the hill.

Donn came out from the rocks to look after them. He leaned against the rock, thinking. He had seen the reluctance of Sean. He had seen the way she had taken his hand, and the repugnance he had felt.

He couldn't quite understand it all, but at least, he thought, I have found out what I wanted to. She is quite safe, now, with Sean.

His face was grim.

Twenty-five

DINO CAME home on a wet night in July.

He scratched on the back door with his nails, and his father heard the scratching and let him in. He was very wet. He wore no cap and the hair on his head was flattened and rivulets of water were running down his face. His clothes were soaked.

His father looked at him wordlessly. Dino took off his wet coat and his soaked shirt. His mother was sitting at the fire.

'Get me a towel,' he said. She rose to do so. 'And get me some clothes to change into as well,' he ordered.

He sat on a stool and started to unloosen his boots.

'Did you get the battery?' he asked his father.

His father came over slowly and sat down opposite him.

'I did,' he said, 'I brought it up on the cart under a load.'

'Good,' said Dino.

'Are you going there tonight?' his father asked.

'Yes,' said Dino. 'I'm sick of him. He better not interfere with me if he knows what's good for him.'

'He stays watching from the window,' his father said.

'What is he like?' Dino asked. He was naked now, rubbing himself down with the towel.

'He's not the man he was,' said his father. 'He has been drinking a lot, they say. He just stays at that window, drinking and brooding. Do you know what you are up to?'

'I do,' said Dino. 'He better not interfere with me, I'm telling you.'

'He's a dangerous man,' said his father.

'Maybe I'm more dangerous,' said Dino. 'I am getting my tractor out of there tonight, I'm telling you, and let him try and stop me!'

His mother came down from the room with clothes over her arm. Dino covered himself with the towel.

'Here,' she said. He took them. 'It isn't true what they say about you and the young girl, Dino?' she asked.

He looked at her. His mother wasn't very bright.

'Do you think I would do a thing like that?' he asked.

'That's what I told them,' she said. 'I said Dino is not the kind of boy to do a thing like that.'

'Your man just loads it on me,' said Dino. 'I'm the nearest one to hand for him. He goes and tries and kills me without asking if it is true.'

'Why would he do it?' she asked. 'He seems a decent man.'

'He doesn't like independent people,' said Dino. 'He comes back here and he wants to lord it over us, that's why. But not me or the Tumelty people. We are our own men. He doesn't like that. We strike out on our own. We don't go around and kowtow to him. He doesn't like that. So he keeps my tractor. I bought and paid for that. It's my living. It belongs to me. I'm going to take it.'

'Why don't you go to the police?' she asked.

Dino gave her a look of pity. He was pulling on the dry clothes. They felt good on his body.

'When did the people of this place ever go to the police?' he asked.

'I hope there will be no fighting,' she said.

'If he wants fighting he'll get it,' said Dino. He hoped your man wouldn't have a shotgun. It would be hard to fight a shotgun, but he intended to get his tractor out of the yard.

It was the thought of the sitting tractor that had plagued him over the weeks. Sitting there, idle, when it could be making money for him. When he ran away down to the other side he had stayed with a cousin in the mountains for a few nights. The first two nights he had slept uneasily. Your man had frightened him all right, he would admit that. Any man who heard the sound of shot whistling over his head and cutting the heather just in front of his nose is entitled to feel frightened.

He had gone away to the other side of the county. He had worked at odd jobs, driving a tractor when that was available, or working in the fields. He didn't last long in any of the jobs. He couldn't stand men ordering him to do things that he knew how to do better than themselves. So he would argue with them, and they would tell him to take off, that he was too talented for them. It annoyed him that he had to go working for other people, when he had his own way of life and his own tractor that could make him a steady income whenever he wanted to go. The trailer and the implements were in his own yard, the ploughing equipment and the hay-cutting attachment, everything he needed to make good money. All he had to do was to get the tractor out of there, hitch up the trailer and get out of the valley.

He didn't want to stay in the valley. It had no hold on him. There were broader pastures on the outside where a man could keep working from dawn to dusk, and after dusk if necessary, when there was a good light on the tractor and he could work fields overtime.

He sat now and lit a cigarette.

'Get me some tea,' he said to his mother. She rose to do so.

His father was smoking a pipe.

'You haven't done us any good in the valley,' he said. 'What did you want to go and do a thing like that for?'

'I didn't do nothing,' said Dino. 'He just said I did, that's all.'

His father wished he was small enough to beat. He had pounded him before when he was young, but it seemed he hadn't pounded him enough. He couldn't give him the fist now or he would get it back, he knew this. Dino was looking at him with sullen eyes.

'We always had a good name,' his father said. 'You made a haimes of that, but you don't care. You'll go away now and you'll leave us here to carry the shame of it.'

'You don't know,' Dino shouted. 'It's my word against his, isn't it?'

'I wish he had got hold of you, and beaten some shame into you,' his father said.

'You will turn on your own,' said Dino. 'You won't listen to me. You won't take my word for it. You'll take the word of that foreign bastard before you'll take my word.'

'Well, what is your word? I'm asking you!' His father was angry now.

'What use is my word to you?' Dino asked. 'You have judged me, haven't you, before you hear my word? What use is my word?'

'Jack,' said Dino's mother, 'what's got into you? You know

234

that our Dino would never do a thing like that!'

'That's the trouble, I don't know,' said Jack. 'I wouldn't put it past him.'

'Don't say things like that, Jack!' she said.

'That's right,' said Dino. 'You'd take the word of a tinker before you would take mine.'

'Everybody knows it was you,' his father said.

'Everybody has been wrong before,' said Dino.

'Come over and eat,' his mother said.

Dino rose and went to the table.

'I'll be glad to get away from here, anyhow,' he said. 'It's a nice state of affairs to be held up like that by your own father.'

'Just say you didn't do it,' his father said. 'Just say once that you didn't do it.'

'What about Sean McNulty?' Dino asked. 'Why aren't they accusing him? How do you think he got a bad leg? And why? Everybody knew the way he was drooling over that girl.'

'If it was him why is he back working in the shop?' Jack asked.

This was news to Dino.

'He is, eh?' he said.

'Do you think Donn would take him back into the shop if he was the one?' Jack asked.

'He's queer, that Donn,' said Dino. 'Everybody knows he's not right in the head. Why would the girl be a half-wit if there wasn't something wrong with the father? How can you account for the queer things he does?'

'If you did what they say,' said his father, 'the man has a right to lay you out. I'd do it myself if it was me.'

'Jack! Jack!' his wife said. 'Don't talk like that. You don't know what you are saying.'

'You don't have to do this,' said Jack. 'I will go over in the morning and ask him for the tractor. I did nothing to hurt him. And I will bring it to you in the street town below, and you can away with yourself.'

'He'd tell you to go and jump in the lake,' said Dino. 'I know him. He is watching that tractor. He knew I would come back for it. Well, I have come back for it, and I'll get it out from under his nose, and be away before he wakes up from his drunken sleep. You leave me alone. This is my business.'

They were silent. He ate his food, stuffing it down because he was hungry, and nervous too, but determined.

Finally he rubbed his mouth and rose to his feet.

'Where's the battery?' he asked.

'It's out on the cart,' his father said.

'You can keep all my things,' he said to his mother. 'I'll be back again for them one night.'

'Dino,' she said, 'don't get hurtit. It's not worth the tractor if you get hurtit.'

'I won't,' he said. 'And it's worth it. I had to slave hard to get that tractor. It's a way of life. I've had enough of a sample of working for other people. Goodnight. I'll be back some time.'

He went out the back door.

They looked at one another helplessly. Jack's jaw was tight. She started to cry, sitting on the chair, the edge of the apron up wiping her eyes.

'Don't do it,' he said to her. 'He's not worth it, I am afraid.'

Outside, Dino found the battery. He chanced putting on the light in the carthouse. He got some rope and made a cradle for the battery and hung it on his back. He hoped that the tractor would start with a fresh battery. The old one would be run down. The ignition might be damp, but he had had it attended to shortly before, and he hoped it would be all right. He looked for a few small tools and put them in his pocket. He looked further until he found the short crowbar with a bend and a slit in the end of it for lifting big nails. He hefted this in his hand. Then he hoisted the battery on his back, put off the light and moved quietly from the house towards the road. There was steady rain. The night was very dark. He waited until his eyes became accustomed to the darkness, and then moved to get into the fields and down the back of the houses towards Donn's yard. It took him a long time. He moved very slowly. He had come back once before and had been enraged when he found the gate padlocked. He had shaken it in anger, but he had taken enough time to look at the padlock. It was a cheap mass-produced one, and it had been no trouble, when he had memorized the size of it, to go to a shop and get one just like it and the two keys that went with it.

After a long time he came to the wall of the yard. It was only chest-high, so he got over it easily. Taking the padlock key from his pocket he crept to the gate, felt for the padlock, inserted the key, held his breath to see if it would open, and when it did, he heaved a sigh of relief, took off the padlock, and freed the gate so that it would swing open at a touch. Then, still crouching, he made his way to the wetly-glistening tractor. He looked. There were no lights in the back of the house. He eased the battery from his back and left it on the ground.

So far, so good, he thought, but he didn't know that eyes were watching him.

Sean came from the lighted kitchen into the dark pub, and stood just inside the door. Then he saw that Donn was there, barely visible, sitting at the table with his back to him. It would have to be a conversation in the dark, he thought, and maybe that would be just as well. He walked a few steps into the place.

'Donn,' he said. 'I want to talk to you.'

There was no reply from him. Sean thought he would not answer at all, then he saw him turning his body towards him a little, obviously trying to see him.

'What do you want to talk about?' he asked.

'I find it very hard to talk about it,' he answered.

'If you find it hard then it might be worth listening to,' Donn said. Sean noted with surprise that his voice sounded sober. You had to listen closely to him to detect that he was drunk. He just spoke a little more slowly, so that his lagging speech could catch up with his still alert brain. Now even that pausing didn't seem to be there. Sean didn't know whether he was glad or sorry. He moved towards the table and caught the back of a chair and pulled it away and sat on it so that he wasn't too close to Donn.

'I want to talk about Nan,' he said.

There was a silence then, a heavy one, and all it did was make Sean's pulse beat a little faster.

'What do you want to say about her?' Donn's voice was almost icy.

'You wouldn't notice,' he said, 'but she has taken to me. I

237

didn't try to bring this about. I did everything I could to avoid her. Now everywhere I go, she is there. But she is very good. If I say: Nan, I have this to do or that to do, she just goes away until I am free and then she comes back again.'

'Does this annoy you?' Donn asked.

'No,' he said. 'It's just that I feel that she should never come near me at all; that I am the last person in the world to whom she should show trust and affection.'

'But she does,' said Donn.

'I know some of the reasons for it,' said Sean.

'Say them,' said the other.

Sean moved uncomfortably.

'You are neglecting her,' he said. 'I know you have something else on your mind, but you have withdrawn from her and so she has sought out me. That is one of the reasons.'

'And what's the other one?'

'You are the cause of the other one too,' said Sean, steeling himself to the saying of it. Donn waited for him to go on. 'When I was wounded,' he said, 'and had to hobble in my walk, it made her notice me. You know how she has always taken pity on wounded things, birds and animals – even fish, which are coldblooded and pitied by nobody at all, except someone like Nan.'

'So you blame me,' said Donn, 'on all counts, for Nan taking an affection for you.'

'No, no,' said Sean, 'I don't blame you. I just say that in a large way you are responsible.'

'Would it therefore make Nan happy,' Donn asked, 'if I sent you away?'

Sean thought over this.

'I don't think so,' he said. 'Since she has fastened on me like this, it might hurt her if I was sent away.'

'So what is this talk all about?' Donn asked.

'I am afraid of annoying you now,' said Sean.

'You won't,' said Donn. 'Sitting here at the window has at least taught me patience.'

'You won't live for ever,' said Sean.

To his amazement, Donn gave a hoot of laughter.

'True,' he said then, soberly.

'And neither will Meela,' he said.

'And neither will you,' said Donn.

'But I have a lot of years on you,' said Sean boldly, 'and on Meela, and what I am saying is what will happen to Nan when you are both gone?'

Donn thought over this.

'It's a sobering thought,' he said.

'Which is why I want to marry her,' said Sean, and noticed that he was holding in his stomach almost painfully.

'What!' Donn shouted and turned completely around, trying to peer at him in the darkness.

'I wish you would think over it and not lose your temper with me straight off,' said Sean hopefully.

He could almost hear Donn's body stiffening and then after quite a while relaxing.

'I want to try and explain,' said Sean. 'This is the way. How can you know what purity is unless you have felt and witnessed lust? That's one thing. Before, I was going to approach a life of purity without even understanding what purity was about. Now I know what purity is. It is something that is attainable, if there is a human objective, since the other way seemed unattainable to me. I want to marry Nan, to protect her always, to make her life as pleasant as ever it can be with her mind as it is. I think I can do this. It will provide me with a reason for living, and since I am of an age with her, I hope I will be here long after you are gone, so that I can look after her.'

'What are you trying to do?' Donn asked. 'Do you want to do penance? Is this your idea of punishment?'

'No,' said Sean. 'I cannot see any punishment in it. There will be only pleasure and satisfaction for me in doing this.'

'Look into the future,' said Donn harshly. 'I can tell you now, there is only one satisfactory relationship in life, and that is husband and wife. This is the closest that two people come in the world to understanding one another, beginning to comprehend what is real friendship, what is real companionship, what is love. But there must be a meeting of minds, even if they clash. You will have no meeting of minds here, ever. Have you thought of that? You will be like a male nursemaid for the rest of your life. Can you carry a burden like that?'

'I think I can,' said Sean. 'I haven't come talking to you about it now without doing a lot of thinking.'

'It seems to me like madness,' said Donn. 'In this case it doesn't seem to me that the punishment fits the crime. The punishment will be lifelong, even if you are let. Do you really think that a priest will marry you and Nan?'

'He will,' said Sean. 'I asked. The Church can't stop us marrying if you and Meela agree. That's not what they are here for.'

'It's impossible!' said Donn.

'Why?' asked Sean.

'You will get tired,' said Donn. 'It will be fine for a few years, but you will get weary, and you will hurt her.'

'No,' said Sean. 'I won't get tired. I will never hurt her. I know of no way I can persuade you about this. You will have to believe me. I don't regard it as expiation, or a mission, or a deed of charity. I'm just telling you that it will work out, despite all that seems to be against it. Because this is the way I want it to be.'

'By God, you have shocked me,' said Donn.

'Will you think it over?' Sean asked.

'Why do I have to think?' Donn asked. 'I have seen more than you know. Now you go to Meela and see what Meela says. If she says it will be all right, then I say it will be all right too.'

'I cannot . . .' said Sean, but Donn hushed him loudly.

He was standing close to the window. Even in the midst of the extraordinary conversation he had been listening and he had heard a tiny sound outside.

'Go away, now,' he whispered. 'Away with you fast. Dino has come back.'

Twenty-six

SEAN WAS surprised when he closed the door and turned to leave. Coming towards him from the shop was a procession of men, walking softly. What surprised him about them was that they were not talking. They were headed by Bartley Folan, who held his fingers to his lips, eased him out of the way and then went into the pub. He watched them in silence as they filed past him cautiously, Seamus Mooney, Mick Dunn, Corney Kelly, Tim Woods, Josie McNally and his father, all the able-bodied men of the village and their sons of drinking age.

He stood back and watched them pass. He didn't know what they were up to or what had brought them. He tried to tell himself that it was none of his business, but it was his business and he had to satisfy his curiosity, so when the last man had passed him he went in too and stood in the darkness to watch them. They had all gone down and stood in a ring around Donn, stretching from the door that led into the yard, right around him where he stood at the window.

Donn became conscious of them.

He had been listening closely to the noises in the yard. If his ears had not been attuned to them he might never have heard them. But he did and he knew, by the tingling of his own nerves if by nothing else, that Dino was out in the yard. It was then he became conscious of the movement behind him, and as they closed on him he even sensed the change their bodies made in the air of the room.

He stiffened.

He heard Bartley's voice, speaking softly, almost in a whisper.

'Donn,' he said, 'Dino is out in the yard.'

He didn't answer.

'We have had him under our eyes since he came in,' said Bartley. 'Every move he made we have spotted. He came with a battery on his back. He climbed over the wall. He opened the padlock on the gate. He is now taking out the old battery and putting on a new one. He is half-lying on the ground, reaching up a hand to do it.'

'You are not telling me anything I do not know,' said Donn. 'I know all that.'

'That's fine,' said Bartley.

'What are you doing here?' Donn asked.

'Will I tell him?' Bartley asked.

'You tell him,' said the voice of Seamus Mooney.

'You are not going out to him,' said Bartley.

'You are going to stop me?' Donn asked.

'Faith, we are,' said Bartley. 'If you could see us, there are a lot of us. There are too many of us to fight. And we'll fight. If we have to we'll beat you senseless. We're not fooling.'

They were speaking very softly, but their words were clear. Donn was clenching the frame of the window with his hands, almost hurting himself. A flame of anger rose in him, so that the wet darkness he was looking at seemed tinged with red. He waited until the spasm passed and then turned.

'Why?' he asked.

'It's simple,' said Bartley. 'He's not worth it.'

'He is to me,' said Donn.

'Look, Donn,' said Seamus. 'Dino is a nit. Dino hasn't the brain of a midge. Dino is just a poor stupid bastard, who'll never be any good to anybody.'

'Whatever he is, I want him,' said Donn.

'You go out there, and you'll probably kill him,' said Seamus. 'All right. Maybe he should be killed, but it's you and all belonging to you who will suffer afterwards, and we don't think Dino is worth it. We think too much of you. We know how you feel, but we talked about it, and we asked who was more important, you or Dino, and we decided that you were; so we waited and now we are here and we are going to make you let Dino go.'

'Who do you think you are, to do a thing like this?' Donn asked.

'We are your friends,' said Seamus, 'all of us. Not Dino's friends, your friends. Dino will leave the valley. If he doesn't we will make his life a bit difficult. We don't think you should ruin the rest of your life for him. So we are here to see that you don't.'

They were massed about him. Donn thought of fighting them. He had no chance. He couldn't fight a mass of bodies like that. He could chance bursting out through the window, but it was all small panes of glass. By the time he had fought them and made his way to the door into the yard, Dino would be gone anyhow.

He thought over all this, resting his closed fists on the table. They were all tense. He could feel their tenseness. He could sense their determination. He tried to think what other reason they might have for doing this. He couldn't think of one. He would have to accept the reason they gave for it.

Suddenly he relaxed.

'All right,' he said.

He felt the tenseness leaving them.

He turned back to the window.

'Let's see what Dino is at now.' He felt them crowding close to him. They could see nothing at all. It was a black night. 'Listen,' he said. They listened. The sounds were very slight. Still, when you knew what he was up to, you could detect their meaning. 'He has the battery changed,' said Donn. 'Now he is going up to the gate. Listen, he is opening it.' They heard the slight creak that the gate made. 'Now he is going back. He will hoist himself up on the seat.' They could hear that, the squeak that the seat made as he sat into it. 'Now, whoever is over near the yard door, stretch up your hand and you will find a switch, and when you find it, use it.' They all heard the hand feeling at the wall, and the silence and then the click, and outside two lights sprang up in the yard, spearing Dino in a bright glare as he sat up on the tractor. They watched him silently.

Dino stiffened. It was almost pitiful to see the look of surprise and terror on his face. He was twisting the starter. They could all hear the slow, slow turning. It seemed to last for centuries, if you were looking at the naked panic and fear on his face. They felt themselves wishing that starter to work, so that they wouldn't have to be looking at Dino's face. When it didn't work, they saw the move he made to leave. They thought he would, that he would get down from the tractor and run screaming from the yard. With a great effort of will, or greed, he stopped himself, and twisted the starter again. This time it whirred and the engine blasted into sound. His movements then were enough to panic the onlookers. He tried to throw her into gear and she jammed because the brake was on. The engine cut out. He took off the brake and tried the starter again. It wouldn't work, as the engine was flooded. He had to pause and pause, with his white face turned towards them. They knew he was waiting for Donn to emerge. He couldn't know that he wasn't going to, and his panic was terrible.

The engine caught. This time he was ready. She was in gear and he let in the clutch and in a set of staggering movements the tractor went out of the yard out of the glare of the lights, and the whole lot of them visibly relaxed.

'That was the worst few minutes of my whole life,' said Bartley.

'It was even worse for Dino,' said Seamus.

'Put on the lights,' said Donn, 'and we'll all have a drink.'

Sean, who was near the switches, pressed them down, and they all closed their eyes and blinked. Then they looked at one another and at Donn.

He was looking at them. He felt that he was seeing them for the first time, as people. They seemed to come into focus for him. Old men and young men with their own characteristic looks. Complicated human machinery, none of them the same, but he saw, and knew that what they had done had been for him, not against him. He could see that. They could have left him alone. They could have felt aggrieved at the way he had treated them, indeed at the way he had looked at them, dipping them all in the one barrel with a fellow like Dino.

They looked closely at him. Bartley thought he had lost weight, but the redness was gone from his eyes. The eyes seemed to be calmer. In a while, Bartley thought, the glint of humour might come back to them.

'Sean,' said Donn, 'set up a drink for our neighbours.' His hand was rubbing his unshaven chin. 'I'll go and clean myself up, and then I'll talk to ye.' He walked to the door, and turned there and looked back at them. 'Now we'll never know what would have happened,' he said.

They didn't say anything. They all knew.

'Drink up,' he said. 'You deserve a drink.' Then he was gone and they looked at one another, and as the first pints appeared on the counter they took them and drank and wiped their mouths and started to talk.

Donn went to his room. He sat on the bed. He felt very tired. He rose to his feet then. He pulled off his shirt and went into the bathroom and looked at his face in the mirror. He let water flow into the washbasin, cold water, and he rubbed it all over his face and his head. Then he let the hot water flow and shaved himself. It was a test of the razor, but when he got the beard off, his jaws looked startlingly pale. He saw that his face had thinned. He wondered at this, because all the time he had felt calm and resolute. Now he knew it had taken it out of him. He looked like a man who had been through a long illness.

He went back to the room again. He chose a clean shirt and put it on, and then a coat, and then he rooted around until he found the duffel bag that had come with him when he returned. He dusted it off and started putting things into it, all that he would need, a few of his books and the copybooks in which he had written, and his shaving things and a change of clothes, and when he had all that done he looked around the room. It held nothing for him now. Meela had emptied it when she had gone. He put out the light and left it. He went to Nan's door and opened it softly. He went and knelt beside the bed watching the light awakening her. It took a time for the sleep to leave her eyes, but when she recognized him, she put her arms around his neck.

'Daddy,' she said.

'Listen, Nan,' he said. 'I want to tell you something.'

She freed him.

'What?' she asked.

'I want to tell you this, I am going away for a while,' he said.

'Going away?' she asked, her eyes wide.

'Yes,' he said. He watched her thinking over it.

'Is Sean going away too?' she asked. Now she was disturbed. He checked himself. He felt no jealousy.

'No,' he said. 'Sean is not going away. Sean is staying here to mind you.'

'Oh,' she said. 'Sean will mind Nan.'

'Yes,' he said.

'You will come back then?' she asked.

He didn't know. He felt that he would not. He felt that this was the right time to go.

'Why wouldn't I?' he asked, which was the best way to put it. 'If I put the light out now, will you go back to sleep again?'

'Yes,' she said. She was half-asleep already. He put his hand on her smooth forehead, then he went and switched off the light. He stood and listened for a while. Her breathing was soft. She was not disturbed.

When he turned in the corridor, Sean was there.

'What's up?' he asked.

'I am off,' said Donn. He saw the dismay on Sean's face.

'They will be expecting you back there,' said Sean. 'Do you hold it against them?'

'No,' said Donn. 'I appreciate what they did. In some odd way maybe they were right. I don't know. I feel they have rewarded me for something. I don't know for what.'

'What about me, and Nan?' Sean asked. 'What am I to do?'

Donn put his hand on his shoulder. 'Do what you want to do,' he said. 'You have a business. It's in debt, but you can haul it out of debt and make it pay and support yourself and Nan.'

'You can't do that,' said Sean.

'I have done it,' said Donn.

'But where are you going?' he asked.

'God knows,' said Donn. He was already walking to the parlour. He was going to go out that way. Sean followed him.

'Can't you take the car,' he asked, 'to wherever you are going?'

'No,' said Donn. 'You'll need that. I want to go as I came. It will suit me fine.'

'Do you know what you are doing?' Sean asked.

'Amn't I leaving Nan in good hands?' Donn asked.

'Oh, yes,' said Sean.

'That's all that matters. I am leaving you a lot of burdens to carry. Carry them as well as you can.'

'But you'll be back?' asked Sean. Donn had opened the door now and was looking at the sheets of rain.

'Who knows?' said Donn. 'Maybe I never came back at all. Maybe it was all a dream. Goodbye, Sean.' He went into the night, pulling up the collar of his coat.

Sean stepped into the rain after him. He called: 'Donn! Donn!' in a bewildered sort of cry. Donn just waved a hand at him and walked on, and Sean closed the door and leaned against it. Who could understand the man, he wondered, and then he listened at Nan's door before going back to break the news in the now loud pub that they were again without a Lord of the Mountain.

Donn saw the lights in the pub and could hear the voices of the men. He was getting very wet, but he didn't mind. It reminded him of the night he had left before, with the rain raining and he pedalling down the hills on a bicycle. He felt drained. What good had his coming back done? If he had never left at all perhaps things would have been different. He wondered if it was his very coming back that had precipitated the things that had happened. Basically he knew that he had come back on account of Meela. Without her now, the place was nothing. He knew this but he tried to put it out of his head.

The mud was deep on the road and he felt his shoes sinking into it. He felt his clothes getting wet. He didn't mind. Rain was rain. It was funny it should be raining again now when he was going away, like the last time. He was sure the tracks of Dino's tractor were in the road if he could see them. It meant nothing now. The few minutes of panic that Dino had gone through were sufficient. He could think of his face like that, if he wanted satisfaction in the future.

He had gone over the gap when he heard the car behind him and saw the headlights in the rain. He pulled to the side of the road to let the car pass, but it stopped.

'Can I give you a lift?' the voice asked.

He stood there without answering. It was the voice of Father Murphy. He saw his face bending down to look out. He had opened the door on the passenger side. Donn hadn't counted on this. He thought over it, suddenly decided and got into the car. He said nothing, just closed the door. The priest started off again.

'I was up with old Sarah Magee,' he said. 'She is dead.'

'Oh,' said Donn, who had been thinking that he might have had something to do with the men's behaviour tonight.

'She just made the hundred by a few months,' he said. 'So she got her five-pound cheque from the President. They had a great party. You weren't there.'

'No,' said Donn. There was silence between them again.

'Well, go on,' said Donn. 'Ask me what's up, where I am going with my bag, what's it all about.'

'I will not,' said the priest.

'Why?' Donn asked.

'You know what will happen,' said the priest. 'You'll say something rude that's maybe right, and I'll have to be hanging on to my temper by the grace of God, and it'll do neither of us any good, so it's as well to talk about Sarah Magee who died like a saint.'

'Well, I'm going away again,' said Donn.

'Oh,' said the priest. 'I'm sorry.'

'Don't be polite,' said Donn.

'It's not so,' he said indignantly. 'I'm sorry you are going. You will take a lot of colour out of the valley. I liked to know that you were there.'

'Corrupting your parishioners?' asked Donn.

'Doing them good in a lot of ways,' said the priest. 'Why, you even did me good.'

'You don't have to pile it on,' said Donn.

'This is true,' said the priest. 'You made me think about a lot of things. For years I have been saying things in my mind and then I would hear your answers to them, and I would have to defend what I said, and in this way I reached conclusions that I would never have reached without your opposition to them.'

'That's something,' said Donn. 'I had reached conclusions too and now it's the same as if I had reached no conclusions at all. I have to start all over again. You needn't worry about

Dino. He came back. He took his tractor. He's gone out into the poor world again, as if it hadn't enough trouble.'

'How did this happen?' the priest asked.

'You'll know soon enough,' said Donn. 'You better wait for the legend.'

They were silent then. The wipers were working hard and still not managing to clear all the rain from the windscreen. The car was jolting and bumping in the ruts. Sometimes the front wheels threw yellow mud on the glass.

'You won't tell me where you are going?' the priest asked tentatively.

'I won't,' said Donn, 'because I don't know myself.'

'You did a lot of good in the valley,' said the priest.

'No,' said Donn. 'Things are changing. There is evolution abroad in the world. Even in the valley, these changes would have come anyhow. I only squeezed them a little. The only monument I leave behind me is hatred.'

'Sometimes,' said the priest, 'hatred springs from love.'

'People-love or self-love?' Donn asked.

'Who will look after Nan?' he asked.

'You know well,' said Donn. 'Sean will. He talked to you.'

'I didn't know what you would say,' he said.

'What do you think?' Donn asked.

'It will be good,' the priest said. 'It will work out. I think Sean is fitted for the burden.'

'So now everything is solved,' said Donn bitterly.

'Nothing is ever solved,' said the priest.

There was silence between them again for a long mile.

'Would you get mad if I said something else?' the priest asked.

'That's the way Sean started a conversation tonight too,' said Donn. 'Was I always so unapproachable as that?'

'You were a bit hot off the mark,' said the priest.

'What do you want to say?' Donn asked.

'Don't go away without saying goodbye to Meela,' the priest said. 'We will be passing her cottage in about fifteen minutes. You went away before without saying goodbye. You ought to do it this once. Maybe it will make up for the other time.'

'You know what she did to us?' Donn asked. 'A time like that and she walks out on us.'

'Tell her that,' said the priest. 'Give it to her good.'

'Everyone goes around seeing me as a big sinner,' said Donn, 'and themselves as great saints. They don't listen to my point of view. It's not a nice thing for a mother to walk out on her own child at a time like that. Do you think that's an inhuman thing to do?'

'I think it was human, but if you think it was inhuman go and tell her so before you leave. I would, to tell you the truth. I would unload a lot on her before you go. Dammit, she can take it. You go in and give it to her.'

'What kind of sight does it make me seem, with my own wife walking out on me at a time like that? Wasn't that the time to stick it out, and oppose me, if she thought I was wrong, not just run out on me at the time I needed her most? Even if I did it before, times had changed, things were different. It wasn't the same at all.'

'If it was me,' said the priest, 'honest to God I'd tell her that to her face. I don't think she should have done it. I think she should have stayed there with you. It was a weak and selfish action and I think somebody should tell her so.'

Donn was surprised. The priest was genuinely indignant.

'You do, eh?' he said. 'Well, here's Martin McGerr's cottage coming up. Let me out and I'll talk to her.'

The priest stopped the car.

'Don't cool off,' he said. 'Give it to her. This is one time, Donn, when I am behind you to the hilt. Goodbye. Some time maybe from some faraway exotic place you might send me a postcard.'

'I'll do that,' said Donn, 'a nice obscene postcard.'

The priest laughed.

Donn banged the door of the car. It drove away. He waited until the red lights had turned a corner, and then, tightening his jaws, he opened the small gate and walked the short path to the door. He pounded the wood with his fist.

Twenty-seven

THE DOOR opened almost immediately. That was typical of her, he thought. She should have asked who was there before she opened the door. How did she know? It might have been somebody come to assault her. That was true in a way.

Inside the door there was a glassed sort of porch with curtains and a door. This was to keep out the draughts. It was brightly lighted so he could get a good look at her. She recognized him. Her face did not harden. She looked different.

'Hello, Donn,' she said as if he had been just down the road to buy groceries.

Suddenly he saw why she looked different. She was pregnant.

'Well, the cute bastard!' he said, turning to look out at the night. All he could see of the priest's car was a dim light in the distance, illuminating a patch of rain.

'Who?' she asked.

'That holy curate of yours,' he said. 'That Father Murphy.'

'Were you fighting again with him?' she asked.

'I should have known,' he said. 'He's tricky. He is like a coloured salmon lure.'

'I suppose you are going away again,' she said.

'What makes you say that?' he asked.

'It's raining,' she said, 'and you are all wet and you have a bag over your shoulder. It's history repeating itself.'

'I came to say goodbye to you,' he said. 'At least I was tricked into coming to say goodbye to you.'

'Well, goodbye,' said Meela. 'Glad to have known you. Call around and see us when you are in these parts again.'

Suddenly he laughed. Well, at least, she thought, in a great surge of relief, he hasn't killed Dino or he wouldn't be able to laugh freely like that. She opened the door and he came in. He passed her into the other room. She closed the door and followed him in. He was looking around. She had made the place very neat, a combined kitchen and dining-room. It was warm.

The ugly night was completely shut out. There were wooden armchairs near the fire with cushions on them. There was a small dresser with glinting delf.

'You've made yourself very cushy here,' he said disapprovingly.

'Why wouldn't I?' she asked. 'Will you leave your bag down for the while you are here?'

He dropped it on the floor.

'How did you manage?' he asked.

'My father left me a little money,' she said. 'I had that. When the school opens in September I will have a job teaching.'

'I see,' he said. 'You are very independent, aren't you?'

'I am,' she said. 'Your coat is all wet. Will you take it off and dry it in front of the fire before you go?'

He thought over this.

'I might as well,' he said, and took it off. He draped it over the back of a chair. Almost immediately it began to steam.

'Here's a towel,' she said. 'Dry yourself.'

He started to do that, wiping his hair, which was still wet. At least, he thought, I dampened the seat of Father Murphy's car for him.

'Will you eat something before you go?' she asked. She wasn't pressing him, he knew. He could take it or leave it. Suddenly he felt very hungry.

'Yes,' he said. She started to do things, neatly and efficiently as she always did them. He stood in front of the fire and held his damp trousers out from his legs with his fingers. The trousers started to steam. He watched her. Her face was plumper, like the rest of her. She hadn't really changed a lot. Why would she, down here having a fine time for herself while he was up there wrestling with demons.

'A man is only as strong as the weakest woman,' he said loudly. Apart from the men, she was the one who really stopped him from killing Dino.

She was working at a small gas-cooker, lighting two jets, putting on a kettle and a pan. She turned and smiled at him.

'That's very profound philosophy. I'm glad to see you, Donn. I would have been very sad if you left without seeing me.'

'You see what I mean,' he said.

'Where are you going to go this time?' she asked.

'What do you mean this time?' he said. 'What do you think I am, a tourist?'

'I'd like to know where you are,' she said.

'I'll send you a postcard,' he said. 'I am also sending one to Father Murphy.'

'That'll be nice,' she said. She was laughing softly.

'What's there to laugh about?' he asked.

'I don't know,' she said. 'I just feel like laughing.'

'It's not a time for laughing,' he said. 'Why did you leave us? What might have happened to Nan? What might have happened to me?'

'Just what did happen,' she said. 'I spent long enough up there. It was time for you to have a go.'

His trousers were steaming nicely. It was just the front parts of the legs that were damp.

There was a delicious smell of frying bacon.

'You lost weight,' she said.

'Bridgie is not a very good cook,' he said.

Suddenly this seemed funny to him. He laughed at the thought of Bridgie's dough.

'In fact,' he said. 'It's revolting.'

'That was probably the main reason you were angry at my leaving,' she said.

'That's it,' he said. 'Bellies and brains, two things that can be undermined by a woman.'

He watched the steam rising from his trousers, he smelt the frying bacon. He looked at Meela. There was a wisp of hair falling over her face. She was smiling. He didn't feel like upbraiding her. Did the priest know this? Just get the big fellow in there and let him have a look at her and it's all over. He felt that he had to fight this.

'I can't stay long,' he said. 'I have a long way to go.'

'Where are you going to, then?' she asked.

Well, where was he going?

'Nowhere,' he said. She looked at him. She laughed. He laughed.

'I don't know why we are laughing,' he said. 'The situation is not good.'

'Is it all that bad?' she asked.

He thought over this.

'Will you let your daughter marry Sean McNulty?' he asked.

She turned to face him. Her eyes widened. She was searching his face to see what he was getting at, how he felt.

'I will,' she said, 'if you will.'

'I will,' he said.

'Then that's all right, isn't it?' she asked.

'I hope so,' he said.

There was silence between them as they thought over the implications of this. The kettle was boiled. She made the tea. She put the bacon and eggs on a warmed plate for him. She put it at the small table near the dresser. He sat down at the table. He was very hungry. He couldn't talk from the hunger. He ate the freshly-baked cake.

'Did you bake that cake?' he asked.

'Who else?' she asked. She was sitting opposite him, drinking tea. At times their knees touched under the table.

'You'll make a great wife for some fellow,' he said. This made them laugh again.

When he was finished eating, she gathered the dishes and put them away. He dried his trousers some more and then he sat on the armchair. He was looking into the burning turf fire. He felt very comfortable.

'Do you like business, Meela?' he asked.

'No,' she said. 'Do you?'

'I can do it,' he said, 'but I don't like it.'

She was washing the dishes in a basin. She looked at him. She could see the side of his face. His cheekbones and jawbones were more prominent than she had ever seen them. She felt sorry for him, but it was more than sorrow. He had always accomplished things with dash and a little violence. He had enough brains to get on without the violent part of him.

'I discovered one thing anyhow,' he said.

'What's that?' she asked.

'For every Dino,' he said, 'there are a hundred or more decent people.'

'That's important,' she said.

'I didn't know, but these people up there really liked me.

They are decent people. Whatever their faults they are decent people.'

'You earned their liking,' she said.

'No,' he said.

'That's only your opinion,' she said.

She was finished now with the dishes. She came and sat on the chair opposite him. They looked at one another for several minutes without any talking.

'I must be on my way soon,' he said.

'That's right,' said Meela. She was smiling.

'You'll be glad to see the back of me,' he said.

'How did you guess?' she asked.

He leaned back in the chair.

'Would you be able to support your husband on a teacher's salary?' he asked.

'I wouldn't know until I try,' she said.

'I'll tell you something,' he said. 'The easiest thing in the world to make is money.'

'I'm glad to hear it,' she said.

'I'll tell you something else,' he said.

'Well, tell me,' she said.

'It's going to be a hell of a christening,' he said.

A SELECTION OF
POPULAR READING IN PAN

Obtainable from all booksellers and newsagents. If you have any difficulty, please send purchase price plus 9d. postage to P.O. Box 11, Falmouth, Cornwall.

I enclose a cheque/postal order for selected titles ticked above plus 9d. per book to cover packing and postage.

NAME..

ADDRESS...

....